THE CONJURE MAN

by

Peter Damian Bellis

River Boat Books
Saint Paul, MN

An excerpt from The Conjure Man *was previously published in* One Last Dance with Lawrence Welk & Other Stories (River Boat Books, 1996), which was a 1997 Minnesota Book Award Finalist.

River Boat Books
302 West Church Street
Lock Haven, PA 17745

PO Box 16521
St. Paul, MN 55105

Copyright © Peter Damian Bellis
Published by arrangement with the author.
Library of Congress Catalog Card Number:

ISBN: 978-0-9654756-6-2
Library of Congress Control Number: 2009939267

Original artwork entitled "Blue Gator, Purple Tree" by Dr. Bob,
3027 Chartres Street, New Orleans. Used with the artist's permission. All rights reserved.

First River Boat Books printing May 2010

This novel is dedicated to my father.

THE CONJURE MAN

when the world was first born, the swamps like the one here they was all bigger then they is now, everything was, the pines they was knocking they blackgreen heads up against the sky, look like they knock down some cloud every once and a while, and they was hundreds of blue snapflies fly about, some days couldnt see or either hear nothing else, and mosquito too, and long as a mans arm, and there was all kind of hawks and buzzards and crows circle this way and that maybe looking for something eat up like a dead hog, and every one of them birds big as a horse is now, and the water it was full up with snake, mostly cotton mouth and black snake, but some rattler too, and they was all maybe fifty foot long slither this way and that in the black-green water, in the grass too, and they was looking for eat up something same as them birds, but the king of that there swamp he was as big as all the rest of them animals put together, and more hungry too, and what he was was a bluegreen alligator . . .

The Island

-1-

I been living on this here island my whole life long and aint never been off, which it dont bother me like some cause there plenty to do. Seems like every day me and Jonas Lee Porter we is stretching out for somewhere, maybe one day is a hog killing and we grabbing a ham hock right off the table, and the next we down to the dock even there aint nothing but tins and wire and pieces of wood stuck down in the grass, but maybe we find we a old boat and head on up the coast, so we down there all the same, and every now and then we be slipping out to the backwater come night, we eyes set on witches, cause Jonas Lee his brother say how there plenty of witches what roam about the wood, them out looking for something to eat.

Today aint no different. Jonas Lee he come along he saying say let we head on out to the tidewater no telling what we might find floating in the shallows, so thats what we done, and is there we seen old man Thaddeus napping in the sand. He look most dead the way he stretch out white as he is, and he must of been that way a while cause there a flock of white gull fish-fighting back of his head a bit, and then a couple them fat gull they come up to the old man hisself and look him dead to his eye, and with that we done bust ourself laughing, and then they all fly off. The old man he dont look so bad close up, nothing like people say, but Jonas and me we quiet up and steady ourself just the same. My mama she tell me say I ever see the old man coming up the road I should keep my eyes to myself and pass on by without saying a word. I use to think he been the devil hisself the way she be talking on and on, and there wunt too many peoples argue the other way. Only thing was, when me and Jonas Lee come along, the old man he wunt on no road at all.

"What you think he doing," Jonas Lee say.

"What you think," I say.

"Maybe he dead," Jonas Lee say.

"Maybe he aint," I say.

Jonas he done know about the old man same as me, but he wunt thinking past his stomach. The old man he had hisself nine or ten string tied round some fish heads or maybe chicken heads, them heads mud-flapping back and forth in the yellow-green water. Aint a crab in the world pass up a meal like that. They go nibble on them heads no matter the time of day and then all you do you just net em. It looked like the old man done netted hisself a few cause he had a cutacoo basket full of some big old blues and all of them pile up claw on claw see which one get to the top. Jonas Lee he saying say it a shame the old man is died like he done, only no sense let all that sweet blue crab meat go to waste, and with that then he flash me a smile like it been his basket all along, but before he even think to grab it he down on his knees and he pointing at something move in the water.

"You see em there, Kilby," he say.

I seen em just the same. Four big blues nibble on a head down in that yellow-green water. Jonas Lee then he saying say they just enough room in that cutacoo basket for maybe four more, and he smiling with his whole stomach now, and before I know whats what I down in the sand, and I pulling them heads into the shallows, and them crabs they right behind, and Jonas Lee all he can do he saying say hurry up hurry up, and the more he talking the more I thinking four more they bound to cost we something, but I aint know what just yet. Then the crabs so close I can maybe catch em with my hands, but all the same I is spitting out sand for where the net where it at and Jonas Lee he say he looking he find it, only just like that it aint Jonas Lee talking at all, it the old man, and he sure aint sound dead the way he cussing and spitting and kicking hisself awake, and look like Jonas he done come to the same conclude, cause he running away like he bleed to death. Well with that there aint nothing else to do but follow his tracks, only my feet they catch a hold of that cutacoo basket, and then me and that basket we both rolling in the sand.

My mama she like to say to me time trouble fall it fall. I knows right then aint nothing more to do but watch them crabs come bubble up out of that basket. They is heading for the wet of the yellow-green water fast as they can go, and I wishing I was with them, only the wishing it dont do no good, and then this net come crash down a top of my head. The next thing I know I see the old man face it hover up above, and it white white like the moon, except it pitted with dirt and grease, and then the old man he bending down close and closer, and then the white white it gone and all I see is his red-devil eyes.

"You see what you done, boy," he say. "They is all gone, every last one of them."

I is pretty much froze by now and watching after them crabs and not saying a word.

"Just what do you think I oughta do?"

Then the old man he shaking that net at them long-gone crabs and then he fling it to the water. Then he do the same thing with that cutacoo basket. Then he look down at me some more. "Get up," he say.

I aint move nothing, except maybe my eyes, cause they watching that basket sink low in the yellow-green water, and seem like it aint never go under, only it does, and then it gone, and all the while I watching, the old man he watching me. It have the feeling like I go under the same.

"Get up," he say again, so I does, and then he grab a hold of my arms and he dragging me along.

By and by we moving through the long grass along the edge of the marsh, which I dont want to cause the marsh it full of snake, only there nothing much I can do. My mama she say ifn you has to choose youself between a alligator and a snake you best choose the alligator, cause you cant see or either hear the snake before it come to strike. The old man he dont seem to know about snakes, or maybe he do and dont mind none on account of he the devil and been a snake hisself what just as bad. Either way Im is holding my breath to see what what, only nothing happen, and then pretty soon we leaving the tall grass and coming up a rise. There some black-green oaks up top with they branches sagging to the ground, and up past that theres a dirt-white clapboard cabin with a tintop roof cover up with rust, and three blackeye window looking out to a porch. The old man he drag me up the porch and open the door, and then he chuck me inside leave me pile up on the floor.

Next thing I doing I telling myself aint nothing be scare about, but I crawling up to the window all the same see what the old man he doing, and there he is sitting hunch over on a old Co-Cola crate in front of the door, and he holding a alligator knife in his hand like so. The knife it bother me some, on account of a knife it big big trouble, but then it come to me how it aint the knife I has to worry about. The old man he whittling down a piece of hickory, and every now and then a dark dark look come to his eyes like all he can do is grab a hold of that stick and laugh, but the only sound be the cut of that knife on wood, which it mean the old man he making up a switch and soon as he done he go beat me good. It then I looking to the door, like maybe I go bolt on through, but the old man he in the way, and with that then I waiting on him he do his worst and talking to myself the while I saying say I the one all right aint no one else done trip up on that basket aint no one else lock up in the old man cabin but me and that the truth, and then I saying say maybe it aint go be that bad, maybe it aint, cause it only a stick.

The old man cabin it aint like people say, it like every other clapboard cabin I ever been. Is a threelegged table and a couple of chair push up against the wall, and this yellowglass lantern resting easy top of the table, only it aint lit up so the room pretty dark, and there some kind a barrel in one corner and a couple bag of beans on top of that, and in the other corner there a fat old blackbelly stove, and a bucket of charcoal and a can of kerosene to one side, and a big black pot on top with a mess of beans inside been cooked and hardly ate and left cold, and with that it have the feeling like Im go be the next thing go into that pot, cause them beans is why the old man done went crabbing in the first place. I just standing there looking at that pot, and all the while Im is wishing some more I was with them crabs, so hard it feel like praying, only the wishing it dont do no good this time neither. Then the old man he slap open the door and step inside. I can see the last line of red in the sky go black with that, and the old mans face look like it going black the same, and then he slap that door shut and turn around give a look around the room. Seem like he waiting on me make a move, only I dont. Then he step over to the lantern and he fire it up and hang it on a hook. Then he turn to stare me down, he holding that switch in one hand, and the light from that lantern washing yellow over his face and his eyes and his teeth, seem like he starting to burn and smoke, and he looking more and more like the devil in that yellow light than the devil ever been.

"You move yourself over this way, boy," he say.

Before I knows what what I moving up from the table just like he say, and then he grab a hold of my pants and he give em a yank like so, and with that I is looking down at the floor, my pants they wrap loose round my ankles, and it have the feeling like the old man he grinning.

"Time we settle up."

The old man he wet that switch on the tip of his tongue and he bring it across my rear with a whack couple time like he done gone butcher up a hog, and it seem like I gone numb all over, except for I can feel two raw welt breaking through my skin. Then the old man he lay that hickory on the table, like maybe he done change his mind, but I aint one test the devil neither, so Im is keeping my eyes to myself and waiting what come. Nothing more happen. And by and by I looking around some and there the old man he over at the stove and grumbling low to hisself about beans for supper how he done had his fill of beans and bread and not even a bit of ham he should of dumped the mess out back for the crows, and then he bending down in front of that blackbelly stove and looking through the grate. Look like maybe he go toss in a couple three more piece of charcoal, only he dont.

"Say boy," he say. "You hungry? Hell, you gonna have to be hungry eat some of this mess."

I aint guess what the old man about to do, maybe he laughing to hisself and then give me a plate or either take up that hickory a second time. But the old man he dont even look up, he just keep on talking into that stove.

"Whyunt you just pull up them pants and sit yourself down. I aint gonna eat these goddamn beans all by myself. I dont like em that much."

It dont sound like the old man he like much of anything the way he talking, but the next thing I knows Im is sitting at the table and the old man he bringing two plate heap high with beans and some bread, and he sit down and say dig in, so we does, and all the while we eating Im is looking at the old man see what he go do next, only I aint exactly sure I want to find out. Then we both done, and the old man he pushing hisself way back in his chair and take out a pipe, and then he smoking some, and Im is watching the smoke curl up to the ceiling with one eye, but I still got the other one on the old man, and he looking at me now like he dont know what to say or either do, like maybe he still thinking on that hickory. Then he lean some closer and start talking.

"Boy, you let me tell you something, on this here earth aint hardly nobody been born who ain't afraid of one thing or another, and most folks got a list. Most folks is so afraid of living they cant wait to go to war. And they is so afraid of dying they cant pass up a church without going inside. Hell, boy, most folks they's afraid of just about everything there is. And that's God's own truth talking."

I looking at him and nodding, only what exactly he talking about I dont know cause aint nobody afraid of everything, not even Jonas Lee Porter his little sister. Im is looking and nodding, and waiting on him say some more, but the old man he done talking. All he do he lean back in his chair, and he seem pretty please with hisself now and looking out the window, and then by and by that pipe slip from his hand, and he sleeping like a mule. I aint move for a minute, just to be sure. Then the next thing happen Im is heading for the door, I aint fool enough wait around see if he go wake up, and then Im is across the porch and past them black-green oaks, and them beans and the bread and that blackbelly stove, they all been left behind.

-2-

The next couple three weeks I aint doing much. I just laying around the house and thinking about the old man. Mama she dont know what to do with me. I aint tell her about them crabs and the cabin, and I aint going to neither.

I figure to let the whole thing lie where it is. But mama she figure there something peculiar going on inside my head, and if I wont talk to her, maybe I go talk to God, so thats when she start taking me to church. I dont tell her I is almost thirteen and aint been to church in maybe two year. I figure maybe it a better thing to go to church and have her praying over me than have her worry about some crazy old man. Besides, there aint no telling what she'd do if she found out about me and old man Thaddeus. She is a pretty big woman, packs a pretty big wallop. There aint no sense even taking a chance.

Church is like its always been. And after its over, me and mama we sitting down by a few womens resting in the shade of a scrub pine, and they all waving they fans like thats all they know how to do, and then there come Delilah, she the fat one in the fade yellow dress, and a fade yellow hat too on top of her head, and she has this I-a-beauty-queen-was-once kind of net hanging down to hide her face, which it all right by me cause her face enough to bust up a piece of granite. The next thing she do she leaning herself up against that pine tree, cause she cant sit herself down on the ground if she want to get back up, and all the while she be fanning herself and cussing out the bugs and the hot and this island and even God hisself, and that scrub pine be about to bust from under. Then she see me and mama sitting there and she start in with the question. The same question she say every time she see me. Like she stuck up in a movie.

"That you boy there Isabelle? He such a fine looking boy for his age?"

Mama she nodding her head and give me a nudge, and with that Im is standing up so Delilah can see, and Delilah she clucking to herself now like she some kind of hen. Then she grab hold of my arm, and it feel like a claw. Delilah she one of the reasons I stopped going to church.

"He sure is. He as fine a looking boy as I ever seen."

"You tell her Delilah," say a voice from the flock, and they all getting into it now they laughing and flapping they wings, and mama she just nod her head some more.

"What you plan on doing with him," say Delilah. "Better have something special in mind the way he look."

Then Tramsee come along, she wearing a slinky red dress and waving a skinny red umbrella in the air, and you should see the rest of them womens struggling to they feet and their arms flapping and they all of them cluck cluck clucking, and then they all fly off, even Delilah, like Tramsee was some kind of crazy, dirty dog looking to get herself a chicken. Then it just me and my mama and Tramsee, and she saying Ty he still in the church, he be coming along in a minute. Then she look at me and wink at my mama and then she saying say now who is this, all the girls they gonna go crazy over him, remind me the next time she throw a party, he go be the guest of honor, then she wink at my mama a second time and give me a smile.

My mama she the only one have anything to do with Ty and Tramsee when they aint having a party. Most peoples talk like them two been live under some kind of hoodoo spell, like maybe she done witch him or he witch her, so most times wont nobody have nothing to do with them. Part of it cause they living out the beach in a shack gets blowd over every time a storm come along. When that happen Ty he race into town let everybody know he need some help put it up again, and everybody go even they aint want to cause when they done they know they go have one hoodoo of a time. There something about Ty and Tramsee bring everyone together, and that the truth. Pretty soon there all kind of people out the beach and they hammering at boards and hanging up windows and sweeping out the kitchen where Tramsee she cook up her peach pies and such, and Ty and Tramsee they watching everything, and every now and then Ty he say how he want a couple more nail in this board or that board so it wont get blowd off so easy the next time, and before he even done speaking there a couple more nail in it, and then he saying he want six layer of tarpaper on the roof he dont want to get wet when it rain, and there it is just like Ty done said, and by and by the work it done and the peoples they all dancing and drinking and eating and laughing, and Ty and Tramsee they doing the same, only they aint have to shell out a single dime.

Mama she been friends with Tramsee since before I was born, and she say Ty the best thing ever happen to that girl. I cant see it, but thats what she say. She say before Ty that girl didnt know the sky was up. Everybody figure she go walk into the ocean sea and drown herself, or fling herself at some alligator get eat up, or something else just as crazy, and then one day she say she was go head up to Charleston, and she was go walk all the way too, and right then everybody figure this was it. Now Tramsee she didnt know nobody there, but all the same she started walking and walking, and pretty soon she found herself up along the East Side. She was five-day hungry, only there wunt no place to eat, and she was tire too, looked like some raggedy old hoodoo doll, and she was thinking how she want to lie down, and was just about to stretch out in a alley when she seen this two story brick church, and before she knew what what she was walking through the doors and sitting down in the back, and by and by she done fell asleep.

Tramsee she didnt know but she was sitting back of the Fourth Baptist Church of Saints and Sinners, which it was the Reverend Otis C. Pettigrew in charge. The Reverend he said he had hisself a church where saint and sinner they was the same, though wunt any saints ever come through the doors, and there was some said how the Reverend Pettigrew he was the worst sinner of them all, though no one seem to mind. Well, time the Reverend he saw Tramsee in the back

of his church he done start to shake, look like he was about
to shake right out of his skin, which was saying something
cause he was a big big man, but he let Tramsee be a while
thinking she go need her strength, and then come the
morning he done slid on up to her and tap tap her arm light
like so, and Tramsee, well she must of been dreaming cause
she jump straight up and grab a hold of the Reverend round
his collar and she was saying say she aint had herself a
cooked chicken in a month or more and ifn she couldnt
break this fat chicken neck then where was the butcher
knife, and then all of a sudden Tramsee she open her eyes
and she seen how there wunt no chicken in her hands, it
was a Reverend instead, and with that she done slid herself
back, and her hands they was letting go of the Reverend
collar and sliding down into her lap, and her jaw bone was
sliding down the same till her mouth open up look like she
go speak, only there wunt a single word come out. It was
then Tramsee she start to cry, the water rushing down her
face like the tide, and every now and then she was saying
say she sorry she sorry, and the Reverend he was smiling
more and more like he was looking at a chicken dinner
hisself, and pretty soon he was chewing like he already
some in his mouth. Tramsee she couldnt hardly see she was
crying so much, and when she did look to that chewing
mouth all she could see was some raggedy yellow teeth look
like they about to fall out.

The Reverend he was a older man, and so fat he had
trouble grab hold of his own hands, but when he seen that
girl crying like she was, he done squeeze them hands
together and then he start to talking, careful and slow at
first, and then faster and faster and faster. All Tramsee done
heard was noise, wunt no sense to it, but all the same she
was nodding her head like so, and the Reverend was saying
he was the world renown Otis C. Pettigrew, and this was his
very own church, and she was welcome to stay on for long

as she like, only she have to help out in the chow line and with the USO dances on account of there was plenty of boys coming home. Then the Reverend he was done with his talk, but he was still looking at Tramsee with them chicken-hungry eyes, and almost bite off his tongue. And Tramsee she was done with her cry, but she wunt looking at the Reverend at all. Her eyes was turned in and she was thinking on them coming-home boys.

Tramsee she done stayed with that church for almost a year. Evenings she help the Reverend Otis maybe serve up some rice soup, or maybe stew and cornbread, and then some shrivel-up fruit, and come every Friday night she be dancing with some soldier boy done come home. Wunt none of them what she expect, but Tramsee she wunt about to give up cause them boys they was all pressing her to dance, and wunt no better way she say to find herself a man. The Reverend Otis C. he wunt about to give up neither on account of he could still taste that chicken-dinner, and he be smiling at Tramsee and wouldnt she help out in the kitchen tonight clean them pots, and then he be smiling some more, and Tramsee she do enough pots keep him smiling, but every Friday night she be off to the dancing floor all the same, and the Reverend Otis he be left with a couple three dozen empty pot on his hands.

Then one night Tramsee she met up with a fellow call hisself Icebox Pete. Wunt no one full up his belly like Pete, didnt matter what, and he told Tramsee all about it too, how he been eat up more than all the boys in his squad put together, how one night they come down to Charleston on a weekend pass, they was most of them from there but it was Pete's first time, and Pete he been eat five stack of rib in ten minute and there been room for maybe five stack more. Then Icebox Pete and Tramsee they was both laughing and dancing across the floor, and when the dancing was done they both went off.

20

The next day Tramsee she come to the church by two, and she was wearing a cream-color picture hat with black trim, and a cream-color dress hang down to her knees, and some square-heel pumps was black like the trim, and the first thing she done she tug on the Reverend arm and she was saying say how she was full up with gratitude the way he done let her stay on but she was heading out with Pete he had hisself a horse farm down Florida and she hadnt even been out of South Carolina fore this but it wouldnt be long she was stretch out in the sun or riding bareback, and with that she done pick up a little black string purse she been dangling, and then she give a hiccup she mean for a laugh and she run out wait on the steps, cause her Pete done said he was coming round three o'clock. The Reverend Otis he knew what she was saying even he didnt hear all the words, and he was feeling sorry for hisself on account of he wunt go have no chicken dinner now, but he didnt know exactly what to do neither time she run through the church door, so he just stood there a while, watching her words where they was hanging in the air, and then the words they was gone and the Reverend he give a heavy, slow rolling slouch with his shoulders like that, and then he head on back to the kitchen to wash what was left of them three dozen pot.

Tramsee she wait on Icebox Pete past three o'clock and moving on to four, but didnt nobody show up except a fellow what come with Pete the first time she seen him. This fellow he didnt bother none about his name, and he didnt smile neither except to say evening, and then he was saying say how Pete he sure was sorry, he been down working the docks most of the day, and he was still there too, even he barely move his arms, but he said he go be a drowning man soon as he seen her and wouldnt she wait on him and Florida till three o'clock the next day. Tramsee she was frown and sore-hip from sitting on them steps, but she like the part about drowning, even it didnt make no sense, and time that fellow he say Florida she was saying say fine that'd be fine, and moving like she a suitcase to pack, and that fellow he just tip his hat and off he went. The next day was the same thing, only Pete he hadnt been to the docks, he been hoofing it through the Battery. Tramsee she want to ask just what it was Pete been doing he couldnt do with her, but before she could say a word that fellow he just tip his hat like so, and off he went again.

Well, by and by it come on seven day of Tramsee waiting on Icebox Pete, and she done give him up already, but she know she want the truth, so time that fellow come strolling up the street, and he was singing to hisself about some girl wearing one red shoe, Tramsee she almost tackle him before he reach the steps. Seem like she too skinny, but time she jump she grab a hold of him with both her arm and both her leg like she some kind of crab, and with that he felt hisself falling, and then he land a heavy thwack on the sunburn brick, and he was hoping he aint broke his back.

"What you mean by coming here every day this week with that same beat-up story coming from out you mouth? How long you think I a fool?"

Tramsee she was sitting square on that fellow chest and looking like she go beat on his face but good if only she could find a loose brick to hit him with, and that fellow he was looking up to her and blinking and he didnt know just what to do cause his back it was pretty sore even it wunt broke, so he allow a what-ever-you-say-I-do smile come creep across his face and he hope for the best.

"You be telling me now."

"Yessum, I is."

"And none of you lies, you hear, aint nothing but the truth come from out you mouth today."

"Yessum, I hear you."

"That better."

"What it is you want to know?"

Mama she say that there how Tramsee done met up with Ty, and he wunt but a bigknuckle tarbaby look like he lost his hat, but Tramsee she done took to him all the same.

-3-

Now the truth is that going to church didnt do no good. God he didnt need no telling. And I still thinking about the old man and that piece of hickory and wondering if he go come after me again, cause a couple of whacks dont seem enough for losing him a crab dinner. I been thinking on him so much it seem like he living up inside my head. Maybe he is. I told Jonas Lee about it, but he just laugh. "You been sitting in the dark of your own room for too, too long. What you need is to get out have a little fun. Why dont we head on down to the dock, maybe wait on the ferry boat come in." And just like that I aint thinking on the old man no more, and me and Jonas Lee we out the door.

The ferry boat been coming to this island two or three time a day for more than twenty year, and that mean there all kinds of junk been left, but aint nobody never done nothing about it, so it just pile up all over the dock, but mostly around the ferry boat company office. There three or four empty barrel out front of a couple mud-dusty window and five maybe six tire from some old Fords roll up against the washroom side, a old buoy out front what rust and crack and look like it nail down to the dock, three or four sign what say Co-Cola shove back in the grass where the road come up and another one nail to the washroom door, and there one more sign say United States Post Office, it hanging from a hook. Is a fine fine place to be out the dock, even you just sitting on two barrel halve look out at the water and the yellowtail jumping, or maybe some mullet, and theres no other place in the world you want to be, and thats just the way it is now.

One time someone from the ferry boat company he come on out to the island and he was saying say the dock was a absolute disgrace there was so much junk laying out, and fill up the office too, and where was the man in charge he want to see him right away. The man in charge was Hugo Brown, he about seventy year old then, and he come out the washroom and wiping his hands on his pants and who was it want to see him what it about cant a man have some peace and quiet he was trying to think. That company man he fire Hugo right on the spot. Then he tried to hire someone else but wunt nobody want the job, even for eighty-cent a day, and so pretty soon he give it back to Hugo. Aint no one from the ferry boat company been back since.

Hugo he have a battery radio turn on to some ballgame, only he aint listening too hard cause his feet they prop up on top his desk and his head it flop over on his shoulder. But me and Jonas we listening. We sitting down the end of the dock and looking out at the water and listen to that game. We aint even mind the heat. Then about the eighth inning Jonas he have a idea. First thing he looking at me with one of his sly eyes and then he nodding his head over at the washroom door and he saying say pretty soon the ferry boat go be in and peoples getting off and some of them go want to use the toilet and wouldnt it be something if we done took a wrench to the drop pipes leading down to them toilets and loose up the joints and soon as anybody pull on them chains why there be water spray all over the place.

I have to say it a pretty good idea, and the next thing I know Im is sliding in back of Hugo I go rummage around his office see what I can find, and Jonas Lee he scrunch down waiting by the door and he telling me say they has to be up under the desk and is they there and whyunt I just grab em now and run, and I sure is glad Hugo he a hard sleeper cause Jonas he have the kind of voice cut through a wall, and he dont shut up neither, he just talking and talking, and Im is looking where he say, but there only three or four box of bent nail and some metal scrap, and then I sliding past the window and then up along some shelves, only aint nothing but some empty coffee cans there, and Jonas Lee he talking so loud he almost drown out the radio, and Im is saying say Jonas I dont know where they is I aint seen em yet, only just then I does, and with that I is out the door with two green monkey wrench in my hands.

The ballgame it over by now but Hugo he still stretch out, he even snoring some, and there a old song call *I Be Seeing You* come on the radio, which it almost make me laugh, only I dont. Then me and Jonas Lee we in the washroom, and first thing he do he point out a black pipe run down along the white tile wall to the toilets, and then he give me a wrench and he say lets we do it, so we does, only I aint exactly sure just what it is we suppose to do so I looking on over to Jonas watch him work. He standing up on one of them toilets, and he having some time of it with his wrench hook around the pipe and he pulling and pulling and pulling, but then the joint come loose and some water come crawl down the pipe, and then the water stop. Then Jonas he off to the next one and he pulling and pulling some more, and I up there next to him and pulling the same, aint go be long now, and then all of a sudden we is blast from them toilets by the ferry boat whistle, and it sound like it pretty close, too close for me. Then Jonas he give me a flat-lip smile and he saying say there nothing more we can do now but wait and see, and then he pitch that monkey wrench into a bluegreen waste-can and he busting out the door, and I is right there with him.

Hugo he almost kick his radio off a that table there come a second whistle, and then he fall to the floor, and his legs they so tangle up with his feet, by the time he make it to the edge of the dock, me and Jonas Lee we sitting on them barrel halves like we been there the whole day. We both looking up at the sky, there some black black clouds a ways off, and there a sick, green color under that, and it seem like the sky it saying say these here the ones, these boys, they the ones done it, but Hugo he dont hear nothing, it dont even seem like he know we there, he just standing on the end of the dock and mumble some about a storm coming in and he glad it aint now cause he aint have his supper. Then he see the ferry boat and he waving his hat, and somebody wave back.

The ferry boat it aint a big boat, it barely hold fifteen maybe twenty people, and every time out the peoples they wondering if it gonna sink, but it aint sunk yet, and every time it pull up to the dock the peoples they waving they hats. They all waving they hats now, and some they laughing, and the wheelman he standing up and waving his hat like the rest, and then he crow-squawking some, and then two boys they toss down a couple three tires keep the ferry boat from smash itself up against the dock, and then they jumping down theyselves with these raggedy old ropes go tie that ferry boat down, only fore they even take a breath, the peoples they all of them already on the dock, and some they shaking mill dust from they shirts or either wiping down they faces and then they off, and some they in all kind of hurry they talking it look like rain just look at that black black sky coming in it go be some storm, and then they off the same, and some they smoking from they pipes and talk about the chickens or the hams or the soup they go eat up at Capn Calloway come supper, and maybe some peach pie, and some they hardly looking where they going cause they just tire as they can be. But they all walking right past the washroom and heading into town, and me and Jonas Lee aint nothing we can do we watching them go, and then it just the wheelman and his boys, and then they heading into town the same as everyone else have a little supper before they go back.

Look like we done loose up them pipe joints for nothing, and we just about to head into town ourself maybe go home when we see a couple three marine they still on the dock. We aint see them get off or either where they been, but there they is now, they standing there all spit and polish in they Sam Browne belts and they flash a couple three leatherneck smiles, it look like they waiting have they picture taken. Then they talking to Hugo up alongside that rust-out buoy, and we cant hardly hear them, except every now and then they up and laugh, and one he step up a foot to that buoy and he pull out some smokes and then they all smoking, except for Hugo, and then they laughing some more. Then Hugo he locking up the office and he saying say he see them at the Capns and then he gone. But them marines they just waiting around, smoking some more, and talking some, only it aint so many words it mostly just hmmming and such, and then they toss they smokestubs to the dock and give them stubs a twist like so, look like they just one black shoe doing it, and then they heading off to the washroom.

Jonas he clap his hand over his face to keep hisself quiet the while we watching, and time they inside, Jonas he say how we best be gone fore they come out again cause they be ready to bust some heads time they does, so me and Jonas we up fast as we can climb on board that ferry boat, and then we both ducking down low in back of the rail. All we doing then we listening, and then we hears some shouting from the washroom and one of them marines he cussing all up and down and then the door it bust wide open and they all come race out onto the dock. Jonas he wave for me have a look and see whats going on, and I shaking my head slow slow like does he think I crazy, only the next thing I know my eyes they up over the rail. Them marines sure is angry. They done come out wet and they shirt tails hanging out and they stomping around the dock like they three knockabout alligator, and one of them he waving a wrench in the air and he shouting out how he go loose up some joints hisself, and the other two they poking through them barrels and roll up tires and shoving at them Co-Cola signs, and they all turning they eyes this way and that look for something to have at, only they aint see nothing but the dock and the ferry boat and the water and them two barrel halve.

Jonas Lee he say again say what going on, and I wave him up have a look for hisself, and then we both eyes up over the rail, but it too too hard not to bust up laughing, so we back down again, we go wait on them marines give up they search. Seem like we waiting and waiting and waiting. Dont know how long, except by and by them black clouds they straight up over the boat. And then Jonas he cant wait no more he up again looking over the rail and then he laughing out loud he saying they been long gone, and with that he climbing over the side of the boat, only he aint have a good grip, and then all a sudden he give a short yell and he waving his hand in the air and then he land on the dock with a heavy thumpump like that.

Well Im is up with that and wondering what what, and I calls out to Jonas, only he just answer with a low moan, so I climbing down have myself a look, and there he is, he all spread out with his leg twist up one side of his head. He look just like some of the junk been left around the dock the last twenty year. But I talking to him anyway.

"Say, Jonas, what you done to youself," I say.

Jonas he just roll his head at me and moan some more. He sure pick a fine time break a leg. Hugo office it been lock up, and aint no one come down from the backwater wood or either up along the road, so I grab hold of him myself and drag him across the dock set him up against that rust-out buoy, and then I saying say how I going to town for help and dont he be worrying none cause somebody go know what to do, but Jonas he just roll his head around some more. All the way into town Im is thinking say what if that storm break and Jonas still out there, maybe it go wash him away, or maybe it aint go be the storm that get him, maybe it go be the witches, cause witches they always out before a big big blow, and even when it blowing, what if they go stick Jonas Lee in a pot, what he go do then, and then it have the feeling like I is the one stuck up in that pot, only it more than a pot now, it a big big cooking kettle, and there a pack of witches standing round and they waiting to eat me up, and with that Im is trying to shake them witches out of my head, I is too too old believe in such truck, but they up in my head all the same. Then there some yellow lights up ahead, and just like that them eating witches is gone from my mind and Im is thinking say it aint go be long now Jonas Lee, you hold on, it aint go be long.

The first place I come is Capn Calloway Bait Shop and Grill, only why he call hisself Capn aint no one know cause he never been foot on a boat his whole life long. The people they dont bother none about me when I open the door so I go on in. Some they is sitting at the counter and eating on they fried chickens and rice or they ham and biscuits and beans or maybe some hog pudding, and they all drinking Co-Cola, and some they sitting in the booths up front and eating and drinking on some of the same, and theres a girl name Shirley working the counter, only there aint nothing for her to be doing till the people they done, so she just sitting up front on this three-legged stool and humming and scraping the dirt from up under her fingernails, and the Capn he standing off in the corner and he arguing with little Fergie Wallace about the best way go catch sheepshead, and hard to say who winning cause they both waving they arms like they reeling in fish. I open my mouth to tell em all what what only there aint no sound come out at first except this rasphuhrasphuhrasphuh, and with that then some they turning they heads so they can see what making that kind of noise, and then they see me stand in the doorway cover up with a pasty, wet dust from running. Some they asking me then if I all right, and I just nod my head and they nod back, and some they asking if I was running and what I running for or either from, and I nods my head some more, and all the while I breathing in and out, in and out, and soon as I done steady myself, I open my mouth again and I saying say how Jonas Lee Porter he done fell from the ferry boat to the dock and broke his leg upside his head, and with that then the peoples they all up talking fast like fire, only that about all they doing, which Jonas Lee he needing more than that cause he still up at the dock.

Is then I hears these voices come from one of the tall red booth near the back and them voices they saying how they knows just about everything there is to know about broken bones and how they better get up to that boy fast as they can fore he done gone into shock, and I just about to turn around lead the way when I see who talking, it them three marines we was laughing at, only they aint wet no more.

"It all right boy," say one. "We know what we doing."

Then the one who closest he shaking me some, get a move on boy, and aint no telling how long he do that, but then he aint shaking me no more cause Im is moving through the door and out, and them marines they following close behind, and the rest of them peoples what been eat at the Capns, and Shirley and little Fergie Wallace, and even the Capn hisself, they all following the same and talking on and on about poor little Jonas Lee what was he doing top

of that ferry boat he wunt suppose to been up there and
that a fact, only they voices is soft as the wind.

By the time we up to the dock, them black black clouds
they everywhere, look like the storm go break in a minute.
And Jonas he still leaning up against that rust-out buoy, only
it look like he slip down some, and he moaning and
shivering like the rain it already coming down. Soon as
them marines see that, one he taking off his jacket throw it
over Jonas Lee, and then they checking him up one side and
down the other and pull on his leg a bit, and Jonas he
moaning some more and roll his head this way and that,
and all the while the peoples they is all crowd around on
the dock to look, and then Hugo he break off from the rest
and into his office and he flick on a couple of light so every
one can see more better, and some they stretching out they
brown rooster-necks cause they aint seen a bust-up leg
before, and some they is shaking they heads they saying say
poor little Jonas he dying for sure what he must of done for
the good Lord to come down on him like that they didnt
know but they glad it wunt them, and little Fergie Wallace
he saying how he wouldnt trade places with that there boy
for a pot of Chinee tea, and the Capn he aint saying nothing
at all, he just trying to stand away from that black black
channel water, far as he can, keep hisself from falling in.

Is just then the rain coming down, and Jonas he moaning
again, only not so loud now, and pretty soon he looking
like a half-drown cat, and all Im is doing I standing there like
Jonas he is died already, and why it aint my leg bust-up I
dont know, and Jonas he roll up his head look at me like he
ask the same question. Then the marines they done
wrapping his leg and they pick him up, and the light from
Hugo office it been put out and the door shut and lock up.
Then everybody they thumping across the dock, and Jonas
he be swinging side to side in the arms of them marines, and
his head it bobbing as he go. Then the thumping and the

peoples and Jonas Lee and his bust-up leg they is all gone, and I is left there standing in the rain.

-4-

The storm it was a big big blow, bigger than what anyone off the ferry boat been talk about, and by the time it done blow itself out it done lay flat most everything from the trees below the bluff to some of the stores down along Front Street. The next day me and mama we out stacking some pieces of board what blowd up onto the porch, and is then Ty he come on up, and he looking like he a blowd-up board hisself. Then he catch his wind and look to mama and me, and then he saying say how Tramsee and he they been working on fix up they cabin, and it be scatter all over the beach and back along the dunes, and how Tramsee she done look for her silks and her fine hats and such and she done hike up into the dunes she scrounging about, and then she down in the marsh flats, maybe she find something there, and wunt too long after that Ty hear something wail and wail and wail, and he head off see what it is and it was poor old Tramsee, only she aint find no silks or either hats, she just find herself stuck up in the middle of one of them bogs back there, she floating in muck up to her neck, and there all kind of flies buzzing by her nose, and she swinging her arms out above her head like she have at them flies, only all that do it make her stuck the more, and all the while she yelling for Ty to get her out, only Ty he say he cant help just hisself, and that why he come running.

Mama she nodding like she cant decide on pray or either laugh, cause she know how Ty he all exaggeration, and then she say for me she say to go on with Ty and keep he and Tramsee company how she be coming there by and by with some people help poor Tramsee out before she sink to the bottom and how I best mind my manners and wait till she come. Ty then he say he oblige, and then he saying say for mama be sure she bring along something to drink cause it be hot out the bog and Tramsee she must be near to spitting foam her mouth so dry, and then Ty he smile hisself and he say how Tramsee she like that sweet rye liquor they selling down at Willies and she could probably do with as many of them bottles as Willie go give up cause it getting hotter and hotter by the minute. Mama look like she smiling inside out cause she know who them bottles for, and then she turn sharp on her heel and head into town.

Well, I wishing my Mama she hadnt up and volunteer me like she done, but she done it anyway, and then Ty he clap me hard on the back and he say for me to get a move on cause Tramsee she been waiting, and so I does what he say, and pretty soon me and Ty we walking out the beach. Now most people they hear the name Ty what come to they mind is a man lost in the desert. Ty he always looking for something to drink, so much so people saying he done drink up more than the devil hisself. Mama she wont never say why Ty he drink so much, and I aint about to ask her cause she a big big women, but I knows it something to do with womens cause soon as Ty he see a pretty one, and he aint like most mens they talking heat soon as a pretty girl come round the corner, no Ty he quiet up like he bite off a piece of kerosene charcoal, and then he looking around for something wash it down, and then pretty soon he a bottle in his hands, sometimes two. Ever since I know him he been drinking most near all the time. Mama she say people just oughta humor him along. What she mean by that she mean people oughta give Ty all the sweet rye liquor he can hold.

The next thing I knows we walking through the dunes and the air it full up with a screechy, whining sound, give me some kind of shiver, but Ty he saying say it only

Tramsee, and aint she sounding some sore thirst, and then a slow-rye smile come creep across his face. All I can think of is Tramsee and I cant hardly believe that her she aint sound human and on and on like that. Then I aint thinking of nothing. Then we coming down a sandy ridge, and there a sandy, grassy place at the bottom, and on one side of that there a thin stand of red-brown sycamore, and on the other theres the bog, look like a kettle bog, and Tramsee she sure enough stuck up in the middle, she maybe twelve foot out, only she dont know we coming. She sure is something to see. She cover up in all that black, black muck, look like she a frog, and all she doing she looking out at the world with two frog eye, and it them eyes what get to me the way they blinking and the mud drip down, and before I know what what I bust up laughing. Ty he give me a what-you-crazy look, only then he looking out to Tramsee, and she looking back, and then she open up her big blue mouth again, only now she angry more than tire, and she saying say what the both of you fools doing there standing there laugh like some kind of hyena, and she flinging some of that black muck with every word she say, look like a sawtooth windmill, and me and Ty we both ducking down in back of them red-brown sycamores, and then we looking to the middle of the bog.

"He aint mean it," Ty say.

"What he laughing for then?" Tramsee say.

"He aint laughing at you," Ty say, and then he looking to hush me up. "Tell her you aint laughing at her."

"I aint laughing at you," I say.

"Well what he laughing at?"

"What you laughing at," Ty say, and he talking hush to me some more, only I aint know what to say, and then Ty he aint give me no time to think about it he just call on out. "He laughing at hisself, how he done walk all the way out here only he just now see he aint wearing shoes," and then

Ty he looking at me some more he want me to kick off my shoes.

"It . . . it just like Ty done said," I say, and I leaving my shoes up under them red-brown sycamores, and then we both hush up. Aint nobody talk or either move, like there aint no such thing as a clock to live by, and then Tramsee she open her mouth again.

"Well, all right then."

And with that, me and Ty we up from them red-brown sycamores and walk across the grass, only it hard to leave them shoes, and then Ty he give me a shove with one of his bigknuckle hands send me a couple step out ahead of him, and there I face up with them two frog-eye again. This time I aint letting out a sound, and Tramsee she asking me say I always go around scream like they is witches riding my back every time I meet up with peoples floating in a bog is that how my mama raise me, and I saying say no maam no it aint it wunt her it was the shoes that all and then would she like for me to get her something what she want anything at all and then my mama she be coming by pretty soon with some help to haul her out. Tramsee she aint all the way satisfy, and she give me a look like she aiming a gun, and then she asking me say I think it a proper set of circumstance a girl like herself she stuck in the middle of a bog without even a towel to wipe her face or either a ribbon pretty up her hair what she go do now there people coming by for a visit.

I aint much of a choice so I saying say no maam that aint right of course she needing a towel I aint blind, only I thinking say what she need a towel for when all them peoples be coming for is pull her out of the muck, and then she asking me say maybe I hike on out to the beach to her place maybe rummage around till I find everything she want and then bring it back so she can fix up her face, cause she want to look good them peoples show up, and Im is nodding my head say a whole lot of yes maam I do just that, only I thinking say aint nothing go help her show off her mud-cover face less it a dip in the ocean, and then Tramsee she give me a thick slice of peach-pie smile, and before I know what what I up over the ridge and then out the beach, and pretty soon Im is wishing on my shoes some more, cause the sand it sure is hot.

The storm it done a pretty good job on that shack. But all the same I poking around, scraping through the sand, shoving through some of the wood pile up, and all the while I poking and scraping and shoving, Im is thinking on how Tramsee she got herself stuck in that muddy black bog in the first place, cause she in there pretty deep, and aint no way she could of just walk on out cause a bog dont hold nothing up that long, and maybe she done jump in, but why anybody do that I aint even guess, and the more Im is thinking the more and more it seem like the only way for Tramsee be stuck like she is is to get herself throwd in, and the only one throw her in like that be Ty. I almost laugh out loud for picture Ty holding Tramsee up above his head and Tramsee kicking in the air and calling him some kind of foolishness and then Ty he letting her sail, but I done lost my shoes for laughing at Tramsee the first time and I aint looking to lose anything else, so I keep it inside. Then Im is ready to go back. I been pretty much over the whole beach with a pine-wood crate in my hands, and it full up with ribbons and small yellow soaps and a crack-handle mirror, but there aint no towel, there a small white bowl with the word candy carve in, or maybe it a dish, and a red lace hat with a button on top, and all kind of Tramsee stuff like that, but there aint no towel, and with that then Im is walking through the dunes to the ridge and whistling all the way.

I is almost to the ridge when I hears a grumbling come from in back of me, and I twist myself around almost drop the crate, cause it old man Thaddeus standing there, he has hisself a empty pail in one hand and some sticks in the other, and he looking at me with his white white devil face and his red devil eyes. First thing he do he scratch the stubble on his chin some and close one eye to the sun, and then he done poke at my crate with them sticks. Then he one big grin.

"Say, boy, what you got in there," he say.

I aint say a word cause all I can think about is them long-gone crabs and wondering if the old man come to give me a couple more whacks, and there aint nobody around go help me get away, just a couple green heron looking for something to eat in the grass, and then they flying off. But the old man he aint have a piece of hickory. Then he talking some more.

"Aint any crabs, is it?" he say.

But I still aint saying a word. Then the old man he put them sticks in his pail and he leaning some closer have a better look see into that crate, and seems like he have a hungry look about hisself, like maybe he aint been eat since them beans, so I telling him say I aint any crabs I sorry about the last time too but like my mama she say what done is done only you want me net some more and give em you I do just that only not now just now Im is bringing this here crate it for Tramsee Singleton she down on the far side of that ridge only she stuck in the middle of a bog which is why she aint up here get it for herself. And all the while I talking, the old man he nodding like so and chewing something I aint know what it is, maybe it his tongue, and then I done and the old man he saying say he know a bit about bogs and not to worry none, and then he tap my shoulder with his stick he saying say we best be moving along, and so we does.

Time we to the top of the ridge, the old man he stop and look to the bottom, and I stop right alongside. Ty he sleeping up under them red-brown sycamores, and he using

my shoes for a pillow too, and he look almost like he a
dead man the way the flies they be crawling down around
his face, and every now and then he give a snort from his
nose it blow them flies clear, and the flies they humming up
above his head a while, but then they come on back. It
almost too hot to do anything. The bog it spitting up muck
this way and that, it almost bubbling over with the heat.
And poor old Tramsee look like she a shrivel up raisin been
chew up and spit out herself, like maybe we too late, but
just then Tramsee she look up, and she give a hollow-out
cry for hello and something it look like a wave, and then
she watching while we climbing down. Soon as we step to
the grass then she waving her hands like so, and the words
they come muck-spitting out of her mouth, and she saying
say how glad she is she see some peoples and did I go like
she done ask and where her things where is they and when
we go help her out of this bog and on and on and on, and I
saying say yessum we glad too we is and this here the crate
and dont she worry none we go get her out, but the old
man he dont say a word, and then we standing up along
the edge and Tramsee she all smile and relief.

The first thing the old man do he give me his pail and
take hold of that crate and he empty it to the ground, and
there go all the ribbons and the yellow soaps and the crack-
handle mirror and the rest. Then he sitting down on top of
it, and when Tramsee see that her smile it gone and she
flinging some more of that muck, only she pretty tire now
from flinging it at me and Ty from before, so it all falling
short. The old man he dont pay her no mind anyways, he
just reach down to a strap on his leg and he pull out that big
big alligator knife of his, and he checking the blade, and
then he look around some, everywhere but where Tramsee
at, and she still flinging muck. Well, it hard to say if the old
man he know what he doing, how he go get Tramsee out
with a knife anyways, but then is like he know my mind

cause he pointing his knife over to where Ty asleep under them red-brown sycamores, and the old man he saying say he go cut hisself a mess of sycamore branches, see which one long enough, and that how he go drag her out.

The moment he say that, the muck stop flying, and I looks out to the bog and Tramsee she aint doing nothing but sit up quiet like some kind of rock, and if you didnt know she was there you be thinking the same with all the muck cover her up from the spitting-up heat and the way she been flinging it about, nothing but her two frog-eye staring out at the world, and even they is pretty hard to see now, except every now and then Tramsee she mud-blinking. Then the old man he step over Ty and he hacking at them sycamores. It sure a lot of work. Aint none of them twenty foot high yet, and they mostly just saplings even they look dead, but a knife it aint the best thing hack at any tree, dead or not. But by and by the old man he cut hisself down a whole mess of red-brown branches, only aint none of them long enough, and he sour and disgust with that so he throw em all away, and Tramsee when she see him do that, she blink back a cry, but the old man he dont notice, he just staring at them trees. Then he grab hold of one it only twelve foot tall and give it a shake maybe loose it up, and then he down to his knees digging and cutting at them shallow roots and cursing, and then he up and trunk-twisting and then he down some more, and then he calling me to grab hold and help, which I aint thinking I just does, and he call out for Ty, only Ty he aint move nothing but his lungs they blowing them flies about, and it seem like we been at it a couple three hour, only it aint been that long, and then the old man he put his knife away, and then he dragging that twelve-foot sycamore over to the bog.

Tramsee she almost drown herself she crying so hard, but she try to shut it off she see the old man with that tree, and then the old man he holding it out for her to grab a hold, only it a foot short, and Tramsee she about to drown herself some more, only the old man he move some closer and reach out again, and Tramsee look like she wishing she had longer arms she strain and strain, only then she catch hold of the tip of that tree, and with that her frog eyes they almost pop, and then she clutching hard with both her hands, and then the old man he haul her in.

For a moment or two Tramsee she stretch out along the edge like she been dead a month, but then she up on her feet, she slow and tremble, and she dripping wet with that black, black muck, and then she smile at the old man, he back on the crate, and she smile at me sitting in the grass, and is then she spy old Ty asleep up under them red-brown sycamore. Tramsee she aint smile none at Ty, but she give him a look like she go be smiling soon, and then she take a hold of his legs drag him to the bog and let go of his feet, and they go plopopp into the black muck like that. Then she settle herself down in the yellowgreen grass and she give her sleeping Ty a sharp sharp shove with both her heel. Aint a thing old Ty can do but roll in face first, and then Tramsee she standing up casual and collect, except she smiling at Ty now, and then she heading to the top of the ridge and then she gone.

The old man he laughing to hisself with that, and then Ty he waking up all cough and surprise and sput sput sputtering he trying to catch his breath, and he wiping the muck from his eyes and nose, and then he up from the edge he crawling through the grass, and then he sitting hunch over and sour and he give a look see what what. The first thing he see is them ribbons and them small yellow soaps scatter round in the grass, and then his eye turn on me and the old man, and Im is wondering if Ty think me and the old man done roll him in, how long we go be in the bog before someone drag us out, and then Ty he grabbing me up around my arm, and I almost feel myself sail through the air, but all Ty do he ask me where his Tramsee done gone. I cant hardly look in his eyes Im is thinking how good it feel my feet on the ground, but then Im is saying say I aint know exactly where she gone she just gone that all, and with that Ty he let go of my arm, and then he running up the ridge, and then he gone the same.

-5-

The sun it almost down now, except for some red burn through the tops of the trees a ways off, and I aint know exactly what Im is go do just me and the old man sitting in the dark, but my mama she told me to wait, so I waiting. The old man he hunch over that crate and grumbling some about his appetite, and every now and then he look over at me, and Im is thinking maybe he want his pail back or either want to talk about them crabs some more, but he dont say a word, and then he pull out his pipe and by and by he blowing smoke. Is then I hears a shout come from the top of the ridge, and then some peoples laughing, and then another shout, and then I sees a couple three yellow ball lantern float down through the shadow, and then there some peoples float down the same, and most they load up with boxes and crates and talking about how much they go drink, and someone he singing bout a couple three fellow what climb up on a roadhouse fence like they straddle up on a girl name Annie Rose, only what happen after that he aint sing about, and then I hears Willie his voice he saying they all come too late for Tramsee, too late cause she done sunk to the bottom of the bog, and why they haul up all these box for someone what knocking on Peter gate this very moment, well he cant say, only they here the same and someone better dig down and pay for all this liquor he brung and the time he done spent carry it all the way out here cause he a man making a living, and is then my mama voice she cut through all that Willie talk for shut his mouth and what he need to blow his hot air up and down people neck, it hot enough, and she know Tramsee wunt in no bog at all, it just Ty talking cause he lonely want someone to fix up his cabin and give him a hoodoo jump, it dont matter who paying for it cause we all in need. Willie he look around like maybe he want to kick something, only he dont, and he saying say he aint a Christian charity give away his liquor unrepent, only mama she act like she aint quite hear him so she saying what, and Willie he aint say another word to that, he just keep walking with the rest of them peoples down the ridge.

By and by all the peoples they be down from the ridge, and the yellow of them lanterns swinging this way and that, and I saying say we over here right here, and the next thing I knows they all gather up around the old man and me and setting they boxes and crates in the grass, and everybody smiling, except for Willie, he looking to the bog like he looking into his own grave, and his eyes they roll up into his bald rumple head, and then he shouting and stomp around the grass and waving his hand in the air, and he asking if any give a thought to Tramsee and why it was they aint and the answer he say it the devil cause only the devil he take you thought, and some of the peoples they looking shift and unease with that like maybe the devil he done stole they thoughts that very minute, and Willie he keep right on about Tramsee and how she aint to blame cause she didnt know more better, but she down at the bottom of the bog now she waiting on the devil come eat her up cause that what the devil do he find a dead body aint been bury by the church, and time the devil he done, well what we think we doing here, cause they aint ever been one body keep the devil he hungry and we all know that, and some of the peoples they aint been hear that kind of talk before, and they surprise and worry, and some they saying the devil he been work that way ever since Elijah born so you just better watch youself, and some they just looking around this way and that over they shoulders, and aint nothing come yet, but all the same they about to run.

The old man he aint bother too much about Willie he just be smoking on his pipe. Mama she crossing her arms and she saying say it too dark we working on anybody's house and anyways it look like Tramsee she got out she ever was in so might as well set up the food and the liquor and have ourself one hoodoo of a time dont nobody worry none cause everyone know Ty he be along soon as he smell that liquor even he ten mile off, and Tramsee she aint be far behind, and with that the peoples they mostly forget about Willie and they slicing up cold chickens and ham hocks and laying out all kind of pie and bread and some they reaching for them bottles of rye and opening them up and drinking and laughing and going on, and some they done make up a circle with them lanterns set shallow in the long grass for maybe some dancing or either some hey-de-hey, and then a couple three start up kind of low and steady with they voices while the rest of the peoples they all eating and talking, and every now and then someone laugh, and then someone he singing about that sweet and pretty sorghum Sal, and by and by everyone singing or either dancing, and the light from the lanterns it dancing the same.

Most everybody they is having a good time, even old man Thaddeus. He sitting on that crate at the edge of the circle and tapping his feet and laughing to hisself and smoking some more on his pipe. The only somebody aint have a good time is Willie. He standing outside the circle of them yellow lanterns and looking at the bog and back at the singing and the dancing, and every time someone cry out,

Willie he look like he go jump up out of his ownself. Then a little while later he watching the old man, and the more he watch, the more his eyes they fulling up with blood and pulling him do something, and the next thing he know he find hisself face up with the old man even he aint want to be, and with that Willie his two eye they bust wide open, seems like there blood pouring out all over the place, and then he stumble into the light and shouting some more and the dancing and singing and drinking and eating it stop right there, and everybody they looking to Willie like they all one trouble eye.

Willie he still scare, only aint so bad with people watching, and then his voice come flash through the lantern light and it saying how we been live with the old man ever since he come to this island only what we know about him we aint know nothing just like we aint know nothing about Tramsee why we aint even see her pull from the bog so how we know she aint there yet and how we know the old man aint the devil hisself and waiting he work up a hoodoo of a appetite and even he did pull her from the bog maybe it just to eat her up some other day cause once the devil he a hold of you he aint let go, and all the while Willie his voice it rant and rattle, and the peoples they looking from Willie to the old man and back again, and then the voice it say how the devil he aint never sleep he looking to eat we all up and that just what go happen we stay here tonight.

Old man Thaddeus he looking more and more now like maybe he really is the devil, what with the light from them lanterns dancing all across his face and the smoke from his pipe, and the peoples they all backing off just a step, they wondering maybe Willie he right, and Im is wondering right along with them, Im is thinking back to me and Jonas Lee and that basket of crabs, and it sure seem like the old man was asleep in the sand, but maybe he was just waiting there try to catch two for one only he didn't cause Jonas Lee run away, and Jonas would of knowd he was the devil for sure I didnt come home, which the devil aint want nobody pin him down, so he let me go.

Well just then there come a scream from up the ridge, it hanging up there in the air, and the longer it hang, the louder and louder it get. Aint nobody know what to do. Some they looking up and up, but aint nothing to see just yet, and some they looking at the old man see if he have a hand in it, but he just smoking his pipe, and some they looking at Willie see what he go do, but he just standing there like a harness-up mule, with the sweat bead up on top of his bald rumple head like it is and then down his back, and all the while he be looking to crawl into one of them empty box or either run off into the backwater wood, only he aint decide which. Then somebody say look, and everybody does, and there something up there, look like a ghost fall out of the sky the way it screaming all blue in the face, but the closer that ghost get, the more it looking like Tramsee herself, and then someone he say how she screaming like that cause the devil done eat her up, bones and all, and how we next we give the devil a chance.

Soon as Willie hear that he give a yelp like he done swallow his tongue, and then he run off into the woods, and a couple three more they run off the same, but most they aint run or either hide cause they just aint sure. Some they edge up close to the old man, only he aint bother about nothing, he chewing some on his pipe and then smoking some more, and some they eyes on Tramsee, her whole face it blue from screaming, only what exactly she trying to say aint no one tell. But soon as Tramsee at the bottom, people see how she wunt floating at all, it was Ty carry her down, he holding her up above his head, he heading straight for the bog, and Tramsee she screaming and kicking cause she already been once and she dont want to go again. Then Ty he feel the eyes of all them peoples stand in the shadows, and with that he dont know what to do so he stop, and Tramsee she stop her screaming at the same time, only she still up in the air.

It then the voices start up for agitation and confusion, like they crabs in a basket they trying to claw they way to the top, and they is all talking about Willie, cause he gone now.

"What we listen him for," say Joe Heywood. "We always been listen him about this or that."

"He sure do like to talk," say another. "Aint a family with twenty female talk more an he do. And that a fact."

"Aint his fault, T-Bone," say Mose Heywood. "It the devil fault."

"How that?"

"I heard it say Willie he born with a lock jaw, and his mama and papa they didnt know what to do they was praying and praying, only wunt nobody listening except the devil."

"So what that mean?"

"It dont mean nothing," say Mattie Simmons.

"It do too," say Mose. "The devil he come for Willie a couple night later, but soon as he Willie in his arms, he trip over his own tail send Willie to the floor. Done broke Willie jaw in two place, and then you aint never heard such a wailing in your life. The devil he cover up his ears he like to run out the door, he aint like a surprise, and Willie he been talking worry and cajole ever since."

"Well he sure do breathe worry just to look at him," say someone else.

And a couple three more voice they chime in with agreement.

"How you think he lost his hair," say Mose Heywood.

And there some laughing from the shadow.

"He a damn fool," say his brother Joe.

"You right about that," say another voice.

"He aint no right talking about folks being dead if they aint," say Joe. "That kind of talk just asking for trouble."

"You right about that too," come a couple three echo.

"What I aint like about him," say T-Bone, "is the way he puff hisself up before he speak, and then aint no one say a word till he done. It like we all scare."

"We is scare," say Joe. "That what I talking about."

"Well, I aint scare Joe Heywood," say Mattie Simmons. "Willie he just words. People hear him talking it like the wind come blow through a pile of dry-up leaves. Before you know it you up in the air and toss about a while. But then the wind it gone and you is back on the ground."

"That aint scare you be blowing around like that?" say Joe. "Well it sure scare the hell out of me. I likes my feet where I knows where they is. Man, you remember the time Willie he talk about we should get off the island before them Nazi Germans come? I so scare then I almost kill a man he come along the beach, and he only come from Georgia."

"That more an ten year ago," say T-Bone. "Willie he aint against Germans no more."

"That right, Joe,' say Mose.

"Well, he has to be against someone," say Joe. "That the way he is."

Then the voices they hush up like they all thinking about Willie some more but they afraid to say, and then mama she move into the circle and break it up.

"What's the matter with you all," she say. "Willie he just Willie. What you doing? We come for something more than scare ourself with a bunch of Willie stories so you all just hush up. Ty, you put that girl down. She been up there long enough. Come on now. This here suppose to be a party."

And with that the peoples they done with they Willie talk, and aint long before they dancing and singing and drinking like they was before Willie open up his mouth, and Ty he done with Tramsee the same and looking for a bottle, and soon as he taste a drop he laughing and hollering and dancing, and every now and then he knock down a lantern, only he aint notice, and Tramsee she all peacock and expectation and she laughing and dancing the same as Ty, only she aint bother with him, she has herself a couple three young mens they pressing up against her one for another, and they all talking how pretty she is and was she a movie star actress, and Tramsee she laugh and laugh and then look to them some more, and every time she do them mens they more and more want to press up against her, and then the first two they rolling about in the long grass they fighting each other now, they saying say she mine she aint she mine she aint, and Tramsee she laugh some more with that and take to the third one, and by and by it seem like everyone press up against everyone else, except for Thaddeus sitting there on that crate and watching what goes.

The next thing I know I is walking through the woods down along the backwater and wondering where Willie run off to, and then I aint wondering a thing cause it too too dark, I has to watch the way I is going. Im is climbing over logs now and brush on past the moss hanging low and kicking up chips and rock, and the air it full-up with marsh frogs singing and the wind it come crisp and warm through the grass, and every now and then a bellow come from out the black, sound like a alligator. Then I sees a tiny ball of fire up ahead, it glowing like the devil's own eye, and next to the fire there a shadow all hunch over and mumble low like a hoodoo conjure man. I aint never seen no hoodoo conjure man before this, so I edge up a little more closer to a couple three water oak, and Im is pretty quiet and restrain cause I aint need a hoodoo spell cast my way just yet, only then it come to me this shadow it aint no hoodoo man at all, it just Willie, and he all huddle up like he scare or maybe tire.

Soon as I see that I moving up to the fire, and Willie he look up he mumbling like he hear or either see me come, only he dont, and then he hunch back down, and then Im is sitting by his side, and he still aint see me so I say hey like that and Willie he jump ten or twelve foot back and land up against a tree. Im is looking direct into his eye then, only he still aint see me, and then his voice come shaking through the air and it saying how it aint his time not yet not yet take them at the bog only leave him be. I crawling to Willie now and leaning close to his face maybe ask him what the matter but he keep on saying it aint his time it aint, and I just about to shout in his ear hope to shut him up, only is then he look down across the top of his nose and he see me crouch in the grass, and with that he aint talking no more, he just caught in a stare, and his eyes they burning a bright bright orange from the fire. Then he nod like so and ask me say what you doing here how come how come didnt you know, only before I say a word, Willie he going on about old man Thaddeus how he really is the devil and there a lot of people know the same even they aint say a word but Willie he tire of waiting it time everyone know, and with that he clear his throat and hunch over real low, and the orange glow from that fire it spread out from his eyes to his face to the top of his bald, rumply head and then up to the black branch of that tree behind him, and all of a sudden I looking at him in that orange orange glow and it have the feeling like Willie he been right about the old man all along, and with that Im is thinking say I in for a whole lot of trouble, cause there something that old man want with me ever since that basket of crabs, only we aint got to it just yet. But I knows now we going to. Once the devil he put his eye on you there aint no where to hide. And that the truth. Then the feeling it gone, and Willie he tell his story.

Willie he saying how old man Thaddeus like to been going the three four mile up the backwater to Pappa Toms when he first come to the island, and Willie he say it the same kind of place then it is now, drinking and dancing and people coming across from the coast in any kind of old boat they lay hands to, and there any kind of girl a man want up at Pappa Toms even he short of cash, a boy too, if he big enough. The old man he use to been drinking every night, only he didnt look like he ever drunk a drop, and most the peoples they done took him for the devil on account of that, and Willie he come to the same conclude, only didnt no one say a word they was waiting on Pappa Tom see what he do. Pappa Tom he wunt thinking on supernatural cause he was a drinking man hisself, and he done figure to let the old man be even he hadnt paid a nickel yet cause he was sure to pay something sometime soon so long as he wunt bother. The rest of the peoples they went along, and by and by everybody done forgot the old man and the devil was one and the same. That was just what he wanted. Every night he done come in he drink some beer, and maybe he leave a dollar on the table and maybe he didnt, and time he was done drinking he find hisself a girl nineteen maybe twenty year old, and if she had on a pair of black nylon stockings he done take her upstairs, and if she didnt he done take her out back in the grass, and sometime it be the same girl ten or twelve night in a row, and sometime it wunt, and every now and then he find hisself a girl with coffee cream skin and pale blue eyes and he take her on up to his cabin for a month or maybe more.

The girls he done took to his cabin they wunt never the same again, and time he done with them they come on back to Pappa Toms, only they eyes was like bits of blue glass glue to they heads, wunt none of them recognize a thing, and some they didnt know what to do and by and by they was walking off the edge of the dock they go drown theyself or maybe up into the backwater be eat up by a alligator, and some they daddys done come catch them up and bring them home, only they was brood and resist like mules so they daddys have to knock them out and slop them over they shoulders, and then they'd carry them off, and some they was angry or either scare, they didnt say which, and then they was on the next ferry boat for the coast. Willie he say it use to been like that for ten or twenty year, and there been plenty of talk too how the old man he done witch them girls with his red devil eyes, only not to his face, and then Willie he hush up a moment he look around like maybe he hear the old man creeping up from behind, only it aint nothing but the crack of that orange ball of fire, and when he satisfy we alone, he hunch over again and tell some more.

Willie he say the last girl the old man done took to his cabin her name was Kiri Girl, and she was the softest coffee cream color anybody ever seen, and her eyes was a pale pale blue, and she had herself a long black braid of hair down the middle of her back. The first night she come to Pappa Toms, the old man he come in and he sit next to her. The whole place it was jumping and the peoples they was drinking and shouting and some they was dancing, and there was a big old boy name of Sam Henry he was wearing hisself out on a old upright Conover piano, and there was a fat-hip woman in a yellow slip, she was sliding up and down the frame of that piano while she singing a song, but the old man he didnt see none of that, he was watching them two blue eye floating free in the dark. Kiri Girl she wunt hardly looking at the old man cause she was singing along with that fat-hip woman, but the old man he didnt say a word yet, he was just listening to Kiri Girl singing to herself the words, and then the song it was done, and that fat-hip woman she was done the same, and then the old man he was asking Kiri Girl where she from. She didnt say nothing right away cause she was looking over her fingernail first one hand then the other, and then she said she was nineteen and didnt have to answer to no one even they was white. The old man he done swallow some of his beer she say that, seemed like maybe this here one girl he wunt go have for hisself, but it wunt long before they was both swallowing they beer, and the old man he was laughing, and Kiri Girl she was laughing the same even she didnt want to, and then come the next morning she was hanging on the old man arm and playing with his shirt and they was heading on up to his cabin.

Kiri Girl she done took to living with old man Thaddeus after that, and every night they be coming to Pappa Toms and dancing and drinking and walk along back by the backwater, only it seemed like she was more and more tire, and maybe even scare, only what it was about nobody knew. Then Kiri Girl she just stop coming to Pappa Toms, and the old man he was carrying on like she never been, and with that some was saying how Kiri Girl she been try to burn his cabin down or either poison what he eat, so he done tie her up from hand to toe and left her back of the cabin for she soften up a bit, and some they was saying how she done run off to the backwater scrub to hide, only the old man he done catch her up in his hands and he eat her only two bite, even the bones, and some they was saying how she wunt but a she-devil herself and the old man he done call her up for a while and then he have to let her go back, and there was all kind of story like that, only no one knew for sure what was what, and wunt no one fool enough to find out neither.

The truth come out one night. The old man he was running into Pappa Toms and he was waving his two arm in front of his face like he was some kind of windmill and shouting out for someone to fetch up a couple old woman midwife cause his Kiri Girl she was about to give birth, and with that the peoples they was moving fast as rain, and the girls they was jumping out of laps and knocking they bottles of beer to the floor, and big old Sam Henry he done bust up his toe against the leg of that piano he move so fast, and must of been ten or twenty other what running around like a flock of hen, only they didnt know where to run. Then the old man he was out the door and running through the backwater wood, and the peoples they was out the door and running the same, and pretty soon they was coming up the rise to the old man cabin, and they could hear poor Kiri Girl she was a bellowing away like she a alligator been stuck by a knife, and the old man he could hear her same as the rest, so he was moving hisself faster and faster, and then he was through the door, and the rest of the peoples they was right behind him.

Kiri Girl she was spread out across the old mans bed, a red-check blanket thrown across her legs, and she was breathing pain and resist, and with every breath her brown-ball stomach it bubbled up and then down and then up and then down again, and the peoples they was looking at her, though mostly her stomach, and the old man he was looking the same. Wunt none of them knew what to do. But was then old Mara Higgins come through the door, and she was hallow and portend even she wunt but five foot tall in her shoes, and she done press her teeth together she see Kiri Girl in the bed, and then she took off her scarf. She didnt even show the mens the porch, they went out on they own for refuge, and maybe a smoke, and then the girls they was getting out sheets and boil up some water, and all the while they was humming and hover up around the bed, and old Mara she didnt say a word, she was just holding on to Kiri Girl arm.

Kiri Girl she was bellowing most of the night, and old Mara she was with her all the way, and the old man he was standing off to one side of the porch and smoking on his pipe, and every now and then he was up have a look through the window, his eyes they was burning red, and then he was talking to hisself, only there wunt no sense to the words coming out, sound like the old man he was coughing up some kind of hoodoo spell only the devil could know. The rest they was huddle up the other side of the porch, and they wunt saying a word while the old man grumble, and then they was betting on what that baby was go look like down to the size of it peanut, and then one he was saying by the sound of that Kiri Girl cry it go be the size of a barrel, and then they was all laughing, and all the while Kiri Girl she was bellowing louder and louder, like she was ready eat up the whole world for breakfast when she done, and by and by it was hard to tell she even catch her breath, and then that bellowing done stop altogether, and Kiri Girl she give a hollow-out gasp seem like it come straight up out of the ground, and then the air was still.

The old man he done looked to the door with that, only wunt no one coming out just yet so he tapped on his pipe some and took a puff or two. The rest of the mens they was looking to the door the same with eyes what was saying get you money out that one big boy or either no it aint, and then the door it open up slow and old Mara she come waddle out, and she done look to the old man like she had something to say, only she wunt able to open her mouth, and then she stepped to the side, and it looked like the old man give her a wicked smile, like the devil does when he done what he come for. Then he went inside, and the rest of the mens they was all crowding in behind, and Kiri Girl she was laying curl up on her side with her arm pull in and that red-check blanket pull up around her neck, and she was all perspire and exhaust, and the girls they was cleaning up the blood, it was all over the place, only they wunt humming no more, and up alongside the bed there was a cutacoo basket and a thin cotton blanket, and there was the child, but it didnt look like a child, no sir, its skin was all a blueblack kind of pebbly color, it looked more like a dried up frog than anything else, and it wunt moving at all. But the old man it didnt bother him none, he touched that little blueblack child, and then he done pick it up and bring it close to his grizzle up face a while like he was trying to tell it something. Then the old man he was moving stiff and slow like he was having trouble even think what he go do, and then he done walk out of that cabin and into the shadow.

Willie he stop a bit, take hisself a breath of air, and then he start saying how a child born blueblack like that one was is a sign of the devil sure as we sitting here only the devil take up such a child in his arms and then how no one know what the old man he done with that blueblack child, only some say he done bury it up along the backwater, and some say he done toss it in the water for some alligator eat it up, and some saying he done eat it up hisself. Most the peoples they pretty much give up talking about the old man after that even they thought he was the devil, and the old man he didnt bother come into town no more neither, so it squared both ways, but every now and then the name Kiri Girl come up, and what done happen to her, cause no one seen her since that devil baby born, and she sure was a pretty girl, and then they'd all shake they heads.

Then one day five or six year later, Kiri Girl she come to town, only no one asked her where she been or where she was going on account of they all took her for some kind of ghost. She was wearing a bright blue dress and a pair of white glove, and a pretty blue hat done up with bits of white lace, and looked like she was going to church, only she was heading the other way, and dragging a black leather suitcase as she went. She walked down through the square and down along Front Street, and then up past the firehouse, was like she saying goodbye to the whole town, only she wunt saying a single word or either nodding her head at anybody she knew, and then she was out the edge of town and then down to the dock, only she wunt alone cause by that time must of been half the town done turn and follow her see what what. All she did she pull up her suitcase and sit down on top of it, and then she was looking out out across the channel. The peoples then they was hanging back and talk some, and then they wunt talking, and then some was looking out out across the channel same as Kiri Girl, but most was looking at her on that suitcase. It looked like a picture with the sunlight bounce off a Kiri Girl bright blue hat, and the wind it come crisp and warm through the channel grass and up across the dock, and a crowd of heads looking on, wunt none of them move or even breathe, and it looked like that for two whole hour till the ferry boat came chugging up the grassgreen channel and blow its whistle a couple three time and then it stopped alongside the dock to pick up a couple of passenger.

Aint no one know exactly what happen after that. Kiri Girl she was still waiting, and the peoples they was still waiting the same, only she didnt move to get on the boat, and maybe fifteen, twenty minute later, the ferry boat it give a quick, sharp whistle, and then it done pulled away from the dock, and then it was gone, and everybody was talking with that they was saying what a fool they been come wait on a ferry boat for a pickle-head girl get on like she suppose to, and they done lost two whole hour, and what she go do about that, just look at her, only Kiri Girl, with her coffee cream color, and her pale pale blue eyes, and that long black braid of hair stretch down the middle of her back, well she was gone the same as that ferry boat, and time the people see that, didnt none of them say another word, and then they was all heading home.

-6-

The next thing I know, Willie he asleep. The fire it almost burn out, aint nothing but a small ball of orange it glowing from the black of the ash, and that ball it getting smaller and smaller, and then it gone, and then something it telling me move along, so I does just that.

It too dark to see or either hear a thing, like I done been swallow up, and every now and then a piece of moss come rap me in the face, but before I know what what Im is back at the bog and looking at the ring of yellow lanterns, only they mostly been knock over or kick in, and there aint but a few strings of light sliding up through the grass like they snakes. Everybody there must of had some time of it. There all kind of empty bottle toss about, and a couple three empty box floating in the bog instead of Tramsee, and shoes and shirts every which way you look. Ty he done sack hisself out by them red-brown sycamores again, and he using my shoes some more, and he clutching a couple of empty bottle like he done married them instead of Tramsee, and Tramsee she all twist up in the middle of them three young men, only two of them look like they went down fighting the way they all cover up with blood, but they holding her ankles all the same. Then it have the strangest feeling like everyone done fell dead from dancing the way they stretch out and tangle up in the grass, like all it take is a nudge to roll them into they graves, and the more Im is looking at all them peoples, the more Im is thinking they really is dead, and with that then I aint know what to think.

I only been face up to death just one time before this, and that was when the Widow Mrs. Baxter her husband die, and his name was Mister. My mama she been knowing Mister and the Widow a long time, since I born at least, and so we was over early and she was helping with the grief-talk. Wunt much but wait around the house, and Mister he was stretch out on the dining room table, so I was having a look. His skin look to been stretch up over his face look like he was a red face hog, and I was tapping on his face like so a couple three time, and then my mama she come up behind.

"Aint nothing anybody can do now," she said. "When death come swooping down most he ever left been a long, white feather."

My mama she was quiet with that five maybe ten minute, and I didnt know just what to say so I didnt say nothing, and then I was heading out maybe sit on the front stoop, but all the while I was thinking about that feather and wondering where it was, only I didnt see it, and then there come some voices gum-greasing through the gate and up the walk past the Widow Mrs. Baxter her chinaberry tree, and they was saying say how you do son this here a time we all grief and perspective but we get over it by and by, only I wunt but nodding my head the while they talk, and then them voices they was up the steps and into the house have a look they ownself and maybe shake on Mister his hand, and then some they was saying say he aint look any more better then when he was alive, and laughing to theyself, and some they was a pasty white and maybe perplex, like Mister he owed them money only they just then thinking how they wunt go see it, but by and by the voices they was gone, and it was just me on the stoop, and I wunt thinking on a single thing except about that feather.

It the same thing up at the bog. Im is looking up and down that tangle of arms and legs and bottles and shoes and boxes, and it hardly seem coincidence how death done swoop on down get all of them peoples and he aint even left one white feather, not a one, but that how it is, and then Im is looking up to the trees and the dark of the ridge and the sky maybe catch me a sight of death his wing when all of a sudden a voice reach down through the dark and grab me from behind.

"Say boy, what you doing there in the middle of all them folks?"

I looking around, only I aint see where it coming from, and I ready to run off to the wood, only it grab me again.

"You thinking maybe they all dead, aint you, boy?"

Is then I see the voice it coming from the old man. He been sitting hunch over on top of his crate and smoking his pipe, and he have his pail back now but he aint bother with it, and then he straighten hisself up and he telling me to sit alongside him in the grass. Well aint nothing to do but run, all this Willie-talk about death and the devil and them peoples tangle up by the bog, that the smart money, but for some reason I aint move except to do just like the old man said.

What go happen then I dont know. The old man he just smoke some more, and then there a flicker from one of them kick-in lantern come snake across his face, it just enough to give his face a hollow-out look against the dark. Then he saying aint nobody dead, not all them folks, not hisself, and me neither, and then he poke me with his pipe stem just to prove hisself, only he aint have to prove about me, and then he smoking some more. I aint say a word but rub my side with that, and I aint move none neither, Im is just watching the old man what he do next, only he aint do nothing but smoke on that pipe, and by and by there so much smoke snaking up around his head I thinking if he aint the devil then there no such thing.

Then the old man he look at me like he reading my mind, but all he do he ask me where I been, and before I know what what my mouth it open up and Im is saying how I been up in the backwater wood, only I aint say a word about Willie how he been saying the old man the devil and eat up his own children, instead Im is saying how I been hunting alligator, only they all must of been asleep or it too too dark cause I aint seen any.

The old man he a knowing look in his eyes now, like he knowd wunt nothing for me to do but lie and now he done caught me, but he aint do nothing about it, all he do he wait till I done, and then he saying say a alligator he aint asleep when most people think, he like to move about in the cool of the dark, but even he look asleep in the middle of the day, he one eye open for whatever come along maybe a wild pig or a heron or even a mule come down to the water take itself a drink, and that all she wrote.

Then the old man he smoking on his pipe some more, it look like his eyes they lost in the smoke, and then he telling me about the first time he ever went hunting a alligator.

This here the story.

The old man was traveling with a flock of them evandalistic preachers, he was just a boy then, and everyone call him Tad. The time he talking about they done set up they tents in this narrow wedge of a field maybe three mile from a town call Barclayville somewhere down along the Yamahatchie river, and Tad he was waiting for the show to start around seven o'clock so he was thinking he head on into town and see the sights. Before he done gone five step he met up with Henry Jacobs and Henry cousin Oliver walking out of a tent. Henry he wunt as big as a raccoon his ownself, and he look like one too he wearing a pair of wire-rim eye-glasses, but he was the only son of the Reverend Samuel T. Jacobs, so wunt nobody go put him in his place. Oliver he was bigger than Henry, but that wunt saying much, and he was down for the summer from Charleston cause his folks they was hoping a traveling preacher show do him good, wunt nothing work so far. Tad he said how he was going into town, and Henry and Oliver they done fell in behind, and off they went.

By the time Tad and them other two boys hit town they seen wunt much for them to do. They walked by row after row of white-wash buildings, and some was shops and some wunt, and the peoples they was dress up with they parasol and they hats and walking in and out of the shops, and they was all talking about the revival coming up. They wunt asking for any miracle, but it couldnt hurt none to pray for some, and wouldnt it be nice see them Everets get that plow horse and plow they been wishing on, maybe if the whole town went out the Lord would see fit to bless them people. But the boys they wunt paying no mind to the talk. The only folks they'd ever seen blessed was them gang of preachers, maybe a girl or two come the morning, but wunt nobody suppose to know about that. So they kept on they walking and walking, and by and by the town wunt nothing but a ball of road dust.

Was maybe a couple more mile and Tad he stopped, and the other two they stopped the same, and Tad he was dog-sniffing at the air, and then he wet his lip with the tip of his tongue like so, like maybe he hungry, and then he was saying say he done smell the saltpeter of a backwater wood, and wherever it smell like that was bound to be a alligator or two, maybe more, and wouldnt it be something they done found theyself a ten-footer they kill it dead, and Oliver he wunt saying a word, he was thinking on them alligators, but little Henry he was saying how the meeting was go start up soon and shouldnt they be getting back and what they go do if they late, his daddy have something to say about that, only before Henry he said another word, Tad he just pointed to a black black clump of wood up by the river, and he was saying over there it over there that the place, and then off they went, with Tad he leading the way.

The boys they must of been walking through the woods of that backwater for close to a hour, they was following the black, slow-moving water of the Yamahatchie, and they was passing by river birch tangle up on the banks, and sweet gum, and water oak stretch out low to the ground and the branches rustle this way and that, and every now and then they heard a bobwhite or some other bird, and always the hum of the flies, and they was walking and walking and walking, only there wunt no sign of a alligator anywhere they walked. Wunt long after that little Henry Jacobs he was fed up to here, and he said so too, he was saying say how he was go head back to camp it didnt matter if he was going alone or not on account of he was sure the meeting done start up already, and wunt nothing anybody could do about that even they did find a alligator, and Oliver he was nodding his head like wunt nothing he could say against his cousin. Tad he didnt hardly miss a step he was saying say the reason they aint seen no alligator was the alligator he the one been hunting them all along and maybe the best thing they could do was to split up head on back to camp that way the alligator only get one of them instead of two or even all three. Little Henry he done shut his mouth with that, and he was looking around like maybe there been a alligator behind every tree, or maybe just down along the bank, and Oliver he was nodding his head some more, but he didnt say a word, and the boys they just kept walking.

Then they done come to a bend in the river, and Tad he done stepped out to the edge, only then he rush back and hush, and the other two they hush the same, and then Tad he was pointing to the far side of the river, and the boys they was twisting they heads for a look. What it was they done seen these knock-knee cypress rise up black out of the water, and up on the bank in back of them cypress they seen this big old alligator. Tad he was saying he aint never seen a alligator long as that why it must of been twenty thirty foot long, and the other two they wunt saying a word. Then Tad he have a idea, he was looking to the other two and saying how they was go swim that river and sneak on up to that alligator from both sides, and Oliver and Henry they was go jump on his back, keep him from rolling into the water, and then Tad he was go hack away with his knife and kill that alligator dead.

Well, the boys they done swim the river like Tad he said, and they come out by them cypress, with Tad on one side and Henry and Oliver on the other, and then Tad he done give the sign, was only a flick of his chin, down like this, on account of there wunt time for more, and with that the boys they done jump on a twenty thirty foot alligator. Mostly they was just hollering, at least at first, and little Henry he was hollering the loudest, and that alligator he done wake hisself up all in a rush and he was trying to shake hisself from the three of them boys, only he wunt able to just yet, and then he was twisting this way and that, and he was looking all hunger and revelation. It wunt pretty. Oliver he was hanging on to that alligator head and his arms was wrap tight around that big old mouth keep it from open up, and Tad he was straddle back of that alligator's eyes and he was pulling out a sawtooth hunting knife, and little Henry he done grab a hold of that alligator tail, only he was so little that alligator hardly knowd there was a boy hanging on the tip, and Tad he was just about to bring his knife down, only just then that alligator he done give a big big belly-shake all the way from his tail to his head, and with that then little Henry he was flying off all ball up like he shot out of some kind of cannon, and then he was gone, and Oliver he done lost his grip around that alligator mouth and before he knowd what was what he was sliding down the bank and into the water of the Yamahatchie, and Tad he was knock up his heels where his head suppose to be, and when he come down he seen that alligator mouth open wide go eat him up one bite, only Tad he was too quick, he roll hisself up under that alligator and he was swinging that knife up and then into the soft part of the neck and grunt some and grind and twist and turn, and then the alligator his eyes was popping out, and then just like that he fell dead to the warm black earth of the river-bank.

It was something to see how big that alligator was, and Tad he was resting a moment on the bank and looking awhile make sure that alligator wunt just playing dead on account of he done heard plenty of story, and he was thinking on how close he done come to lose his head, and then he heard Oliver climbing up the bank, and Oliver he was breathing heavy, but he still wunt saying a word, and then they was both resting they heads in they hands and looking at that alligator, they was both retire and relief. They didnt know exactly what to do next they'd never been that close to a deaded alligator before, and maybe they'd of been there the rest of the day except they heard some shouting from off in the distance, and it sounded like little Henry hisself and he was saying over here over here over here, only he wouldnt say exactly where here was.

Both Tad and Oliver they was looking up and around, only they had no idea, and then Tad he was moving hisself along the tangle of the bank and he was calling out little Henry name, and Oliver he was moving along the same, and every so often Henry he'd answer up, only he was sounding weak and confuse and didnt even know what day it was, but Tad and Oliver they was coming closer with every step, and then they seen little Henry, he was up in a big black oak maybe a quarter mile down the Yamahatchie river, but this oak was maybe forty foot high, and there was little Henry up at the top. When Tad and Oliver seen that they wunt able to move nothing except they open up they mouths let em fall to like that, and all they could do they was wonder how little Henry he done got hisself all the way up there, and then why he wunt climbing back down, and little Henry he was saying say was something wrong with his arm, like maybe he done broke it, and with that then Tad he was saying how he and Oliver they'd be coming right up.

It done took the both of them two whole hour for they done carry little Henry down from that tree, and little Henry he been talking the whole way about wunt that alligator something to see, only he mostly seen it from the air, and did they get him or did he get away, and wunt he lucky he only done broke his arm and not his neck, and is they hunting up some more before they go cause there just has to be a couple three more alligator lay around here hiding in the weeds in the grass this being the saltpeter backwater like Tad done said, and maybe all they need is a bag of pig feet sprinkle some out along the bank and watch them alligator come rushing up, and little Henry he was looking up and around like maybe he was go tackle some more of them alligator by the tail, and by and by, Tad and Oliver they done carry him all the way from the top of that big black oak all the way back to the alligator, and little Henry he could see the knife how it was stuck up in the neck and the blood all around, and with that little Henry he done shut his mouth.

It was then Oliver he done open up his mouth and he was saying say what we go do now, meaning the alligator, and Tad he was saying how they was go knock out some of them alligator teeth, one for each of them there, cause a alligator tooth it close to the most prestige charm on the face of this here earth, and then they was go set that alligator on fire burn him to ash and bone, and all the while that alligator was burning, they was go say how they was the ones kill him dead, just so there wunt no mistake about who done it.

Then Tad he reached up under that alligator head and pull out his knife, and it was scrape up with blood, only Tad didnt mind, and then he was knocking out them alligator teeth, just like he said he would, and there was one for

Henry and one for Oliver and one for hisself, and then he was telling the other two to wear they teeth up around they necks till the day they died or the charms wouldnt work at all, only with that Oliver he was asking just how them charms knowd if a fellow go take it off tomorrow if he wearing it today, but Tad he was saying that just how charms work, and damn if they didnt always guess right too, and then he was telling how one fellow he done heard about he had hisself a alligator charm only it wouldnt work and it wouldnt work and damn if that fellow didnt throw that charm away, what only went to prove it for the real thing all along, and then Tad he was up gathering some wood and dry brush for the fire, and Oliver he was doing the same, and Henry he was looking from the alligator to the tooth in his hand and then back again. Then Oliver and Tad they was ready, and Oliver he done pick up his cousin from the black, black earth, and Tad he done set the wood and the brush on fire, and then the three young boys they stepped back from that alligator to watch it burn on a bank above the Yamahatchie river, and the fire it was burning bright and then brighter, and the smell of alligator meat it was rising up with the smoke through the black-green of the trees and swirling around the branches and into the night sky, and then the alligator it was gone, wunt nothing left but some black ash and some bone, and little Henry he jump down from Oliver to have a closer look, his broke arm dangling by his side, and then he was saying how that there alligator he done gone up like old Elijah hisself, and the other two they didnt say nothing they was nodding they heads just so and watching the smoke some more, and then the smoke it was gone, and the three boys they turned they heels and they was heading on back to camp.

With that then the old man he done with his story and he arch up his back give it a stretch. Then he smoking some more on his pipe, and the smoke its curling up around the old mans head, and Im is thinking on a alligator charm, how it the most prestige there is, and then I trying to see around the old mans neck if he wearing his like he done said, only there too much smoke to see and too much dark. Then the old man he saying when it his time he want to go up just like old Elijah, how there aint nothing like watch what a fire can do when it catch a hold of a body, it the hand of God hisself come down to take up the dead, and then the old man he aint paying me no mind at all, which it all right by me, even if maybe he aint the devil.

The next thing I know I is heading for home. It so late now it almost early, which means there aint nothing more to do anyway. Let all them dead folks be even they aint dead. And by and by I is coming through the dunes and then down along the beach, and the sky it kind of a pale blue by now and spreading itself thin along the water, and then the sun it coming up. The beach it cover up with a pack of fish stretch out dead on the sand from the storm, and some they been half eat up, and some they aint, and there a couple three shark belly up the same, and plenty of seagull walking in and around them fish, they fighting among theyself over a scrap of fishmeat. I aint never been up a whole night before this, and maybe that why, but I aint tire or confuse a bit, at least not yet, and then Im is laugh and laugh, and chasing them gulls back to the sea, only soon as I pass by they back at them fish and I chasing them some more, and then Im is walking down along the shore, and the waves they coming in gentle and lap lap lapping up over my toes, and there must be ten, twenty fiddler crab running in and out of the waves and up over the sand and the shells and the fishes and the seagrass and then back again, and then Im is thinking some more on the old man, and maybe there aint nobody know for sure what he is or what he aint, not even Willie, but maybe that aint nothing to worry about, and then Im is thinking on old Elijah and cutting out them teeth and it sure would be nice have a alligator charm like the old man, aint nothing I wouldnt do have me one, and then I aint thinking no more, there aint nothing more to think about, the sun been up a couple three hour, and I is just now heading home.

. . . now this here bluegreen alligator he know'd he was the most powerful animal ever come out of the swamp, and the rest of the animals they done know'd it the same, and ifn they done got too close why he'd just gobble them up, so the alligator he done set hisself up on a big old black stump of a log stick up from the blackgreen muck, and every morning he'd be sunning hisself his eyes half close like he asleep, only he'd be waiting on one of them animals, and sure enough, down come a coon or maybe a pig get hisself a drink of water, only before they done open they mouth that alligator he'd just gobble them up, and wunt nothing nobody do about it neither, and then that alligator he'd look up from his log to the rest of the swamp, and his head it'd be rolling up and around, and then he'd give a roar come rumbling all the way from his belly, and he'd be saying say just me and my world, and with every word come out of that alligator mouth, the rest of them animals they'd be scrambling through the long grass and hiding up in the trees, they was plenty of cover what with all the moss hang about, and they was doing like that for the longest time, but all the while they was wondering say just what was they go do cause they was getting awful damn sore and tire of living up in them trees . . .

Ghosts

-1-

A young man squatted stiffly in the damp grass in front of a small, canvas tent, the flap of the tent tied back and the just-rising sun flashing against the exposed corner of a small wooden cot, and a pair of roughed, brown workboots underneath the cot. There was a strange stillness about the camp this morning, a waiting kind of silence which filled the air like wind-blown ash, making it difficult to breathe, and which suggested, among other things, the unblinking vigilance of God.

The young man's name was Thaddeus Jacobs, and he was thinking about the past few days and a girl he'd only just come to know, only now he was wishing he hadn't, and all the while he was thinking his grayish-blue eyes were flashing about, impatiently, aggressively, like fish flashing about in the cool of a river. What the hell had he been thinking. It was one thing to head off down by the river. Maybe go for a swim. But to go back to her tent in the middle of the night. Then again it was only supposed to be the two of them. How the hell was he supposed to know. Then he thought of a few other things he should've done or should've thought and he became angry and his mouth filled with a bitter, coppery taste, and then a few minutes later the taste was gone. He did not see the older man approach, stand to one side of the small, canvas tent, elbows hanging at odd angles, and a prayerful uncertainty etched in a thin, weather-worn, oblong face. He did not hear the words angling down, quiet words, almost subdued in the morning blue, lingering.

"Thaddeus, hey Thaddeus, you okay? They're ready for you. They're up in the tent. Come on Thaddeus, you know aint nothing else you can do, come on."

The young man said nothing. And the older man, having delivered his message, smacked his lips together, a look now of almost prayerful anticipation spreading across his thin, oblong face, then stuffed a wad of tobacco into his mouth and chewed, chewed, looked to the young man and chewed some more, and then headed back across the field through the wet, wet grass, the young Thaddeus watching, thinking, watching, remembering,

the revival meeting a couple of nights before and the sheriff and the main tent collapsing and him and her ignoring the commotion and heading down to the river for a while. but not to swim, the two of them talking softly, a lazy kind of talking, the commotion of the camp a distant echo, her moving closer, asking him if he really loved her and when did he know and him not knowing what to say at first but then the words rolling out his mouth of course he loved her he had loved her since the moment she and her father had joined the Reverend, since that very first day they rolled in and he saw her there sitting up in the front of the wagon with a red-letter bible plopped in her lap and her father on the one side and the good Reverend Jacobs on the other, and she smiled at that, and all Thaddeus could look at was the brownish-pink color of her face, and every now and then a flash of something white when her skirt caught up above her knee, and then she was asking him to say it again, and he did, and now he was smiling also, he had never thought they'd even get to talking, she troubled him too much for that, every time he got near her he couldn't seem to get his mouth to work right, her giggling at that and telling him his mouth was just fine, and then the two of them not talking, and then the commotion of the camp had quieted and they headed off to her tent, the soft, hazy light of a single lantern

*on a hook, the girl slipping inside, slipping out of her dress,
her soft lace girdle, the pink of her skin budding up and the
arc of her hips flashing in the lamp light, and then she was
stretched out on the cot, her clothes scattered about the
ground, motioning for him to join her, which he had done,
losing himself in the emotion of the moment and the
nakedness of both of them, like losing his entire soul, he had
thought, which was all right by him, but then the flap of the
tent had blown open suddenly, or been thrust open, and the
two of them had looked up to see what it was, the warm
dark shell of the night exposed, a warm wind then blowing
through the opening, and there they saw the Reverend
Jacobs himself in the dark of the opening, a large black hat
on his perspiring, balding head, an oil lamp in his hand, the
yellowish, oily light mixing with the light of the other oil
lamp, the light too much now, the girl and the young man
blinking in the sudden glare, but as the good Reverend
stepped into the tent he was unaware of the two on the cot,
or so it seemed, the canvas flap still flap flap flapping with
the wind of his presence and the Reverend trying to grab
hold and pull it shut but unable to and then setting his
lantern on the ground and getting a firmer grip and then
tying the flap securely, and still unaware, for he wasn't
looking directly at the cot even then but past it to the heap of
the girl's clothing on the ground, the girl herself only half-
recognized in her nakedness, and the young man seeming a
part of the girl, the Reverend flinging his own coat onto the
pile, then loosening his tie, his shirt, his pants, and all the
while the Reverend's mouth was flap flap flapping also, how
he knew it was late, he'd have been there sooner but the tent
was down on account of that blithering, bumbling fool of a
young sheriff, still down as it turned out, but he'd given up
on it for the night,*

Then the memory faded and Thaddeus put on his boots
and followed the other, older man across the sunny, dew-

grassy, tent-dotted field towards the waiting reverends, towards a long, black table and a narrow white tent. He could almost see them. The Reverend Jacobs and two other ministers of the camp walking slowly towards the long white tent, the day just breaking, the good Reverend mumbling to himself about wagging tongues, the other two a step or so behind, their tongues wagging in agreement, and then they would be through the white canvas flap and inside, the interior strangely dark with the sudden morning blue breaking full across the field outside, and within the dark dark tent the loamy, earth smell of brushed leather and Castile soap, and then the Reverend Jacobs sitting down behind a long, black table, the other two following, still a step or so behind, lighting the lanterns on either side of the table and then sitting down also, and the darkness inside somehow darkening in the lamp light, deepening, the three talking amongst themselves for a moment then stopping, looking up at the open flap, the brightening triangle of morning blue outside but not entering this place of the long long table, the three waiting reverends, each rigid in his silence, each burning with the self-righteous infallibility of men who see with the eyes of God.

Thaddeus walked into the tent and was instructed to kneel, which he did, his body swaying slightly on the uneven earth, and then he looked up at the waiting reverends, at the light of infallibility shining from the shadows. He asked the good Reverend and the others what it was he had done that they wanted to see him. The others looked to the Reverend, and the Reverend said he knew the moment he'd laid eyes on the boy, from the moment Thaddeus first came into his care, he'd known the boy was no good, but he had turned a blind eye, so to speak, in the fragile hope he could mold the boy, tear him loose from the rigid, inexorable grip of the devil, but to no avail, he could see that clearly now, there is no excuse for your behavior, such a wild and utter disregard for the sanctity of the laws we live by, I will not tolerate it any more, I will not tolerate such moral turpitude, what did you think you were doing with this girl, good Lord, son, to shame her so beneath the umbrella of my care, the umbrella of this ministry, my ministry, and her father, the good Reverend Fillmore, a witness to this shame, what you have done Thaddeus, you have committed an unspeakable, an unpardonable sin, and I am sorry for you, I truly am, but I suspected all along this day would come, and here it is, I have no choice now but to see that you never set foot in this camp again.

On and on he went, his words flickering in the tentshadow like the yellowish, gloomy light of the oil lamps, and every now and then the other two would nod in instinctive, tacit, simultaneous agreement, particularly the girl's father, the good Reverend Martin Fillmore. And the young man heard the words, or so it seemed, but they had little effect. He was beyond the angry incoherence of this man who was not his father. Him thinking again, remembering again,

how the good Reverend had moved towards the cot and then stopped, a black shadow against the light of two lanterns, the blackness deepening with rage, and then a moment of inarticulate, gurgling sounds, as of someone being strangled, and then a rush of anger, you harlot, you harlot, the words rushing also, the young girl squirming out from beneath the young man and then up from the cot, screaming, then running past the shadow, past the words, struggling with the flap then into the night, and the young man after the girl, but the shadow grappling with him, grip of the devil it seemed, then the young man breaking the grip, the rage, you harlot, you harlot, then the shadow stumbling into the side of the tent and the tent falling and the lanterns falling also and the fire scattering upon the ground, spreading, the canvas beginning to smoke, and the young man looked to the fire and then to the shadow of the Reverend, which was not moving, then to the fire again, the fire speaking, leave him be he belongs to me his bone his flesh his soul are mine they are not yours you do not need him alive you do not want him alive to save him would be a mistake you know that you must know that he will not thank you so go and leave him to me go and the girl is yours no one will ever know, then the fire burst into laughter, a taunting, eviscerating laughter, the flames becoming brighter and brighter, but in spite of the warning, the young man grabbed hold of the Reverend's arms and pulled him free of the burning tent, the glint of the fire showing itself on the dry dry grass and the two of them there and no one else, not even the girl, and him thinking why, why had he done it, why had he pulled him out, maybe he could put him back, but the moment had already passed and the next thing he knew a crowd of men and women stood in a ragged half-circle behind him, behind the Reverend, the tent fire burning just a few yards away and the cinders showing themselves orange against the sky, and then the men and women moved closer, wondering at the young man's nakedness, wondering at the heavy, unmoving heap of the Reverend, also naked but seeming clothed, the impenetrable shadow of righteousness blurring the line between faith and reality, or so it seemed, and then slowly, even painfully, with an almost theatrical flourish, the Reverend opened his eyes and looked at the wondering men and women, some of the men shaking their heads and slipping off into the crowd, but the rest crowding closer and offering the Reverend a chew of tobacco or a snort from a jug, and the women crowded around too, pushing the men aside and sneering at their offerings and wiping the Reverend's brow with aprons or scarves and their voices piping up with awe and indignation, what happened, was he all right, how did the fire start, was it Thaddeus, what's the matter with that boy, no wonder you

*was in shock Reverend, here let me get you something, Lord
a mercy, what got into that boy's head do you think, and as
the voices merged with the cinder-filled dark, the Reverend
turned his eyes from the crowd to the young man, the eyes of
the crowd following, then falling upon his naked young skin,
and Thaddeus looked first at the grim-standing crowd
assembled there, the yellowish glow of the fire showing itself
on their faces, and then he looked into the face of the silent,
raging, recuperating Reverend, the fire showing itself there
also, but only in the eyes, for the Reverend's face was
strangely obscured by shadow, and in that instant, the young
man knew that the fire had spoken the truth,*

Again the memory faded, the Reverend still speaking, the
others still nodding, have you nothing to say, your actions
alone are reprehensible, but that you have nothing to say is
surely cause for concern, the devil himself could boast no
greater apathy for good than you, Thaddeus, are showing
now by your silence, well I am done with you, I've done
my best, but it is no use. Then he stopped speaking, sat
back in his chair, arms folded across his chest, and he stared
at the young man from the glinting shadows, the young
man nodding now, but indifferently.

Then the other two leaned forward, a head on either
side of the good Reverend Jacobs. They looked to the
young man and then spoke, quietly, almost inaudibly, first
one, the good Reverend Fillmore, having returned from
Jasper county the evening before and only then finding out
about his daughter, first the Reverend Fillmore, and then the
other filling in.

"Son, you must know you're heading down the road of
the Devil."

"Yes, Thaddeus, you must know that."

"And you must stop."

"Yes, you must stop."

"Turn back to the Lord."

"Yes, turn back."

The voices stopped a moment, waited for the young man to respond, and when the young man said nothing, the voices continued.

"Thaddeus, I'm not blaming you for what you did, only God knows I've a right. She is, after all, my only daughter. But I am not a vengeful man. What's done is done. All I ask is that you repent of your sinful ways."

"Yes, Thaddeus. Repent."

"Do not mistake me, son. Think on this carefully. It is not too late. Though you may no longer remain here, and I agree with your father, the Reverend, on this, it is not too late to save your immortal soul."

"Yes, Thaddeus. We are all concerned with your salvation. Your father most of all. But listen now to what the good Reverend Fillmore has to say. Who better to instruct you than the father of the very girl you have tried to corrupt?"

The young man looked up at the men who were speaking to him, the dim, dark, heavy light of the lamps burning on either side of the table but now the light was not shining beyond even the glass, or so it seemed, the waiting reverend faces obscured by the darkening darkness of the tent, and all the young man could think was he is not my father, this one, you have mixed it up, and so he said nothing.

"Do you think he understands what is happening here?"

"Yes, Martin. I think he does."

"Then there is nothing more we can do. Is there?"

"There is nothing."

So the voices stopped again, and the two men sat back in their chairs and folded their arms and stared out from the shadows. Still Thaddeus said nothing. There was nothing to say. Always he has been against this one who was not his father, but up until the last few days it had been an unexpressed, groping sort of opposition, something felt but not known, as a small child feels, but now he knew, they both knew, they had both been in the girl's tent, and they both knew why, but nobody else knew, you would've thought different with the Reverend laid out on the ground as naked as he was, but nobody would ever know, you couldn't say anything against the man, not so anyone would believe you, so why would they believe their own eyes, and then the young man looked up at the unblinking face of this one who was not his father, could not really see the face in the oily gleaming obscurity of the lamp light, but he could have tried to make them see the truth, yes, he could have, but then he hadn't, and then the young man was filled with a rage and a longing and an emptiness and fear all at once, but still he said nothing.

Then the meeting was over, and Thaddeus walked from the tent of his banishment and he was thinking of nothing in particular, not even where he might like to go. The strange, watchful silence from before had given way to the shock of a morning already there, the men and women now stumbling from their tents, the grumble of put-upon voices, a "where's the wood" and a "hurry up with that there water there's coffee needs making," and the cookfires smoking with the smell of side meat and bread. But Thaddeus was not hungry. And he had nothing to pack.

So he left.

-2-

A small white child was born in the spring of the year a thin caul across his face and the mother and the father of the child removed the caul and cleaned the child as best they could and then they kissed the child and looked into his eyes and they asked themselves what name they could give the child but they could not agree on a proper name so they decided to bring the child to a preacher a minister a man of the cloth and ask the good Lord to name their child then they wrapped the child in an old blanket for there was still a chill in the air then carried him through the alleys of the town to the edge of the town and into a large green field and in the center of the field a large white tent had been raised a tent that housed the word of the Lord and there were many wagons gathered around the tent and many horses pawing at the ground and some snorting and some eating grass and there were many people gathered around the tent also some standing outside in the evening light for the service had not yet begun some talking the last time they had a minister come preaching in town half the congregation came drunk started throwing empty bottles at the podium then some laughing some just nodding their heads some smoking then a man dressed in black stepping outside calling to the people waving then inside and the mother and the father smiled and walked across the field and they were not the last ones inside the tent and then they sat themselves down on a bench near the back the child in the mother's arms and they let the music and the words of the service wash over them and they did not try to understand what they heard and saw they did not sing or pray as if just coming to the tent and sitting on the bench was enough to cleanse their simple souls and so they sat with unconscious acceptance as the people around them sang and prayed then the Reverend a man of the cloth stepped to the podium and raised his hands and spoke and he spoke with the voice of God or so it seemed to the people gathered before him and the mother and the father of the child felt the power of his words and so they listened to him and the Reverend called out to the men to the women to the children and he asked if any were in need of the Lord and some did say they were and their voices were heard save me Lord save me Lord save me from myself and the Reverend then asked them to come up to the platform and bow down before the Lord and one by one the voices with need became men and women and children and one by one they stood up and walked to the platform and bowed down before the Lord and the mother and the father stood up also and they walked down the aisle with their child in their arms and they stopped before the platform then they laid the child upon the platform and bowed their heads and the Reverend looked down upon the men and women and children before him and he called to the Lord to save his people and the people called out also and the air was filled with the cries of intolerable suffering and some were rolling about on the platform and some even on the ground their holy roller arms and legs flailing in the air and some were moaning and speaking gibberish their words rising from the black of their souls and some fell down upon the earth and prayed in silence their suffering caving in on itself and when the frenzy had passed the Reverend raised his arms a second time and blessed the people gathered in the tent and he said the Lord is surely among us then the people on the platform walked back to their benches some shaking their heads some smiling many more not smiling then the Revered looked down and saw the child on the platform and he picked up the child and looked to the people before him and he asked whose child was this and he held the child up in the air but no one answered for the mother and the father of the child had left the tent and were walking across the field to the town where they lived and the Reverend asked a second time and a third time and still no one answered so the Reverend lowered the child and looked out to the crowd and he said he would claim this child in the name of the Lord and then the spirit of the Lord descended upon the child and the people gathered in the tent were witness to that spirit and they cried out hallelujah Lord hallelujah and with that the child with no name opened his eyes and looked first to the people gathered below him and then to the Reverend looking down upon his face and the child's eyes shone with the fire of God a white fire a too-hot fire and the Reverend recognized the fire for a moment and he was afraid but then the fear passed for it was only a newborn child before him and so the Reverend left the platform with the child in his arms and gave the child to his wife and told her the child was a gift from God, and thereafter the child with no name was called Thaddeus.

Thaddeus sat in the rear of the lead wagon, looked from the morning blue fields, the morning blue woods to the Reverend, the Reverend smiling, sitting next to a young girl, the young girl smiling also, then the Reverend expounding upon his virtuous mission to bring the word of God to the poor people of South Carolina, his arms pointing randomly to the fields and the woods passing by on either side of the wagons as if the poor of South Carolina were hiding in the grass or behind the black line of the trees, the Reverend going on and on, his voice deepening with every word, the voice of God, or so he seemed to think, and the young girl listened to his words, not quite believing he was God but willing to try anything once, had tried, perhaps, hallelujah then hallelujah again, and the young Thaddeus wondered why she was carrying on like that, what hold did the Reverend have on her, he didn't understand, he didn't want to understand, and for a moment he imagined the Reverend and the young girl sitting naked in the front of the wagon, the driver whwhwhipping his wrists, the horses clopclopclopping, and the young girl wrapping her legs around the Reverend, the Reverend nibbling on her arms, her breasts, her neck, taking all of her in a single breath, the girl wrapping her legs tighter and tighter, the good Reverend nibbling faster and faster, and then the Reverend was gone and in his place was the young man name of Thaddeus, the two, the girl and the young man, clipclopclipping, their naked bodies moving faster and faster and faster, and then hallelujah one final time, and then the vision was gone, and the wagons were off to the side of the road down in a shallow gully, the horses tied down, the wagons empty, the men squatting in the shade of the wheels in twos and threes, some chewing on grass, some talking, some listening, seems like folks aint showing much interest in religion these days, not like they used to, aint enough faces to fill a tent, sure aint, aint enough pockets to fill a plate neither, sure aint, seems like folks have turned their backs on the Lord, seems like, and the women cooking soup in a shallow gully, same old scene, same old same old, three black pots each hanging from an iron rack, a large fire underneath, the women watching over the pots and the pots boiling anyway, the women talking, also talking all at once, hope we fare some better up in Barclayville, we always do well there, sure hope so, we aint made enough to buy a ham, to buy a goose, seems like folks have turned to buy a new blue dress have turned their backs to a new white hat seems like seems like the same old scene, and then a single woman's voice, soups on soups on, then a single line, the men and the women and the children each with a bowl and a spoon, then sitting down in the grass, the men in the shade of the wheels, the women by the pots, the children scattered here and there like stones, and the young man name of Thaddeus sitting away from the rest, sitting with his back to the road, then the young girl sitting in the grass beside him, not quite smiling, then warm and wet her blue blue eyes looking at him as if she thought he might know God, or so it seemed to him, and he fell in love with those blue blue eyes, and then the two of them eating their soup, the young man looking into his bowl, almost thoughtfully, the young girl's eyes looking still, then the bowls empty and the young man and the young girl walking through the grass to the wagons, talking softly, quietly, and that was the first time they talked, and then later they talked some more, and the next night also, and then they were in Barclayville and the tents were set up and the big tent and the show was over but they didn't care, arm and arm they walked through the dark wet grass, dark wet smiles spreading across their faces, the huddled clump of ghost white tents sinking into the ground behind them, and then they were into the trees, pine, oak, some redbud mixed in, dark wet smiles and warm wet wood, a moonless night, then sitting down along the root-worked bank of a slow-moving river, the black sky mixing with black water, the two staring into the blackness, not daring to look at each other just yet, listening vaguely to the wash and ripple of the current, and then the young girl spoke and the young man answered, back and forth, and back and forth again, their voices drifting down and across the black, black river,

why did we have to go so far from camp

you afraid

no im not afraid I just wondered why

i don't know you want to head back

no not yet I just wondered thats all

i wasnt really thinking about where just wanted to get away from all the tents and the voices and the people moving in and out and the shouting and the lanterns and the horses and the trucks i didn't say nothing before but i was standing outside the big tent when the trucks pulled up i saw the sheriff come down with his men the sheriff he even come up to me ask me what i seen but i didn't say nothing i was just standing there on the outside looking in but i didn't say a word

the young girl moving closer now, looking with blue blue eyes at the young man staring at the river, the young girl pulling his arms around hers

is that why you brought me here

the young man still absorbed in the ripple throb of the river thinking of an answer perhaps the girl repeating herself softly now a ripple throb herself

is it

the young man shifting now moving his free arm to rub some warmth into his suddenly cold hands then the warmth returning spreading

no that's not why

i didnt think so

the young girl rippling some more her dress pulled up to her knees and then a little higher the young man noticing pretending not to but wanting to see more then the sound of the river flooding his thoughts the wash of the water along the bank sucking surging damping the black black earth the young man standing up moving to the edge the darkness of the river flowing past his boots sliding into the wet

do you love me

the young girl's eyes now swimming with the wet of the river

do you love me

the young man climbing back up the bank, falling into those blue blue eyes once again

do you love me

her thoughts now swimming with his thoughts or so it seemed

and then their thoughts became a dream revealed, the very same recurring dream that had plagued the good Reverend Jacobs from the first moment he had looked into the eyes of young Thaddeus, a dream that would wake him in the middle of the night in a cold sweat or a hot sweat and the flies swarming and the mosquitoes, unable to get back to sleep, sometimes for days, and he told no one about the dream, it became a dark, private, hidden thing, but not from

Thaddeus, for it was his dream as well, or so it seemed to the good Reverend, the dream taking root deep within the boy, too deep to root out, a dream of becoming, a too hot night, profoundly hot, everyone awake could see the steam rising off of their own skin, which was everyone in camp, there wasn't anything to do but toss and turn on their cots, maybe walk through the dry, hot grass a while, maybe down to the river, then head on back to bed, and then, as if on cue, a respectful silence descended upon the camp and the men and women bowed knee and prayed for deliverance from the all too oppressive and yet potentially edifying heat, their bodies bent in stiff homage before their God, wouldn't He send them a nice cool breeze off the river, give them a chance to get some sleep, and of course their prayer was answered, and quickly too, in twenty-five minutes a cool breeze was indeed blowing through the camp, but along with their prayer-provoked breeze came the largest bluegreen alligator ever seen in South Carolina, the alligator also prayer-provoked, and particular too, for it spent a good hour moving from tent to tent, stopping, then sniffing at the air, then moving on to the next tent, then, finally, coming to a smaller tent set up under three shaking aspen, the only tent in the camp with the soft yellow light of a lantern burning through the canvas, through the black-green branches of the shaking aspen, the soft yellow glow somehow making the whole night seem darker, blacker, even hotter, and the alligator stopping, then sniffing, almost tasting the air around the tent, then snorting at the flap, its head a shadow stuffed up against the white-yellow glow of the canvas skin, and then the alligator gave a prayer-provoked bellow, the alligator's prayer answered now, burst into the tent with an almost religious fervor, bellowing, bellowing some more, the two inside up and bellowing, also with an almost religious fervor, two chasing one then one chasing two, the alligator knocking a lantern on its side with a thrust of its tail, the white-yellow light spilling out, *catching hold of the grassy floor, the white canvas cloth, then a bellow of voices gathered round outside the tent, the voices saying whats going on who's in that tent aint sound like nothing human do it, then the voices circling closer, stepping over one another, moving to the front of the tent to get a better look, then the whole of the canvas-skin etched with flame, smoke curling out from under the flap and then up, the Reverend running from the midst of this unforeseen conflagration into the midst of a waiting, intent-around-the-tent congregation, also unforeseen, a bible in his hand, of course, the Reverend waving it in the air like he might wave a weapon and calling out to the alligator in the tent stand back demon stand back, the word of God stands before you, the word of God in the naked flesh, and quite literally too, for the good Reverend was dressed only in a pair of black church boots, and then he was running from the tent, from the crowd, a pretty young girl running out the tent and after, a step or two behind him, without even the black church boots, and then the bluegreen alligator, jaws snapping at high-stepping heels, then the awestruck congregation giving chase, some running to their tents for guns then off into the wood, every now and then a shot ringing out, then a couple more, then a whole rattle of shot, the woods smoke-full of shotgun revivalists hunting alligator, the alligator hungry for the tang of girlmeat, or so it seemed, the girl just running for her life, the good Reverend now forgotten, him in his black church boots standing once more in front of the now smoke black tent beneath the quaking aspen, the Reverend watching the tent burn to the ground, the bible still in his hand a dream of what was to come, perhaps, or what was, or what might have been, or so it seemed.*

-3-

It is hot, he thinks. Going to get hotter, too. He is in shirt sleeves, brown pants, the brown workboots from under the cot. He has been walking long enough for the fields to pass by one into the next, the same sun-burned grass growing in clumps, thick like the bristles of brooms, the same small white stones scattered here, there, the same live oaks, their giant black limbs stretching up to the sky, black silhouettes against a pale arc of blue. He has been walking the back country roads of Barclay county for hours, or so it seems, a couple of cars dusting past now and then, an old black woman in bib overalls and a mule and a cart and the mule with an ear lopped off, a prison chain-gang working up ahead and then the trucks and wagons moving on. But these country roads offer young Thaddeus no comfort from the suddenness of his banishment, and no escape into the future either. He suddenly wonders where he is going and what he is going to do, and then it occurs to him that the only life he knows is back among those Saturday night penitents and the small, canvas tents and eating soup in a ditch by the side of the road and then moving on to the next town, maybe he'd have to go back, maybe there wasn't anywhere else to be, and this thought leaves him with a burning sensation in his stomach and again the bitter taste of copper in his mouth. But he does not turn around, and then in the heat of his bewilderment he hears a wagon coming up the dry dry road, coming up behind him, the steady clop clop clopping of two horses, the wagon slowing, stopping, and the ghost of the present becomes the past.

"You need a lift, son?" He was a skinny man, unshaven, his face twisted into a kind of perpetual snarl, but he seemed unaware of his disfigurement. When he spoke the words seemed to roll out of the side of his mouth. "You're more than welcome. I've plenty of room. Besides, I could use the company."

For the longest time neither man spoke. The brownish green of the fields on either side soaking up the heat of the day, the black line of uncut woods shimmering in the distance, always in the distance, it seemed. Every now and then the skinny man would lean forward, soberly, earnestly, give the reins a jerk and yell at the two browns to giddyap there and get a move on, but the two browns ignored him, clop clop clopping steadily, unimpatiently, as if the only time were now, the only place here. So the wagon moved on, past the fields on either side, past the unattainable woods, the skinny man not quite in control.

Then a disfigured face turned towards Thaddeus.

"Just like women they are."

The young man nodded, looked to the horses.

"Worsen being married."

The young man nodded again. He had never been married.

"I knowd this fellow once, wasnt much older than you is now, and this fellow had hisself a wife just wouldnt stop talking, jabbing like a jaybird about what she done that day what she hadnt done what she shouldve done when was they going to visit her mother when was he going to buy her that silk scarf from out the catalogue her mother had told her about marrying a fellow like him and on and on and on."

The skinny man started laughing and spitting through his teeth.

"Of course it come to this fellow that if he stayed around much longer his ears was going to be hanging down to his knees, so one night, had to been around midnight cause that women she wouldnt shut up till most everyone was asleep,

so one night this young fellow packs up heading he dont
know where he dont care, and by and by he come on some
railroad tracks, so he figures to wait on a train. He didnt
wait more an twenty thirty minutes fore one swing into
sight, and then this young fellow he was running long side
it, and then he hopped on board. He stayed on that train
for three whole nights and three whole days before he even
thought to get off. He figured he wunt the marrying kind."

The skinny man stopped speaking a moment, his wrists
jerking the reins, a giddyap here and a get a move on, the
two browns ignoring his efforts, then a shrug of his
shoulders and a settling back into his seat.

Then he continued.

"Well, wunt but a month went by and he found hisself
with a quiet boarding house room. Found hisself with a job
hauling bricks. And then he found hisself with another wife.
He didnt remember how it happened, but it did just the
same, and this second one was worse than the first. She'd
talk and talk until her head would just sort of pop off and
fall to the floor, and then she'd pick her head up, wipe it
clean with a damp towel, set it back on her shoulders, and
then she'd start talking all over again. Wunt long before this
young fellow he figures it time to go, so early one morning,
had to been just after dawn this time cause that second one
she liked to watch the sun come up, he packs up, leaves his
room and his job hauling bricks and his matrimonial bliss,
and heads out into the woods, and by and by he come on
some more railroad tracks, and before he even think on a
train one come swinging into sight, and this young fellow he
was running not a thought in his head, and then he hopped
on board."

Again the skinny man stopped speaking. He jerked the
reins a little bit harder and cursed the browns under his
breath. Then he winked at Thaddeus and went on with the
rest of his story.

"Well that fellow he stayed on that second train for seven nights and seven days. Wanted to leave his second wife even further behind than the first one. Which he did. Found hisself another room like before, only it wunt as quiet. Found hisself another job too, only it wunt bricks. And then he found hisself another wife. Or just about. There they was standing at the altar, and this one was worse than the first and the second tied together. Took her ten minutes just to say 'I do.' She'd just about talked his ears off before they even got out of the church, so he left her on the steps. She didnt even see him go she was so busy talking about how hot it was in her wedding dress she was soaked clean through hoped he didnt mind none but she was going to peel it off soon as she could hang it up to dry, and then she was laughing and talking and talking some more. By the time she seen she was talking to herself, he was already down the road to the train yard, and the next thing he found hisself an empty boxcar on a train heading south. Folks they say his ghost is riding that train to this day. Only way he ever found some peace and quiet."

And with that the skinny man stopped speaking altogether and his disfigured face twisted itself into a smile. The young man returned the smile. He wondered what life in an empty boxcar might be like. A life of unending freedom, he thought, a life where who you were and where you were going was never a question, a life of going and going and never returning. It wouldn't matter then his parents had left him in the tent of a traveling preacher show the day he was born. The Reverend Jacobs used to tell him how lucky he was not to been thrown in a ditch. But it wouldn't matter any more. He'd be out on his own and no one to say a word, and then the Reverend Jacobs and what he used to say, and everything that had happened with the girl in the tent, none of it would matter.

"We almost there."

"Where?"

"Up ahead there."

A skinny arm hung in the air, wavering, pointing, a couple of side-rail trucks in the heat-shimmering distance, and also some wagons, and Thaddeus could see a group of men, some squatting along the side of the road, looked to be black, looked to be eating from tin plates and drinking from tin cups, then some standing in the ditch, some on the road by the trucks, some in back of the wagons a ways down from the squatters, looked to be white, well-fed, finished with their own plates, looked to be holding shotguns, arms cocked, ready, vigilant, watching the squatters eat. The skinny man pulled in his arm, and Thaddeus caught the glint of a deputies badge on his shirt, which he had not noticed before.

"Hey, Hurly. What been keeping you?"

The voice came from a burly sort, reddish beard, belly lapped over his belt, a shotgun dangling from his hand. The man stepped to the side as the wagon slowed, stopped. Hurly nodded. The young man name of Thaddeus looked to the reddish beard, the shotgun cradled in the burly man's arms.

"Hey Bill."

"Hurly, you sure the slowest sombitch I ever know. Them browns still giving you trouble?"

Hurly smacked his lips together and grinned.

"Worsen being married."

"Who you brung along?"

"He didn't say. Just some fellow I give a ride to."

"Where's he going?"

"He didn't say about that neither."

Then the men drew closer and spoke in low, guttural voices and looking over to Thaddeus and then a burst of gruff laughter. And beyond the laughter of these two Thaddeus could hear the guarded almost inaudible murmurings of the blacks, like the sound of a river at night, and there was laughter too, but softer, almost like sighing. Then the heads drew apart and the one named Bill motioned to Thaddeus with his gun.

"Say, boy. You hungry?"

Thaddeus smiled weakly, nodded, his eyes on the seemingly poised shotgun. Then the gun pulled back and another burst of gruff laughter.

"Hell, boy, I wasn't gonna shoot you. Just wanted to know if you really was hungry, that's all. Go on, get something to eat if you've a mind. It wont kill you. Long as you dont mind eating after all them niggers."

So Thaddeus climbed down from the wagon and made his way past the squatting blacks to the back of the dinner wagon and a plate of beans and a scrap of pork and some cornbread and a tin cup of water. He was mostly thinking how hungry he was, but he was also aware of the black squatters watching him, silent now, uneasy, wary, waiting until he had moved on with his plate before they continued eating and drinking and talking and laughing, as if he alone were responsible for putting the chains on their feet. He sat down in the dry dry grass and began to eat, far enough away, and again there was the quiet murmur of black voices. Then one voice swelled above the rest and began to tell a story.

This was the story.

"Seems dere was dis convic wokin on dis here chain gang some years pas only he wunt so happy like we all is about all de tasks dem bosses had fuh him to do an de whippins dey done give out when dem tasks wunt done de way dey wanted. One time he come in and dey axed him how much cottin he done picked and when he tole em dey said dat wunt good enough so dey laid him flat across a table whip him bloody wid a strop. Dere was so much blood seem like Noah an his ark be coming long any minute, an dem bosses dey was lookin roun fuh ol Noah like maybe dat nigger he was gonna climb on board get away."

The other blacks started laughing to themselves with that, but Thaddeus wasn't sure what they were laughing about. The whites with the shotguns weren't listening.

"Anyhows dis here nigger he wunt so happy about all dat like i said an he started talkin to hisself bout what he was gonna do. First one side of his mouth open up like so, an den de other side, an de first side sayin was about time he done scape from dis here prison farm an de second sayin how he gonna do dat and de first sayin de nex time dey wokin out de swamp he gonna take off an de second sayin what he gonna do bout dem chains round his feet and de first sayin dat once he done reach dat swamp de bosses and de hounds dey wunt never gonna fine his trail so he take his time about dem chains and de second sayin how if he done met up wid some hungry ol gator and de first sayin he be better off dead in de belly of some gator den wokin de res of dis here life wid dem chains on his feet an de second he sayin he dont know about all dat but he willin give it a try, an den dey was both grinnin at each other cause dats what dey decided to do."

And the voice stopped a moment, the blacks nodding, some looking to the long grass of the field like they were trying to gauge the distance to the nearest swamp, not at all bothered by the possibility of meeting up with an alligator, or so it seemed.

Then the voice continued.

"Well de nex time dat chain gang was wokin out de swamp dis here nigger he was ready to go. Come time fuh dinner dem niggers gather roun de kettle den eatin an all de bosses dey standin roun an hardly watchin what goes so dis here nigger he done slip away easy as pie an den he was runnin fuh de swamp. Wunt long he done foun hisself smack in de middle of some black water an dere wunt much to see cept some black green trees risin from de muck an some moss hang down from de branches and a couple heron poking dis way an dat trough de grass, and den dey fly off. Well wid dat dis here nigger he done set hisself down on a big ol log and he start a talkin to hisself again about what he was gonna do nex.

"First voice sayin he tired of runnin so he jus gonna rest up a spell on dis here log an de second voice sayin de middle of a swamp aint no place to be restin and de first sayin dere aint nothin he can do he feel de need to shut his eyes dey gonna shut jus like dat an de second he was about to answer somethin smart when a blackgreen gator come bustin up trough de grass its mouth wide open its teeth sparkle in de black black of dat niggers eyes, an he give one look an he shut dem eyes he hopin dat gator wunt after him, only it was, an de nex thing happen dat gator come chomp down wid dem teeth.

"It was sure some lucky day fuh dat nigger cause all dat gator done was bite trough dem chains. But when dat nigger he open his eyes, he wunt thinkin bout chains or no chains, no sir, wunt no time fuh thinkin at all cause when he open his eyes, all he see was dat gator open up his mouth take a second bite, and wid dat de nigger he was gone running fas as he could go, so fas he done lef a trail of fire burn trough de grass, and it wunt long fuh de whole swamp was burnin, an dat gator he wunt able to see from all de smoke, so he let dat nigger go, but dat nigger he aint know dat, so he runnin an runnin an runnin, an fuh he know what what he done run all de way back to de chain gang. De rest of de niggers dey was done eatin by den, an de bosses dey was roundin em up send em back to wok. Poor ol nigger. He foun hisself wokin right along wid de rest. Had to wok on a empty stomach too. Dem bosses never did fine out he done run off. An he never tole em neither. But dey did see how his chains was broke, an by de by dey done slap some new ones on his feet fuh he took another step. Aint nothin like a new set of chains on a niggers feet keep him in one place. And dat de truth."

And with that the one voice stopped, the hum of the words suspended in the air, and some of the blacks were nodding their heads some more, and some were laughing to themselves or maybe talking softly, and some were rubbing where their own chains cut into their ankles.

The story was over.

"Thats enough of that now. You niggers back to work."

"Yes boss."

"Get them kettles and them plates and all back on the wagons."

"Yes boss."

"You niggers get a move on."

"Yes boss."

"We gonna work a field down the road a piece."

"Yes boss."

And the young man name of Thaddeus looked to the road, to the two trucks moving out, to the wagons moving slowly from the ditch, kettles bouncing about in the back, to the blacks moving along, slowly also, steadily, moving but unmoved, a thin black line wavering in the heat of the day, chains dragging in the dust, and then to the whites, some walking alongside the blacks, shotguns lowered, waiting for one or two to make a break for it, perhaps, and some walking a step or so to the rear, not so eager, laughing softly, and some not laughing, and then the trucks and the wagons and the blacks and the whites were gone.

-4-

And then he was moving again. He had spent two days holed up in a barn, sucking down a few pilfered eggs in the shadow of a loft, but mostly sleeping, for in the excitement of the girl and the raid and the first day of his banishment he had not slept at all. But now he was moving again. In his gray-blue, unblinking, eyes there was something fierce, obsessive, inevitable, a madness in the sense that youth was a madness, all this urging him on. He wouldn't go back. Not that he was afraid. He just had to move on. Like that fellow running away from his wives. Or that other one trying to escape the chain-gang. Hell, he'd rather get his head caved in by a lop-eared mule, and he laughed grimly at the thought. So he left the road, a dusty reminder of everything his life had been, and abandoned himself to the dark, steaming, shimmering woods, deeper and deeper through the pine and oak and the clutching undergrowth. By late evening he had come upon some old railroad tracks.

He sat down on the ground below the tracks and decided to wait for the next train to come down the line and then hop on board and be on his way. Going and going and never returning. A life of relentless freedom. Then evening became night. In the distance he heard the low rumbling of wheel on rail, a lonely sound in the cool of the evening, but a welcome sound, also. He stood up, and a moment later he could see a train, a smoky blue ghost of a train rattling its chains in the dark, a yellow, unblinking eye, the rush of a thousand tons of iron straining as it slowed to round a curve. He caught his own breath at the sight and sound and stumbled up the dusty embankment with arms outstretched, his hands ready, the blue of the train now moving slowly past, and then he saw an empty box car, the door half open, caught hold of an iron side-rail near the door, his two legs rattling against the side of the car. Again he caught his breath, sure that he could not hold on for long, sure that he was not sure how to swing from the rail to the door, the blue of his face blending in with the color of the train. He would have fallen had not an arm reached out from the half-open door, a bony arm, half hidden in the blue shadows of the empty car. He reached out to the arm with his nearest hand, then hand clasped hand, and when he felt the strength of this one-arm grip he forgot that his legs were rattling against the side of the train and he reached out with his other hand. Almost immediately his legs bounced off the gravel of the embankment below, but before they bounced a second time he grabbed hold of the bony half-hidden arm and tried to pull himself into the car, hand over hand, slowly, but the bony arm straining, his hands slipping, then his legs bouncing off the gravel once again. Then a second bony arm reached out from the shadows and hauled him inside.

Slowly the two arms released him, pulled back into the blue-black shadows of the no longer empty car. The young man name of Thaddeus stumbled away from the door to the opposite corner of the box car and sat down, the hard wood floor a welcome support. He felt the light of the moon wash across his face, the light drifting through the cracks in the roof of the car, drifting downward, mingling with the shadows. He looked to where the two arms had been, but saw nothing, as if those arms had reached out from some other world into this one, for a moment. He looked again, and he thought he heard the sound of laughter, a hollow sound, a faraway sound, as if it came from another world, also. And then the laughter began to swell, no longer otherworldly, a sound from this world now, an ungentle sound, slightly mocking. Then the laughter stopped and Thaddeus could see a man standing in the middle of the boxcar, the man looking down at him now, close then closer, the white moonlight washing across his face also, black eyes sunken like craters.

"What you doin here?"

The young man did not know what to say. He was sitting there. That was all he was doing.

"I said what you doin here? You hear me?"

"I heard you."

"You aint so good at catchin trains. Is you?" And the caricature came closer still.

"No. No I aint."

Thaddeus readied his arms to swing at the man with the crater-like eyes, then remembered the strength of those two bony arms and relaxed his fist.

"I didnt think so. Didnt think so."

And with that the man stopped talking and squatted down next to Thaddeus, slowly, still grinning. He reached into his pocket and pulled out a small black bag full of nuts and began eating. He was an older man, graying hair cropped close behind his ears, a bit of stubble growing on his chin, narrow shoulders flattened by age, narrow hands, narrow fingers, shaking slightly as he brought each nut to his mouth, as if he were curious about what was inside, but also slightly worried. Then he turned and fixed his eyes on the young man.

"What you doing here?"

Again the young man did not know what to say, so he said nothing.

"I been riding in this here car for more years than I care to count on account of these chains on my feet. I been riding round hope to come across someone help me break free." Then the older man paused, leaned closer, the black of his sunken eyes deepening, swelling. Thaddeus could smell the bone-rot of his breath. "Is that what you doin here? Is you the one?"

Thaddeus blinked stupidly at the question, but then he was strangely alert, for it suddenly seemed that he'd been asking himself the very same thing his whole life long. "Is you the one?" Maybe not in those words exactly. But toss in a why and you were close enough. Why is you the one? Or just a plain old "why you?" Growing up in the Reverend's tent and always the Reverend shunting him aside and then Little Henry was born and it only got worse. He was the one all right. The one got shunted aside. But why the good Reverend had picked him out with his almost biblical hatred he never knew. Not exactly. Not the why of it. It was like he'd come direct from God himself just to keep an eye on the old bastard. At least that's how the good Reverend took his being there. Or seemed to. Yeah, he was the one all right. And now he was out on his own, sitting in a railroad car going he didn't know where, but then again maybe he didn't care neither, and there it was, the same goddamn question getting in his way.

"Is you the one?"

His face almost caved in with uncertainty. He didn't know what to think. Then he looked down at the feet of the older man and saw they were bound by chains. He touched the chains lightly with one hand, and the older man nodded, so he took a firm grip with both hands and then, with a growing sense of rage and despair that surprised and frightened him, he tried to tear the links apart. But they did not break. He tore at the chains a second time, and then a third, and still they did not break, and he was about to try again when the older man grunted, shook his head, slowly, purposefully, his eyes no longer grinning.

"That aint the way to break them chains son." The older man carefully regarded the younger man. "Them chains was forged by the hand of the devil and they gonna bind me to this here earth till I find me someone with the fire of God in his eyes. You got that fire? Is you the. . ."

And then the older man suddenly stopped speaking and a seething, wild look came to his eyes. "You better be. You goddamn better be." And in that instant he reached for Thaddeus, two bony white hands shining in the heavy boxcar dark, the younger man stumbling to his feet, his eyes focused on the black of the half-open door, then a step, then the older man grabbing hold of the younger by the shoulders and spinning him into the corner. For a moment the two men stared at each other, the older man with stern, unmoving eyes fixed on the young man's face, and the younger man blinking his gray-blue eyes in bewilderment, but also he seemed strangely willing to accept whatever the older man dished out. But then a second change came over the older man. An unearthly calmness settled about his stern, hawkish features, a look of satisfaction, as a dead man is satisfied. Then he stepped away from the corner and squatted down in the center of the box car and went back to eating nuts.

But Thaddeus was not satisfied. He could still feel the bony, determined grip of the older man and trembled slightly from it, and then the way he broke it off, Thaddeus wasn't sure what had happened there, but it left him with an unsettled feeling, like trembling on the inside instead of the other way with that bony grip. He looked at the older man and took a couple of deep breaths and slowly his trembling stopped. But still he didn't know what to think about the older man's sudden transformations. Too much like the lunacy of a madman. Then again, he'd go crazy too if he had to wear chains like that. And it must get cold living in a box car all the time. In the winter. Freeze your balls off when you take a piss. Yeah, he had to be crazy. And then suddenly Thaddeus saw this ghost of a man as an older version of himself. He rested his head against the side of the car and tried to comprehend this thought. The hum of the wheels on the rail echoed beneath him. The warmth of the night air began closing in. And then Thaddeus closed his eyes, the image of this older version of himself fading into the darkness. Swirling. Mixing with the swirl of box car shadows.

And then nothingness.

How long Thaddeus slept on the floor of the boxcar, his idiot companion eating nuts in the corner, he did not know. Perhaps time did not matter here. Perhaps time had ceased to exist. At least this it how it seemed. Perhaps Thaddeus, in coming aboard, had entered a myth of his own making, a place outside of time where he could reshape the riddle of his past. Here he would either come to terms with the impulsive delirium of his young manhood and take strength from that and move on, or he would be abandoned, as had happened to his idiot companion, to the bewildering isolation of an old age without end.

"We here now. We here."

Thaddeus woke suddenly, painfully, to the almost gleeful words of the older man.

"We here. We here."

"Where's here?"

There was no further explanation. The older man grabbed hold of the young man's shoulders and started dragging him towards the black of the half-open door. Thaddeus tried to move, to maybe twist himself free, but his groggy-from-sleep self did not respond. Then the older man paused in his dragging and wiped his brow and Thaddeus broke loose and stumbled back to the corner. But the older man followed, and grabbed him from behind once again.

"We here. We here."

Again the young man heard the words, again they meant nothing.

"What do you mean we here?"

This time the older man grunted impatiently as he picked up the young man, a firmer grip this time, carried him towards the half-open door, his chains rattling with each step, and he stopped in the doorway, a knowledge of time and place burning in his eyes. Or so it seemed. Then he looked to the young man and grinned. "I mean we here." And before the young man could reply, the older man tossed him from the train, the young man bouncing down the gravel of the embankment, and then the older man followed the younger, bouncing down the embankment also, and when the two men stopped bouncing they found themselves sitting on the cold ground below the now empty tracks, sitting and then staring after the blue blur of the train vanishing in the distance, blue into black, the thin wail of a banshee hanging in the air, and then silence.

The two men sat at the bottom of the embankment for a time but did not look at each other. The young man moved his legs back and forth, sliding them along the ground, his hands massaging the ache of being tossed, brushing away the dirt. He wondered what the older man meant to do next and what could he do to stop him, for he remembered the strength of those bony hands. Maybe he could hit him over the head with a rock, if he could find one, a piece of granite maybe, or a crowbar, but he didn't really think that would stop this one, hell, his head its probably made of stone itself. The only comfort, he supposed, was there wasn't a train to get tossed from now, he'd just wait and see and maybe run if he had to, if he only had a crowbar, come on you old bastard, he thought, what are you gonna do next. And in the very next instant, as if in response to this silent and bitter question, the older man unfolded, got to his feet, shook the dust from his clothes, looked up to the black of the trees edging up to the embankment, and again there was that unearthly calm about his face, again the satisfied look of a dead man. Then this older man of the disquieting face disappeared into the blackness of the wood, only the sound of his chains rattling in the dark to suggest where he was.

Of course the young man followed, but not at first. He looked to the cold white of the moon and then to the black iron of the tracks shining in that light and he listened to the sound of those chains echoing softly through the wood. *Them chains was forged by the hand of the devil.* He heard the words distinctly, the words of a madman. Yet he couldn't rid himself of the idea that he and this lunatic were mirror images of each other. Again and again he heard the words, and the bitterness and rage he had felt only moments before emptied into the loamy soil beneath him. Even the physical hurt from being tossed from the train was gone.

He started up after that, walking through the woods, the branches slapping at his face and the midges and mosquitoes swarming, and he wondered what had become of the older man, for even the sound of the chains rattling had faded into nothingness. Then the trees parted and a white square of moonlight broke through and he saw the older man standing on a ridge over-looking the black of a river. On the other side of the river he saw a backwater honky-tonk, a couple three cars parked in the tall grass to the side, some bright blue lights strung around the outside of the building, clapboard walls, unpainted, some of the planks rotten, giving way, a tin roof, rusted, holes here and there, the wood and the tin and the wire shaking with the sounds of music and laughter. The younger man stepped to the ridge. The older man looked on in silence for a moment. Then he turned to the young man and nodded.

"This here where we gonna begin."

Before the young man could reply, the older man raised his arms, and with that they were both standing in the back of that honky-tonk by the river.

"This here what happened."

The older man nodded to the younger, then to the swirling memory of smoke and laughter and music. The younger man nodded also, absently, his eyes following the older man's tacit direction. Everywhere he looked he saw men and women, black ones mostly, silk ties and satin shoes, like they had just stepped off the streets of Charleston instead of wading through the muck of a swamp, the men eyeing the women, eyes up and down and up again looking to get a closer look, the women knowing just how far to let those eyes wander. The young man found his eyes wandering, also, and he took a step as if to follow his eyes, but the older man put a hand to his shoulder and the young man stopped. Then the older man pointed to a fellow in a checkered vest playing a piano, a fellow with fat fingers plucking on an old bass, the rest of him fat also, a snake-hipped girl sitting on top of the piano, the girl singing somewhat hoarsely about some Charleston gals how they danced with holes in their stockings, the men and women listening to the music, singing along, some talking and smoking and talking some more, some on the floor dancing, most drinking. One woman took her shoes from her feet and said she had a hole in her stocking just like the girls in the song. The men sitting by her snickered at that, and one said he know'd her take off more than her shoes and he'd bet five dollar cash too she'd do it again before they went home for the night, and then they all laughed. Then the song was over, and a tall man in a red hat and a red bow tie walked to the middle of the floor and waved the men and women to silence, for he had something to say. "I is gonna introduce y'all to a man I knows was born with a horn in his mouth and been blowin dat horn ever since, a man I knows been in most all de juke joints from here to Chattanooga, and he done blow'd de roof off a every one of dem places too, and now he done come here tonight see if he can do de same, a man y'all know by de name of Gabriel Dupree."

With that the men and women clapped and shouted the roof the roof and the man in the red hat and red bow tie smiled like he knew he was going to do a brisk business that night, at least enough to buy a new roof, and then he walked from the floor. The older man looked to the young man and nodded, his face etched with thoughtful expectation, and then he spoke.

"This here's the first mistake."

The young man stared blankly at the words as they fell from the older man's mouth. They were the words of a man who can see the train coming but cant jump off the tracks. Like he'd seen that train coming a thousand times. Then the older man nodded in the direction of the band and the young man followed the nod. A small man stepped from the blue shadows of the corner, a square jaw grinning in the swirl of smoke and light and laughter, a smartly polished brass horn in his hands. Then he stepped to one side of the piano with the girl on top and began to blow, narrow hands holding the horn as if it were a part of his bone his flesh, narrow fingers tapping out the rhythm of the notes. The men and women sitting at the tables jumped up with the first note, silk ties and satin shoes shouted, play on Gabriel play on.

And so the man name of Gabriel blew on his horn with every breath in his body, and when his breath was gone he blew some more. Play on Gabriel play on. And the men and women shouted some more. And some clapped their hands. And some danced on the floor. And some drank from their glasses and looked to the roof with redoubtable anticipation. Play on Gabriel, play on. Then the fellow with the fat fingers and the fellow in the checkered vest joined in, the one pluck pluck pluck on the strings of that bass, the other bang bang bang on the keys of that piano.

Then everything and everyone began to shake. Or so it seemed. The girl on top of the piano was the first. She smiled down at the man name of Gabriel, him blowing on his horn, smiling back, and then she stood up on that piano and shook, she shook her shoulders her hips her head, anything that would move and a few things that wouldn't. Then the girls all around stood up on tables, on chairs, and shook shoulders, hips, heads, and more. Some of the men shook just watching. And every now and then the man name of Gabriel looked up to the shaking girl on top of that piano and smiled with his eyes, and every time he did, she looked back and smiled with her whole body. Then the older man, who was not shaking, looked to the younger man, who was, nodded again, and then spoke.

"This here's the second mistake."

Again a blank stare from the young man, again the image of the coming train, again a nod from the older man. And when the young man turned to listen to the music of Gabriel and his horn he found the music had stopped. Hours had passed. Or so it seemed. The young man looked from the tables the chairs to the floor to the bar in back. Most of the dancing men and women had left. Those who remained were asleep, some in chairs, heads hung back, arms stiff by their sides, some on the tables, hands gripping empty glasses, empty bottles, and some flat out on the floor, silk and satin soaked with liquor. The man with the fat fingers slept on the floor next to his bass, an arm draped across, his fat fingers quivering some, but no longer plucking. The man in the checkered vest slept on the piano bench, his body bent awkwardly towards the piano, his face unceremoniously plastered against the black and white keys. The only two not asleep were the girl on top of that piano and the man name of Gabriel. She was resting easy now, her legs stretched out behind her, her shoulders, her hips still shaking, but ever so slightly, her head bent to one side, and then she looked down at Gabriel and the polished brass horn and smiled softly. Gabriel smiled back.

"You wanna go somewheres else? Maybe give this horn of mine a blow?"

"I sure do."

"Well come on, then."

And before Gabriel said another word, the girl spun her legs around, slid down to the floor, took the brass horn from the still smiling Gabriel's hands and set it back on top of the piano. Then she slid up into his arms, her whole body smiling as before, and wrapped her legs tightly around his waist. For a moment nothing happened, as if time itself had stopped. Then the man name of Gabriel carried the snake-hipped girl out through the door of the honky-tonk. And then time stopped again. The young man name of Thaddeus looked to where Gabriel and the girl had been, looked to the door, thought about where they were going, thought to trade places with Gabriel, have the girl blow on his horn a while, and then he moved to follow the two, but remembered the strength of the older man's grip and stopped. The older man simply stared at the brass horn on top of the piano, thoughtfully, hopefully perhaps, and then he turned to the young man yet again.

"This here's the third mistake."

The younger man looked from the older man to the door and then to the older man again, a look of impatience, a look of unwilling complicity, a look of why-dont-we-get-off-the-tracks-before-its-too-late. Then the older man nodded a third time and the smoky, bright light swirl of the honky-tonk was gone and the two men stood inside the door of a tarblacked shack at the bottom of the ridge on the other side of the river. There was a stove in one corner, unlit, a dresser shoved back against the wall, the middle drawer missing, a dirty wash basin on top, and a single bed in the center of the room, a single cotton blanket, and no pillow. The two stood silent near the door, the older man waiting, stoic, unperturbed, the younger man wondering.

Then they heard voices.

"Aint much farther. Come on."

"I is coming."

"What the matter with you anyway?"

"I tire out from thinking on you. But don't you worry none. I is coming."

Then the girl from the top of the piano ran through the door, giggled, slipped off her dress, then lay down on the flat of the bed, nothing but her skin to keep her warm. Gabriel ran through next, stopped in the doorway, breath bursting from his lungs in short gasps, and then one long gasp and he stared down at the girl, forgot to breathe. Then the girl asked him where his horn was, giggled again, and before she said another word Gabriel had climbed out of his clothes and onto the bed and then onto the girl. Once again Thaddeus thought to trade places with Gabriel, once again remembered the strength of the older man's grip, and climbed out of his clothes anyway, a look of willing complicity now. Then the young man climbed on the bed. Or he almost did. For as soon as he stepped towards the girl he heard the rumble of a voice outside, a loud voice, a ways off still, but coming closer, and because the voice sounded angry, cornered, unpredictable, the young man stepped quickly back. And then Gabriel. He, too, had heard the voice, and so he slipped off the girl, off the bed, and into his clothes. But the girl sat up, a curl of legs and hips and smooth brown skin, and she asked him did he think he was through and where was he going, but Gabriel just shook his head and said it sounded like trouble coming and he wasn't one for trouble. So the girl became angry, hurt, or pretended to, said how all men were the same wasn't he ashamed of himself running out on her like this what was she going to do now, and on and on and on, her words blowing through the air like she wanted to blow on his horn even then. Then the older man turned to the nakedness of the younger man.

"This here's the end of it."

And before the young man could ask the older what it was he meant exactly, the door of the tarblacked shack shattered with the impact of a train, and the man in the checkered vest rumbled in, the forgotten horn of Gabriel in his hand, and he shook the horn in the air and shouted.

"This here it the last time I ever gone be made a fool," he said. "This the very last time. I gone take care of things my own way now."

Then he shook the horn again and looked to the bed, to the girl, and the girl leaned forward on her knees and said she wasn't his wife what was he thinking she was planning go off with sweet Gabriel here and who was it gonna stop them, and then the man in the checkered vest stepped towards Gabriel, towards the girl, the horn raised and ready to come down on top of the head of whoever was closer, the man name of Gabriel Dupree looking to the girl in disbelief, then knocking the man in the checkered vest to the side and running out the door. For a moment, the man in the checkered vest didn't move. He looked at the girl now crying on the bed, an angry but self-indulgent look about his face, as if he had known all along that he would catch her at it, and then another look that said he'd be back to see she got what was coming to her, and then he was out the door after her understandably shy morning pastime.

Then the crying stopped, and the girl lay back in the bed, still naked, and wiggled herself into a comfortable position, but there was no time for Thaddeus to even consider what to do with her because the older man then raised his arms, and the girl and the bed and the backwater shack were gone, and the two men found themselves in the black, black wood, the older one walking slowly through the darkness, chains rattling, the younger one following a step or so behind, no longer naked.

-5-

They were back in the black, black woods now, in this myth of the young man's making, and at first the young man was thinking about the snake-hipped girl and the regret of a missed opportunity, but as they walked deeper and deeper into the wood, with the thickening, suffocating heaviness of the air and the swarming mosquitoes and the midges and Spanish moss flapping in his face and the smell of a swamp somewhere up ahead and the possibility of snakes or worse, the snake-hipped girl was forgotten. All that was left was the weariness that comes from walking too much.

"Where we going now?"

"We going the same way ol Gabriel done went the day he done left that shack in a hurry."

"Why're we doing that?"

"Ol Gabriel he still out here somewheres. Got his horn with him too. Folks round here say they can hear him blowin that horn every night from just after midnight till dawn. The sound of that horn it rises up gentle through the woods, through the swamp, then up the river, the notes they is wavering in the air, and then they's gone. Some say he trying to let folks know he was done to death by that fellow in the checkered hat. Some say he gonna keep on blowin that horn till someone come along set things right. Eye for an eye they say. I dont know nothin bout all that. What I say is ol Gabriel he just got hisself lost in these woods and died before he could find his way out. What I say is ol Gabriel he just want someone come along and bury his bones in a proper way. When someone do that ol Gabriel he'll stop blowin his horn. Thats what I say."

Then the older man stopped speaking, his words fading into the silence of the black wood. The two men walked on, the older intent on leading the way, the younger obliged to follow. The trees were crowding closer together. The black becoming blacker. Everywhere he looked he saw the ghost of Gabriel Dupree. Or so it seemed. He could almost hear the sound of that horn. Almost. Then the older man stopped, abruptly, eyes peering into the blackness ahead. The young man stopped also.

They stood on the edge of a swamp, the prison-bar look of many cypress trees rising out of the stagnant, dead water, and also many dead ones at odd angles in the water and leaning on each other and covered with moss. But they did not go into the swamp. Then the older man nodded in the direction of a great bald cypress up along the bank, this one also dead, the weight of the great tree sending its branches into the water, the suddenly exposed roots brittle and white from age and the lack of cover, and there in the shadow of the roots the young man saw the white almost phosphorescent bones of a dead man, and beyond the bones the tarnished brass of an old horn.

"Thems the bones of Gabriel Dupree."

The younger man nodded, staring at the whiteness of the bones, staring and wondering how the older man knew whose bones they were, how long he had kept the secret to himself, why he had chosen this particular moment to reveal what he knew. Perhaps he had heard old Gabriel blow on his horn one night. Perhaps he had spent his life searching for those bones. Then the young man shivered, and not from the cold. He knew how the older man had known about those bones.

"Aint nobody gonna hear that old horn blow around this swamp no more. Not after tonight."

The young man said nothing.

"Once we buries them bones old Gabriel he gonna rest them lips of his. He sure is. Till the good Lord come to call him up. And thats the truth."

The young man shivered again. He believed in the good Lord calling up the dead. Then he opened his mouth as if to speak, the words inaudible, almost.

"You sure about these bones?"

But the older man only grinned, a broad grin that seemed to fill in the black spaces between his teeth. He moved to the fallen tree and squatted beneath the mass of exposed roots, and then he looked into the ragged black hole where the tree had once stood and breathed in the smell of the earth and felt the earth with his hands and crumbled it with his fingers, and then he motioned to the young man and the young man joined him. For a moment they looked at each other, a moment only, each aware of the identity of the ghost reflected in the young man's eyes. Then they looked at the hole again.

"This here gonna be the place."

So the two worked to make the hole into a grave, hands digging deep into the moist, black earth, palms cupped, digging deeper and deeper. Then deep enough. Gathering up the bones, putting them into the grave, silently, carefully, even reverently, as if the fate of the older man's soul depended upon the proper and precise burial of his bones. Covering up the mistakes of this one-time trumpet player with the black, black earth. Then the startling whiteness of the bones was gone, and the young man felt that he had been given a glimpse of the future. Or maybe it was a warning of some kind? Was he going to end up like Gabriel? And what did that mean, exactly? Everybody ended up dead. But the young man could not untangle his thoughts. Then the older man set the tarnished brass horn on top of the earth to mark the grave and both men closed their eyes, as if in prayer, and then the younger man thinking, "It's no good, there aint no prayer in the book would do justice to what old Gabriel went through." And in that instant the younger man heard the sound of Gabriel's horn rising in the air, hesitant, wavering, the last gasp of a ghost, and then nothing, the younger man contemplating the sound of nothingness, and then another glimpse of the future in the guise of a dream, but whether it was a future like Gabriel's, or something as yet undetermined, he could not tell,

him running through the black mossdraped wood mudstumbling over root and rock but not feeling the straw of the branches sharp and sweeping against his face just moving moving forward his hands thrusting leaf and twig aside his shoulders slipping into the shadows and then out again long shadows resonating with the whistle of crickets the whine of cicadae and then he came to the edge of the wood and there was the slowmoving backwater warm water black like the wood reflecting nothing not even the stars and he stopped and looked at the water and wondered why he could not see his face perhaps there was nothing to see perhaps he was looking beyond his face perhaps he was looking into the slowmoving water of his own soul murky water that and though he was not quite sure just what he was looking at he was untroubled by his uncertainty for the blackness of the water brought also a calmness of breath a sense of tranquility as gentle and rhythmic as dying and then he stopped wondering his eyes peering intently into the dark dark air his eyes glowing bright blue like two blue moons and he started walking along the black wash each step measured precisely as if he knew where he was going he walked until he came to where the slowmoving backwater narrowed into a grass-choked channel and there he found a hollow place up from the waters edge and in the shadows of the grass there was an old rowboat scraped clean of paint by wind and age cedar planks damp with the smell of rot one oarlock missing the other heavy with rust and he dragged the boat through the soft black muck a gully where the keel had been and then down to the waters edge and into the water and for a brief moment he looked at the boat and he noticed how low it lay in the water the curve of the bow how it barely broke the surface but then he smiled anyway perhaps the boat had lain in that hollow for years just so he could find it and now all those years had come together in a single moment perhaps the boat had been made just so he could use it that spoke of some kind of eternal purpose or so it seemed and then he smiled again and climbed into the boat his hands on the oars one in the rusted oarlock the other balanced firmly on the rim and he began to row down the grass-choked channel and then the grass giving way and the channel widening slowly he rowed gauging the depth of the water following the steady drift of the current beyond the black shadows of oak and cypress and pine beyond the lazy whisperings of the long marsh grass beyond even the briny mire of the naked coast and then out out into the cool salt air of the open sea and the sea was strangely calm and the sky was black and steadily he rowed his eye to the horizon the chop chop chop of the oars echoing in the blackness of sea and sky and the old rowboat moving like a shadow among shadows chop chop chop and after a time he wondered how long he must row how far before he could stop but at the center of all that blackness such concepts as time and distance seemed to have little meaning perhaps he had already stopped rowing perhaps he had never begun perhaps he had been sitting in that boat his entire life all his experience neatly expressed in a single gasp for air and when that gasp expired so too would his life and his empty empty body would sink to the floor of the boat and the boat would sink to the bottom of the sea perhaps he said to himself but he kept on rowing chop chop chop he kept on until he came to an island rising white and suddenly from that black black sea and then he heard a voice from inside his head say stop rowing so he stopped the oars trailing easy in the water the boat rocking slightly in the shallows and then the voice said get out of the boat and follow me and with that the voice from inside his head leaped out through his eyes and there it was dancing and laughing in the dunes follow me follow me so he got out of the boat and waded through the shallows and then dripping across the mooncooled sand and into the long grass of the dunes follow me follow me follow me the voice said and he thought it was the voice of God which spoke and so he followed it through the grass through the dunes shaking the dust of sand and shells from his feet he followed the voice along the edge of a marsh the smell of salt still in the air and then up a grassy rise and three oaks at the top but everywhere this grassy rise was covered with crosses even up beneath the oaks white crosses wooden crosses a thousand of them shining beneath the moon a thousand and a thousand more and he wondered how there came to be so many crosses on this particular slope who had put them up who lay beneath them why had the voice led him here and then the voice pealed with laughter a laughter that seemed irreverent in the presence of so many crosses and yet not irreverent and the laughter grew louder and louder and then it was not the laughter of a single voice but of a thousand voices a thousand and a thousand more follow me follow me follow me and in the din of so much laughter he became confused which one should he listen to which one should he follow and so he waded through this patchwork sea of crosses the waves of laughter swelling swelling and then the laughter was gone and he found himself standing before a single cross a little smaller than the rest and there was an old iron shovel leaning up against this cross the handle broken the spade a bit rusted an omen he thought at least as far as omens go and then without another thought *he took up the shovel and began digging deeper and deeper the smell of the black earth heavy with moisture the smell of his sweat pungent just a trace of wine perhaps the smells mingling surging upwards and then he stopped digging and put the shovel down and looked into the now open grave and there he saw a tiny coffin made from pine a tiny coffin suspended untouched by the blackness surrounding it or so it seemed a childs coffin he thought and then suddenly he felt that the child was not dead for the aura of young life emanating from the coffin was too strong so he took up the shovel once again and set it to the edge of the coffin and with three sharp thrusts he pried loose the top and back and looked into the coffin and there he saw a small child wearing a white cloak a child with black hair cut close skin smooth like porcelain the lips with a touch of color the hands finely chiseled delicate a beautiful child he thought and he wanted to wake the child for he was sure it was merely asleep and so he reached out and touched the child on the forehead but the moment he did so the child vanished and now he was the one in the coffin now he was the one in the grave and he wondered how he came to fit in such a small coffin and then he wondered where the child had gone and then as if in answer to this second silent question he heard the sound of a child singing and he looked up from the grave and he saw the child from the coffin looking down at him the child now singing in the cold white light of the moon and he tried to speak to the child but his words were frozen the child still singing now taking hold of the shovel and he tried to move to reach out to the child again but his muscles were frozen as well then the child began shoveling the heavy black earth falling upon his legs his arms his face and all the while he heard the child singing a happy song a song of innocence and then the last of the earth fell upon him and he was surrounded by its heavy warm blackness and then the singing stopped.*

And when the dream had passed, Thaddeus opened his eyes and saw that the older man was gone. For a moment he could think of nothing. The image of the ghost had fled, fading into the grave of Gabriel Dupree, it seemed. He looked to the grave, to the rusted brass horn, then to the fallen cypress and beyond. The night was fading also. He could see patches of light filtering into the swamp. He wondered if it was Gabriel had sent him that dream of the future, and was it really his future he had seen. But he could think of no answer. Once more he looked to the grave. Then he moved down the steep of the bank, past the dead, graying wood of the cypress and the shadows there, then the shadows flickering away in the steamy sunlight, and then he was past that and into the morning blue of the swamp and beyond, a voice now beckoning, now urging, now laughing, the voice from the dream   *follow me follow me follow me*

So he did.

. . . and then one day along come a big big man, maybe seven foot tall, and his arms they was ripple sharp like he was made from granite, and when he done heard that alligator roar, he come looking, and when he seen that alligator up on that log, he smile wide, and then he was saying say he done come to wrestle that alligator and when he was done it wunt go be no alligator world no more, and with that the animals up in them trees they was blinking they eyes in the mossdark look first to the granite-man and then to the alligator and then to the granite-man again, and they was all hoping how he was go tear that alligator head clean off, and then the granite-man he was stepping to the log he was go grab hold of that alligator head, and he did, and then he was squeezing hard as he could, only it wunt doing nothing stop that alligator thrash this way and that, and the granite-man he was squeezing harder and harder, and the alligator he was beating his tail up against the log was going dthunk dthunk dthunk, and the animals in them trees they was holding they breath for watching what goes, and then the alligator he was rolling up in the air and back like so, and the granite-man he was rolling up in the air and back the same, and then they was both in the blackgreen water, only the granite-man he done lost his grip, and that alligator he was diving down for gobble that big big granite-man up, and then he done just that, and then he was out of the water and back on his log, and he was roaring and roaring some more he was saying say just me and my world, he was roaring till the dark settle down, and the animals up in them trees all they was doing they was shaking they heads for disbelief and saying say what was they go do now, only they knowd wunt nothing to do but stay up in them trees till morning, so that's what they did . . .

The Festival

-1-

Me and Ty we been sitting down on the stoop out front about an hour now, we waiting on Mama and Tramsee, and Im is wondering just where they at and what taking so long. Ty he saying say that how womens is, most likely they standing up front that old brass mirror hang on the wall in my mama keeping room and they primping with they hair the way they do it up and color they faces like they is thinking they still eighteen year old, only they aint, and Im is listening to Ty, only I really aint cause I looking up at the sky, and it almost dark and we go miss the parade they aint hurry up. Mama she and Tramsee been talking on that parade the whole while they been dressing theyself, and they voices floating out and down the porch like a shadow come before the rain.

"I aint live a day I be the one miss this parade," Mama say. "Why, we aint have one in eight or nine year now. You wunt here the last time."

"Well, I here now," Tramsee say, and sound like she smacking her lips together.

"It the cost of things what done most of them parades to death."

"Long as there a marching band, I aint mind the cost."

"You aint listening. You know how much it cost they hire out a marching band? Every dollar it worth you paying five."

"I heard a band one time up in Charleston. They was blowing they horns and dancing em up in the air and then down, and then they gone down the street, wunt nothing left but the drums. I'd a paid five dollar then and there, only I aint have to."

"Well, you aint paying for this one neither?"

"I aint mind."

"You know who is?"

"Who?"

"Willie, that who."

"Willie! Who twist off his arm?"

"No need. Mose Heywood he say he let Willie ride up in back of that old rust-out firetruck of his and smile and wave to the folks ifn he pay the bill, and Willie he take him up, only he having a couple sign hang down the sides the same. He say he need the advertising."

"He do, huh. Who he advertising for? He have the only store anyone go to."

"Well, all the same he want the signs, and that how come we a costume parade and a marching band, even it is just a high-school band from over the coast."

"Ever we need a mayor, he the only one go run."

"He running for it now."

And with that the voice-shadow it gone and Mama and Tramsee they laughing, and then come another shadow, and then some more laughing, and it been going on like that so long they aint never go see or either hear that marching band, only time they come to that bridge they be looking on someone else to blame. Ty he tire and thirst he waiting so long and he go inside, and then he back on the stoop with a warm Co-Cola in his hand from out the pantry and he saying say he aint mind none no sir he done heard plenty of marching bands in his time he aint go hurry about this one, only just then Mama and Tramsee they come stepping out the porch, and they both done heard what Ty just said.

Before I knows what what Tramsee she all over Ty saying say what he mean about that crack aint he know this here a regular brass horn marching band come all the way

from over the coast and it aint go cost him a plug nickel to
see it neither, and then what he doing a Co-Cola in his
hand, aint he enough sense to know he making people late
sitting there drinking some and talk some like it a regular
Saturday evening, and then Tramsee she shoving him off the
stoop, and he trying to catch up a last swallow from out
that bottle, only she shove him too hard and that bottle spill
out in the grass. Mama she letting Tramsee do most of the
talking and the shoving, but she angry just the same, and
soon as Ty he up on his feet and walking down the walk,
she shoving me the same.

Mama she wearing a blue shirtwaist, and you can see the
cross of Jesus Christ hang round her neck, and Tramsee in
something white seem to move around her whole body like
air, and they both chewing they lips some about slow,
monkey-butt men, and ifn they done miss that marching
band, well, they aint know just what, but they is reliable for
doing something, and that a fact. We lucky we aint been
walking long before Mama she say hear that girl, and she
talking to Tramsee, and it the marching band blowing brass,
only we aint see it, and then Mama she looking back she
saying say you catch up you want to but you stay out of
trouble, you hear, and now she talking to me, and then
Mama and Tramsee they hard feelings they melt off like hot
butter and they running after that marching band, only it
aint exactly running say it more like a twitching, and they
aint looking back neither. Ty he watching them go, but
mostly he watching Tramsee white behind twitching this
way and that, and then mama and Tramsee they gone, and
that white behind it gone the same, and me and Ty we left
to walking by ourself.

"They sure is crazy," Ty say.

I aint know what to say so I aint say a word, and Ty he
shake his head and laugh to hisself, and then he give me a
narrow look and he start up again.

"You ever been with a woman, boy? I aint mean a little girl, now. I mean a full-growd woman. Tramsee she been a woman since she twelve year old. She what I mean."

"I been thinking on it."

"You is what?   Boy you losing some valuable opportunity you spend all of you time thinking on it. I must of been with damn near forty women I old as you. Some of them girls too. I aint waste none of my time thinking on it." Then Ty he stop talking, like maybe he thinking on it all the same, and then he give me a eye full up with confoundment and exaggeration.

"Boy, you making me thirsty something more than a Coke."

Time we up to the square, the festival lights they already on. The parade it done with, and most the folks they done circle back to the tables. I aint see Mama or either Tramsee for too many folks, but there Willie in front of the barbecue, and he smoke-shouting for everybody step on up and get some, and some they doing just that, and some they knocking about in the street and talking, and some they sucking down oysters or they eating a piece a pecan pie, and there all kind of laughter coming from the center of the square, only what it about I dont know, and Ty he walking past the tables and the laughter and the smell of barbecue smoke, and then he stopping in front of the volunteer firehouse, and I is stopping the same.

Five or six volunteer they sitting back on some rickety wooden chairs they done pull up to the edge of the street, and they got they feet prop up on some old wood crates and they drinking and talking and some they smoking and some they checking out the people go by. Aint much else to the place. The firetruck it back now from the parade been park up alongside the house maybe ten minute, but it still have them two sign hanging down the sides saying "Buy From Willie." It aint really a firetruck, just a old Ford pickup they done load up with a couple three ladder and some axes and a rust-out water tank almost empty in the back and about fifty foot of hose. The firehouse itself it just a one-story white cement block with a couple door been painted black and a couple three window cut out and that it, except there a small black bell hang on the wall out front for ringing ever there is a fire.

"How do you do, Ty?"

"How do you do, Mose," Ty say.

"Where you been?"

"Aint been anywhere different, tell you that."

"You want some of this here bottle," and Mose he pouring some rye straight down his throat.

"You done read my mind."

Then Ty he sitting on one of them rickety old chairs hisself and he drinking and smoking same as all the rest, aint no one talking now, and I sitting on the ground, my feet curl up beneath my knees, and Im is looking up to them volunteers and watching what goes. Aint nothing happen for a while. Then Mose he pull a deck of cards from out his back pocket and he slap it down direct on top of one of them crates.

"Who in," he say. Then the rest of them volunteers they all pulling they chairs up around that crate they saying say they in they go win them some hard cold cash before the night over, and Ty he saying he in the same, only he looking down he asking me how much change I brung, he know I a pocketful of dimes, but he aint say another word neither he just holding out his hand, and before I knows what what my pocket it empty, and Ty he playing poker with seven eight week of my working Mr. Fludds truck farm, and every now and then he throw a dime into the pot.

I is wondering how long I go be there before Ty give me my money back, but Ty he aint even look at me he so busy raking in pot after pot. Some of them volunteers they mumbling say maybe he good with cards but what about women, and then they giving Ty a sour mean look, but Ty he in such a good mood all he do is smile and rake in some more. Then Mose he start passing round another bottle of rye, and Ty he about to faint from waiting he want to feel that rye go down his throat, and then he doing just that, and that bottle going round and round and around, and Im is hoping Ty go shovel me some of my dimes before that bottle go round again, cause there a good chance he go forget about the game it do, but he aint pay me no mind at all.

Aint long before Ty he talking while he playing, he talking back to when he was in the United States Marines up at Montford Point, and them volunteers they just nodding they heads and letting him talk on and on. Ty he saying say the first day he come to boot camp, the sergeant, his name was Whitlow, he come on up to Ty and ask him did he like full grown women or little girls or maybe both, and Ty he was grinning with that, his teeth they was press down around his tongue, and he was saying say where was they at and how many and he like em both kinds every inch they head to they feet only he aint never make it all the way to they feet, and then Ty he was laughing with that, only Sergeant Whitlow he didnt see the joke, he start barking up in Ty face about how there wunt no women nearby, no little girls neither, how there wunt go be no one talk about the female half for the next eight week maybe more, wunt no one even think about them neither less he give out permission, and was about then Ty he start getting weak in the knees, and he was praying to the good Lord say dont let it be true Lord not eight week Lord knows he aint never been without a woman that long not since the day he was born, only the praying it didnt do no good.

The next seven week Ty and the rest of them boys they was marching all over the sandy flats and into the pine woods and up and down hills, and then they was wading through all kind of creeks and ponds, and then more woods or maybe a bog, and tripping over vines and pushing they way through briers and blood on they hands, and it was bad enough living in a tent city in them ten-man tents, never mind the flies biting you up and down, or maybe you walking in a black black creek and you falling into a trout hole you aint know how to swim somebody has to pull you out, and the next thing you know you sitting up under some birch pine and you shivering from cold and eating supper out a K-ration tin, and then the tin it empty and you back at it.

Seem like all they was ever go do in the marines was march, even it raining, and when it wunt raining the sun it was laying on hot and thick like barbecue smoke, and the boys was all dragging, and then dragging some more, and they arms they was dropping to they sides, and then Sergeant Whitlow he was telling them all say they aint raise they arms keep them rifle butts over they monkey-butt heads they go be marching the whole night through, and then those arms they was coming up, look like everybody want to surrender, but they didnt know to who. It wunt at all like Ty done bargain for, the rest neither, but they all kept to it, only there wunt a day gone by Ty he wunt thinking about a woman, and he say the rest of them leather -heads they must of been thinking on women the same the way they was talking into they bedrolls every night. Wunt hardly no one getting no sleep at all.

Well by and by them boys they was fed up to here, it didnt matter there was only three day left of them sorry eight week, and there they was sitting on they cots or stretch out and they was all of them tired from marching sixteen hour. Some was saying how they wouldnt mind it none if them yellow Japs come all the way to North Carolina, if they wouldnt make em do all this marching, the

Germans neither, they got there first. Some was saying there wunt no such thing as the Japs or the Germans, that was something made up to keep them out in the field, no, the only enemy they had to worry about was the United States Marines.

Then a couple was saying say it was Sergeant Whitlow to blame, he didnt have no idea what he was doing, hell he was a private hisself ten week before, then a couple more they was saying hell it could a been worse, but the first two didnt think so, and then just like that the four of them was going at it on the ground. Then this big brown boy call Icebox Pete he break it up, and them four was back on they cots, and then Icebox he was saying say he just hope he get a hold of the sergeant just one time take his head clean off, and if he didnt swallow it up in one bite it sure as hell wouldnt take more than two.

Ty he wunt so full of outright pugnation like Icebox, but all the same he was tire of the marching and thinking he go on over the fence that very night maybe head on down to Charleston, just for the weekend, he knowd a couple of pretty girl there, only he aint seen them in a while. He aint never had the chance. Soon as he think that Sergeant Whitlow come into the tent, and this time it a surprise inspection and the sergeant he was looking at a couple footlocker, only they didnt measure up so he turn them over dump everything out he was saying say maybe they do a better job they start from scratch, and then he was walking up and down some more and smacking the palm of his hand with a swagger stick and all the while his tongue was running up around his mouth like he a mad dog licking foam, and then he was telling them boys say they wunt never go measure up, none of them they keep on disregarding regulations, no, he was go teach them once and for all, they had fifteen minute, then they better be outside with full-packs and rifles, they was going on a little march, maybe take part in some maneuvers, the whole damn camp was turning out.

Whitlow he march them boys down across some river and into the black of some river marsh, and they must of been out in that black black muck the better part of the night, and they hadnt seen or either heard of nothing but some gray hoot-owls talking death, and the sloshing of they feet, and maybe some moaning, and some they done figure they was marching straight into South Carolina, maybe they was heading for Charleston anyway, and some, the ones worry about them owls, they was for turning back right then, and some they just figure to find a good place to stop, have something to eat or just lie down, and then they come up from the water to a sandy, grassy flat stretch cover up with mostly pine, and them boys why they stop right there. Whitlow he come on back for a look see what what, look like he want to kick everybody head in too, only he knew he was too small, so he was telling them all he say you all better pick up you rifles and you packs and get a move on you hear aint no time to wait any of you monkey-butt boys thinking the other way I go bounce you out of this outfit so fast you think you back in the jungle. Whitlow he was shouting loud as he was able, only them boys they wunt none of them listening, they was lean theyself back against them pines and some they was falling asleep, and Whitlow he was about to pull a gun, only just then Icebox Pete he was standing up look down at the little man.

"Aint none of them boys gonna foot it no more till they had some rest. They dead like dogs." And then Icebox Pete he done ruffle up his shoulders so he was big as he could be, which was more than enough empty out Whitlow courage, and then he was saying, "You aint like it none, you going through me."

Whitlow he was looking up to Icebox Pete, only he wunt smiling with what Pete done said, but he wunt saying nothing neither cause he didnt relish the idea of going through that big brown boy, so he stood there underneath them pines and he was sputtering to hisself the while, and then Icebox he decide he done spend enough time in the woods he want a real bed under his back, even it only a cot in a tent, and with that he say come on, and then him and the boys they was heading back. Whitlow he wunt so much a fool as he a little man, but all the same he was following those boys through them pines, and all the while he was planning what to do about Icebox Pete and the rest, and telling them so too, how maybe they'd be breaking up rock the rest of they natural lives, but only if they was lucky, but every now and then he was telling them say he didnt mean what he said he forget the whole thing they just turn theyselves around and follow him some more, only wunt none of them listening, and Whitlow he was about to pull his gun again, maybe use it on hisself, only just then the sky was rip open with light and smoke, and a couple three shell come crashing down through the trees.

Icebox he was the first to hit the ground, and the rest of them boys they done the same, only then the air it was raining with hundreds of them shells, look like the sky was bleeding to death, and then there was some more shells and some more blood, and with that them boys they was running like hogs every which way look around for someplace to hide, wunt no one particular, and after a while wunt nothing to see but smoke. Ty he was the only one wunt cover up, and he was wiping the smoke from his eyes and wondering what he was go do, and then he done seen a oak tree been rip up from the roots and it look like a good enough place crawl to and hide, only was just then a shell burst over his head, and that was that, cause the next thing happen he was waking up in a hospital room.

Ty he thought he was in heaven, cause everywhere he look he seen white, and he wouldnt of been surprise to see

Peter hisself coming through the door and he was thinking what to say what all done happen how he wunt look as bad as all that, maybe Peter just hold him up to the light see his good side, but the next thing he seen wunt no angel at all, was a crop-hair nurse standing up by his bed with a basin in one hand and two towel in the other. She was waiting on Ty to open his mouth, only Ty he couldnt get a word out he looking at that nurse, and she seen he was having trouble so she was telling him say he must of had one sweet angel watch over him cause by rights he should of been dead, and Ty he was asking the nurse what she was talking about, only she didnt answer except to say how she wunt the doctor she wunt go talk about what happen it a too too delicate matter he just have to wait, and with that she done set the basin on the bed table and then she took up a towel and full it up with soapy water, and then she was washing Ty all over.

Ty he was a bit confuse and tire, but he sure didnt mind what that crop-hair nurse was doing, and by and by he was feeling pretty good. He didnt remember the last time a woman been touch him like that, it didnt matter how old she was, but all the same it seem to Ty there was something missing, and with that he was sitting up on his elbows and smiling at the nurse try and catch her eye, but she wunt interested, and even she was laughing some to herself, and then Ty seen why. He could see where she was washing, and there wunt nothing there except her hands and the towel and the soap and his own two skinny leg. There wunt even a char-black stub grab hold of for luck, and when Ty seen that, well he wunt sitting up no more. He let his head fall straight back to the pillow, and then a black-ice look come full up his eyes.

The nurses at that hospital they was as nice as they could be, and bringing him soups and sometimes a piece of peach pie, and every morning they'd be washing him down but good, and sometimes they'd just come for relax and some talk, but by and by, Ty he was done with the hospital and them free-talking nurses, and then he was standing up along side the rest of his squad in a oak-panel room. They was all line up, and Ty he figure they was all about to get theyself a court martial, running out like they did with Icebox Pete, and he was waiting on Sergeant Whitlow come in and then they go hear the worst for sure, only it was this square-jaw captain instead, and he was talking how sad he was they walk into them shells, there wunt suppose to be no artillery for two or three more hour, someone got the times mixed up, but they done showed they was first rate the way they handled theyself been wounded like that, he was proud of them all, like they was his own, and Ty he was looking around some more for Whitlow and hoping he didnt show up just yet, cause he knowd the sergeant have something more to say, but then the captain he was talking how sad he was about Sergeant Whitlow, it was a damn dirty shame he been kill dead by them shells, and the only one too, he'd have been proud like the captain, wunt too many sergeants have a whole squad getting they purple hearts, didnt matter it wunt exactly the enemy, the captain he'd seen to that, and then he was talking how he was go find out who give the order on that artillery, even it the last thing he ever do, cause men like the good Sergeant Whitlow they was hard to come by. Then the captain was done with his talk and pinning on medals, and then he give them boys a white-glove salute, and then they was all out the door.

Ty he done talking now, and the volunteers they all nodding they heads like they done got purple hearts pin to they shirts the same, and then Mose he say for everyone to ante up a dime, and with that Ty he looking down at his pile of change, only there aint no pile, cause all the while Ty been talking he been losing, and then he looking down at me again and he asking me say you any more change, and I say I dont, and then Mose he say again for everyone to ante up a dime. Ty he give Mose a hard look with that, and look like Mose he turning blue too, only he dont say another word, and then Ty he the one look discomfort and disbelief in that blueface silence, dont know what he go do, and then he reach into his pocket and pull out his purple heart and he lay it on the crate. Well right off some of them volunteers they asking Ty what he do that for, that his only medal, whyunt he take it up, forget about this here poker game and sleep it off, he only lost a pocketful of dimes and they wunt even his to begin with, but Ty he full of determination now so much so he almost shake, and then that blueface Mose he asking what it worth he always wanted one hisself but he never got the chance they bounced him out of boot camp the very first week, and Ty he nod his head and then he saying say it worth more than the crown jewels of the state of South Carolina. Aint no one know what he mean by that so aint no one say a word, and then that blueface Mose he nod his head and deal up the cards, there aint no more betting this time on account of Ty, and then everybody spreading they cards out face up on the crate have a look see whats what, only Ty he more hesitate and expectation than the rest, and just like that Mose he break into a blueface smile and then he raking in the pot, and the last thing he do he fix that medal to his shirt.

Poor old Ty. He just staring at them cards, he aint move or either say a word, and when Mose see that he reach over give Ty a bottle all to hisself, even it almost half full, and with that Ty he up from that rickety old chair, he a little rickety hisself, and he look around a moment like he see or either hear someone he know come across the square, only aint no one there, and then he sidle up to where that old Ford firetruck it hunker down and he climbing in with all them ladders and axes and that fifty foot hose, and then he tip his head back and start pouring that sweet rye liquor down his sorry sorry throat.

   The next thing that happen Im is walking from the firehouse to the square wish on something to eat, and I know I aint never go see my dimes again so I just put it out of my mind, and I just up to the barbecue grill when this voice it come and full up my ears with a rustle feel like smoke. It Jonas Lee, and he standing up under a string of white light he swaying back and forth and back and forth, cause he up on some crutches, and he laughing all the while like he go beat the tar out the devil his hide on account of he has hisself another idea.
   I know the best thing to do is keep on walking cause Jonas he trouble and Mama she tell me say keep away from trouble before she done run off after that marching band, but Mama she aint here, and Jonas he is, and before I thinking what what we both walking down along the square to Front Street, and then we standing up front of Willies. I knows what Jonas he wanting now, cause we been here before, he wanting to get inside. Willies it a whitewash dry-goods turn liquor store out front, and a two-story weather-beat warehouse been add on out back, only aint nothing up on the second floor but some old newspaper, some empty cans, and some empty bottle Willie been collect the last ten year. Me and Jonas we been try to get inside a couple three time, but Willie he always come up behind. Jonas he saying this here maybe our best chance cause Willie he eating barbecue, and before he say another word we both around back in the alley have a look. There a small flatbed wagon shove up against a double black door and a couple black-out window up the second floor, and Jonas he saying say all we do we pull that wagon up under there, and he pointing to one of them window, and then we climb up and in, and

Jonas he so impress with hisself he almost fall over his crutches. I has to say he a pretty good plan, but Im is wishing it was more better cause I knows Jonas he aint go be pulling or climbing cause he on them crutches, and besides, he too small to reach up to them windows even he standing on two three wagon piggyback.

Aint nothing come easy. I has my hands wrap around the hitch of that wagon, and I pulling and pulling, only the wagon it aint move to breathe, and Jonas he saying say what the matter what I doing now why dont I quit my fooling and do like he say, and I like to knock Jonas his mouth shut right there, only I too busy pulling, and what keeping it I aint know cause the wagon it empty but feel like a team of mule dug in at the other end, maybe worse, maybe it the devil hisself dug in, and Im is thinking say maybe I better give up while I can cause aint nobody win against the devil, and that what I about to do, only just then the wagon it pull loose with a lurch, and I is landing in the alleydirt. Jonas he laughing now and over to the wagon he bend on down, and then he holding up a piece of chain link iron and he saying say this here what you been pull against it chain up to the side only it broke now, and then he laughing some more, and I feels like maybe I should knock him around double, only I dont. Then I pulling that wagon to one of them black-out windows and Jonas he pointing the one he want, and then Im is climbing up. Willie he done put in a brand new pane of glass, but he left it up, so I grab a hold of the sill and then I poking my head inside, and Jonas all he can do he saying say what you see anybody there what it is, but aint nothing to see cause it too dark. Then Jonas he saying he gone go around front and wait on me to open the door, and with that he hobble off, and I hears the scratch scratch scratch of his crutch on the gravel as he go, and then I aint hear it no more, and then I climbs on in.

It too dark to see much of anything, so I hugging close to the wall with every step. Im is walking through some newspaper scatter on the floor, and I kick a couple three empty can smell like coffee grounds, and then Im is coming to a gray box shadow, which turn out it the stairs, and the next thing I sees is Jonas Lee and he at the front door and grinning like some poor Joe strutting around the marsh found hisself something to eat, and he saying say come on come on, so I lets him in, and then we looking up at the shelves see what what. It aint hard to see now cause the light from the festival it pouring through the plate glass windows out front like soft yellow smoke. There everything from glycerol cream to red bricks to beans to hand soap and potatoes, but we aint after none of that, and then Jonas Lee he stop he pointing to some shelves in the back, and there twenty maybe twenty-five carton of fireworks line up in a row.

Jonas he saying say them fireworks they time has come, and with that then Im is grabbing hold of them cartons and stack em up by the door, and Jonas he saying hurry on up hurry on up aint no telling about Willie he might be footing it over maybe get hisself something to drink, and I trying not to listen to Jonas Lee cause sometime he a aggravating way about him, but all the same Im is thinking how what we doing go cost something, and what I go do if Willie come through that door, and I almost drop a couple carton with that only I dont, and then them cartons they all stack up by the door. The next thing Jonas Lee saying say where that flatbed we better move along while we can, only by we he mean just me on account of his leg, so I around to the back go pull that wagon to the front, and then I loading up. It one thing break into the back of a store come night maybe see Willie ghost hover up in the dark, it another load up with twenty twenty-five carton been stole up under the festival eye, and look like Jonas he thinking the same thing cause he keeping a lookout for Willie or either anyone else come along from the square. Every now and then he waving his crutch in the air, which mean stop, so I does, and when he satisfy aint nobody seen us he wave for me to start up again, which I does that too, and then the cartons they all up on the wagon, and Jonas Lee he hop up into the front and then he sitting, his broken leg prop up against the hitch, and his crutches laying up by his side.

Jonas Lee he say the best place to shoot off them fireworks is on the other side of the square by them live oaks lean out over the Governors Wall, so thats where we heading. Then he say what he would and wouldnt give see Willie face time we fire his rockets, and then he laughing some, and then he saying say it a swampblack sky we about to full up with some jolly-roger smoke outdo even Willie his barbecue, and then he laughing some more, and the more and more Jonas he talk to hisself, the more better he impress hisself the same. We a long way to go, but by and by we come to the other side of the wall, and that wagon it pull up under a big old live oak with moss hang down. I is already tired. It have the feeling like my arms still rolling with that wagon, and I is thinking maybe I should stretch out and sleep, but Jonas Lee he have other ideas. He hobbling through the grass now and he saying say what you doing now aint go be no show we dont set it up, and with that I is lining up them rockets, and it don't take too long, but long enough, and then Jonas he say it sure go be something, and then he shove a couple box of matches into my hands and slip behind one of them oaks and aint nothing but his two eyes blinking out through the moss, and Im is looking at Jonas a moment, and it come to me again what we doing go cost something, but I shake it off. Then Im is looking to the flatbed wagon and the shadow of the wall and them fireworks line up and that box of matches, and I aint know if I angry or either scare, but something inside of me about to bust out, and with that then Im is striking them matches, maybe one for every five or six rocket, and them rocket tail tips they glowing red and hissing and spitting, sound like snakes, only I aint bother none cause I moving down the line, and then I done with them matches and I double up behind the wall go watch a couple three hundred snake hissing and twisting they way through a swampblack sky.

I aint never seen nothing like it.   Like God hisself laughing at the world. Some of the rockets they aint go up high enough and they clipping folks up one side and down the other, and some they angle too high and they is heading for the low side of the square down along the Front Street stores, and there all kinds of dogs yapping they heads, and some of the folks they yapping they heads the same, and some look like they bleeding with the light from them rockets and then down on they knees and they praying the Lord go take them up cause seem like maybe it judgement day at last, and the ones from that marching band they aint marching now they all running to the dock, and aint but a couple three hang on to they instruments cause there all kind of horns and drums and pipes and even a brass tuba been left in the grass, they gone, but most of the peoples they running back and forth across the square, and back and forth again, and tripping over horns and such and cursing, they all in a panic like pigs, aint nobody have no idea what they doing or either where they is, and then Im is thinking say there aint no reason be standing by a couple empty box say fireworks on the side, and Jonas Lee he must of come to the same conclude cause he already gone.

The smoke it just starting to lift, and I see a shadow-crowd of people gather down along Front Street, and then I hear a couple shadow-voice come floating through the air, and they talking hush and disbelief.

"It a damn shame it go up like this."

"Poor ol Willie. He wunt but eating his barbecue twenty minute ago, now look what happening."

"Who you think done it?"

"Aint no one burn Willie down on purpose."

"Then how it happen?"

"It just happen. Thats all. It the hand of God."

"What God want to burn Willie down for?"

"He have something in mind."

Then Im is pushing my way up to the front of the crowd see what what, and everybody looking at Willies, which it on fire now, and they all watching the fire grow higher, higher, and then a couple more voice they mumbling by my ear.

"It aint them fireworks thats the cause of all this infernal combustion."

"It sure aint."

"It the fellow set them off."

"We oughta be out there right now looking see who done it. He cant be too far."

"He aint have no sense, tell you that much. Didnt he know the wind catch that fire, spread it around some of them stores, they all be melting like butter."

"You got that right."

"Someone oughta be looking."

"Oughta be is right. But what you go do?"

"Aint that the truth."

I aint hardly move the while they talking, I aint want to give myself away, and then they done and we all watching Willie his warehouse burn. Seem like the fire done eat out the black of that swampblack sky with a couple three hundred red and yellow tongue licking up and out, but aint nobody move cause they watching the same as me till the bell from the firehouse it clang clang clang clang, and with that then the peoples they move a couple three step back and that old Ford pickup come rolling by, and then it stop, and it still has them two sign hanging down say "Buy From Willies."

Mose Heywood he the first volunteer off the truck, he still wearing that medal, and he telling folks say stand back stand back, and then the rest of them volunteers they jumping off the same, and some they out with they ladders and they axes, though what good ladders and axes go do aint no one know cause that fire it burning so hot aint nothing to see pretty soon but ash, and Mose he trying to hook up the hose to the water pump, only every time he pull on that hose it pulling him back the same. What it is there a body curl up in the back of that Ford, and that body it Ty, and he tangle up in that fifty foot hose, he hugging a empty bottle too, and look like he aint about to wake up even he been on fire hisself. Every time Mose he give a pull, he rolling Ty forward, and then Ty his dead weight pull his ownself back, so Mose he aint getting nowhere. All the same it take him five or six pull make him convince, and then he looking in back and see Ty tangle up, and then he call the rest of them volunteers and then they all tugging and tugging at poor old Ty, seem like nothing go make him budge, and then all of a sudden, Ty he come flying through the air, it lucky a couple of them volunteer they catch him, and that fifty foot hose come rolling off the truck.

Them volunteers they done lay Ty down in the dust of the square with that and then they working get a hold of that hose, and some from that shadow-crowd they looking at Ty and shaking they heads with disengagement and they saying say what he doing the back of that truck he cover up with so much liquor he reliable catch on fire hisself well that what come of folk like him yes sir he and that Tramsee girl they should of been a law against folk like that coming here dirty up our town, and look like a couple three they about to kick Ty in the head, only is just then Willie his whole place seem to heave up a shudder like it go explode, and then it does, and then everybody down on they knees they cover up they heads cause here come a flock of bust up wood and bottle glass and window glass and some broken plates, and even some wicker baskets, and all of that come sweeping over the street and then down, and then maybe five six hundred potato sweep down the same, only it aint sweep exactly cause them potatoes aint small, and they coming pretty hard, and knock some people out too, and then someone saying say the fire must of got to all that liquor aint nothing feed a fire like whiskey and rye, and some they looking to the fire with that, like they wouldnt mind being fed some whiskey and rye they ownself, but aint nobody move from they knees, not even them volunteers.

The next thing happen Mose Heywood he standing in front of that old Ford pickup and he calling for help, and then some of them volunteers they climbing up on top pump out some water, and some they holding on to that fifty foot hose, and Mose he pointing the way, only nothing come out but a snake-squirt of water, which the fire it just swallow up, and they give a couple three more squirt, only each time they do the fire open it mouth and swallow some more.

Everybody they back to they feet now, aint nothing to do but watch Willie warehouse burn to the ground, and some they saying it a awful thing, they glad they aint him, but it sure do look pretty, dont it, and some they saying say it a shame some of them other buildings dont catch, aint nothing in em, and they nothing but eyesores anyhow, and then all of a sudden aint no one talking, except maybe to theyself, and they taking a couple step back, some one way, some the other, and from out the shadow of they faces come Willie hisself, and he stop in back of them volunteers, they still feeding they snake-water to that fire, and he breathing heavy, and look like his eyes go fall out of his head.

Willie he furious and uncontrol at first, he looking up at the fire and the smoke, and pressing his hands up to his rumple-up bald head like he trying to squeeze a orange, but by and by he feel the folks they eyes prick up against his back, and he know he have a crowd waiting on him to talk the talk, and with that then he climbing into the back of that old Ford pickup he face up the crowd. Then he open his mouth and the words they come rolling out, they black like the smoke billow up from his warehouse, and Willie he saying say the devil he the one done all of this here the work of the devil it always been mark by fire ever since the Jews they done left the Pharaoh look at this here fire look it you aint never seen a fire so bright as that so red it red like blood you aint never seen the sky bleed like this no you aint but it bleeding now and that the sign of the devil sure as you and me standing here only what we go do about it the devil he go swallow up this whole island with fire we let him so what we go do we aint do nothing.

Everybody know what come next cause Willie he aint never talk about the devil he dont get around to old man Thaddeus, and when he do it hard not to believe he talking truth the way he get everybody work up. He talking anger and revenge now, and everybody listening they all full up with angry and revengement, even they aint know they feel it. Then Willie he open his mouth again nail them folks eyes and ears back to the bone, and with every word come rolling out of his mouth he bigger, bigger, bigger, and pretty soon he big as the fire itself, and with that I aint sure maybe I dead or either dream cause   *Willie his bald rumple head it curl up under the black-burn thatch of the sky, and his words they sounding like the voice of God sit in judgement, and Willie his eyes they burning brighter, brighter with the snake-dance flick of that fire, and everywhere he look folks they all falling dead to the ground, they all burn up aint nothing left but a pile of ash and some bone, and Willie he saying say we* done burn the devil burn him right out of them folks, and I aint move to breathe cause I waiting he turn his snake-dance eyes on me and thinking say what it feel like be burn to ash and bone, only Willie he aint look my way cause he happy enough for burning the rest of them gather-up folk, and some they done try to run, they fighting the urge of them fire -happy words, but they burn up all the same, and then they all burn except me, and Willie he open up a cat-shriek mouth and laugh with that, and he laughing say he done burn the devil from out of his tree aint no where the old man devil he climb to now, only then Willie he aint laughing no more, look like he cover up with fire, and then all I see is a shadow use to been Willie and a piece of that fire it break off and I sees it the devil, and then the devil and Willie they both have at it, they wrestling harder, harder, harder, and Willie he cat-shriek some more he the devil in his hands now and he aint about to let go, and then the devil he throwing Willie to the black wood-ash what left of the warehouse floor, and then old Willie he back on his feet and it his turn throw the devil, and the fire burning brighter and brighter, and Willie and the devil they rolling this way and that through the flames and back to they feet only aint no one turn the advantage yet, and then it look like the devil he a grip around Willie neck but then Willie he has the same grip,

and then Willie and the devil they gone, like they been swallow up, and all what left is a devil-eating fire burn my eyes, and maybe I know better, and maybe I dont, but all the same Im is stretching myself up to that fire to look at it, to know it, talk it, breathe it, taste it, only just then a voice it grab me from behind, and then the fire it gone the same.

"Say, boy. You sure as hell aint gonna find what you looking for in there."

And with that it like I been wake from the dead, and I looking up, and there the pasty white face of old man Thaddeus hisself, only aint no expression to his eyes, and he done caught me up around my collar with two hand and he dragging me back from the smoking black wood and the glass and the brick, and then we back to the grass edge of the square like we waiting on something to happen.

"This a better place," he say. "You see what you want from here, and then we moving on."

Most the peoples they done give up watching now and they walking back across the square in twos and threes look like clouds of smoke drifting up through the haze of them festival lights, and then they gone, but some they still shaking they heads they saying they glad they aint Willie it a god damn shame a fire swallow up everything a man own what God he have in mind let something like that happen must of had something in mind but wunt it a good show all the same it sure was that, and then they looking around maybe grab some half-cook potatoes before they head off, and then there the volunteers they all cover up with black wood-ash hard to see who who, but they too sleep-hungry mind about that and packing up that Ford with they ladders and they axes and they fifty foot tangle hose, and the last thing they lifting into the back is Ty hisself, look like nothing go wake him up a fire dont, and they cover him up with one of those signs say "Buy From Willies," and then they all rolling on back to the firehouse.

The only thing left still burning is Willie, only he walking hush and intent through the hot hot ash and the black wood chips and the soft smell of burn whiskey linger on, and all the while he mumbling to hisself about he aint done yet take more than a little fire to finish him off thats what it was a little fire no he the one go finish off that old man and it dont matter he the devil not one little bit, and then Willie he see me and the old man standing back in the grass, aint nobody move or either say a word we watching each other a while, and then Willie he squatting down into the thick of the wood and whiskey ash, he watching the smoke float straight up into the sky, and over and over and over he saying the devil, the devil, the devil.

-2-

The devil he come for eat my bones,
See he coming up a railroad track.
Been so long I coming home,
Slept last night in a brakemans shack.

Lay my head in a roaring fire,
I aint know I been so tire.
Devil he fixing some barbecue,
Aint nothing left for me to do.

Watch my bones they burn and crack
Devil he eating in a brakemans shack.
Watch the devil he wiping his maw.
Watch me stick in that old mans craw.

The next thing I knows the old man he dragging me from the square, and he moving a pretty good clip so I doing all I can to keep from dragging down in the warm, moist street-dirt behind him, and pretty soon we done left the streets of that fire-stain town behind. The old man dont say what he want, and Im is thinking say maybe he go finish what start with them crabs, and I aint want to bother about that even he aint the devil, but look like I aint got a choice. We coming to the dock now, and then we up to the edge we looking out on the black black water of the channel and watching the grass sway back and forth, back and forth with the wind, and then the old man he pointing down to a old rowboat tie up in the water.

"Get in there, boy," he say.

I aint know what else to do so I climbing down the ladder and into the boat, and the old man he doing the same, and then he pick up the oars and we moving through the water. A couple time Im is looking down at the heavy black water and thinking maybe I go dive in swim for the bank, but I aint ever learn me to swim, so I dont even try, and pretty soon it too late even think about learning to swim cause we moving through the deep wood now, past the black shadows of water-root sycamores, and oaks, and pine, brushing past moss hang down from they branches, and every now and then some hoot-owls come rustle-wing through the air and crying they death-talk.

The old man he talking to me the while he rowing.

"You sure a quiet boy. What's the matter? You afraid of something?"

The old man it like he read my mind, but I aint let on. "No, sir. No, I aint afraid of nothing."

"Thats good, boy. This here wood cant hurt you less'n you afraid."

Then the old man he quiet up, look like he trying to think of something more to say, and while he thinking Im is looking to the black of the wood and worry how the wood maybe go hurt me, and then I sees a bluegray steam rising up from the water for drift on through the trees, only look like ghosts been talk about by them hoot-owls, and every time a owl he open his mouth, them ghosts they scatter back to the black of the oaks and sycamores and cypress and pine wait for them owls fly away, and then the ghosts they drifting some more. It almost more than a body can stand the owls and the ghosts and the black of the wood, and I just about to dive into the water anyway, I dont care what happen, when the old man he talking some more, and this time he talking how he know about the wood, which it help keep me in the boat.

The old man he use to been hunting alligator a couple night a week time he first come to the island, and every time he done it he been camp out of this shack in the middle of the backwater wood, only he aint been maybe thirty year on account of Long Jim. It happen like this. Thaddeus he done hooked up with five maybe six boys been with him regular hunting alligators and they done left town about four o'clock in the afternoon. They was taking the short way up across the island, save time, was walking through the long grass with they gear strap tight across they backs and then skirting up through a couple grave-hump hill, and all they all talking about was how many alligators they was go get maybe sell they skins up Charleston maybe go all the way to Market Street, and then they was coming through the trees heading down to the black of the backwater channel, nothing to lead the way but the sun dance through the leaves of oak and redbay and maybe some pine, there was sun-print all over the ground, and they was climbing over stumps and down past some water oak and some more pine, and was a couple still talking, but the rest was chewing on they words, and then they was down to the shack.

Wunt much to see. The shack it leaning back on the flat of the bank, had some holes look up from the roof and some cracks running to the moss-leaf ground, and it wunt but one room with a old pine table and no chairs and a small red lantern missing its glass, but the boys didnt mind none, and Thaddeus he didnt mind neither, and so they was dragging they gear inside and lay it out on the floor. Was then this long legged boy call Long Jim he put some fire in the belly of that lantern and he start talking about who the noosemens was go be and who the gig and someone be carrying the knives and a couple of lantern, and Long Jim was saying say how he was go be walking the lookout, and then maybe he the gig too, and them boys they was all anticipate for jump the devil and pressing they teeth together like they was all grinning alligators theyself, and Thaddeus he was grinning the same, and then they was all out into the heavy wet green of the wood.

They was following close to the water, some was in, and every step they was moving slow even it early yet, but all the same they was looking for alligators rest in the grass or maybe up under the hammock or maybe slide through the green black muck, and they was keeping they feet ready to run they have to, only wunt nothing to see or either hear but blueflies and gnats skimming the surface, at least at first, and then Long Jim he done give a owl-whistle what meant there a alligator up ahead. Well them boys they done freezed up with that for looking to the blackgreen of the trees up ahead of Long Jim, and Thaddeus he the same, like they was all a flock of blue herons aint know enough to fly off or not, and then there was all kind of shouting and hollering and raking at the water with hands, and then them boys was knee-stepping up along the bank they want to have a hand in the kill, and Long Jim his eyes was iron and he was telling his noosemens to keep they nooses pull tight cause that alligator he was halfway down the bank a twisting and turning try to get to his hole, watch out now he maybe knock someone in the water on the way, but he wunt fast enough for them boys even he was swinging his head around try and take a bite out of someone, no sir, no matter what he try Long Jim noosemens they was holding on tight, and wunt long before that alligator he was out of breath, wunt hardly even give his tail a twitch, and with that Long Jim he took up the gig and come down, and then he done smile cause he seen he done split that alligator head in two on the first strike.

That was all she wrote for that there alligator, and them boys they done whoop it up and was waving they arms in the air like they hadnt been dance since the juba days, and some they was laughing about how small that alligator was, wunt more than twelve foot long, only didnt it put up a fight like they was fighting the devil hisself, and then they was spreading out in the grass to catch they breath. Long Jim he was resting the same up against this big black sycamore and scratching up at his head, like maybe he was thinking some more how he come down a top of that alligator head, he impress hisself with that, and then Thaddeus he was out with his skinning knife go cut that alligator down to the bone, and then a couple more they was cutting the same, and then they all done pack up the meat. With that then Long Jim he was up and saying say it time they move they feet go find theyself some more they full up they sacks, and then they was all slogging they way through the black backwater like they was before, only this time they wunt moving so slow cause they eyes was all fixed with the blood of that first alligator.

Now by this time the sun had gone down and the backwater it was turning blacker with every step, and the trees they was like one black shadow been stretch out all the way to the edge of the bank, so the boys they fire up they lanterns and was swinging em back and forth, back and forth, but most of the light been swallow up by the waiting dark. Even the air it was heavy with some blood-wet predictiment, like the whole world waiting take a breath. And every step them boys was taking they was come on some alligator hiding in a hole or lay out in the shallow, only it all in they homeless heads, and then all of a sudden there come a bellowing from somewheres out of the dark, only wunt no one sure just exactly where, it sound like it was everywhere, and them boys they was straining they eyes they was looking to the trees and the moss and the water and the hammock, they was straining so hard the blood in they eyes come pouring out, and the next thing what happen this big blackblue alligator come a rumbling through the blackblue shadow of the trees, must of been thirty foot long too, and the branches they was breaking off been kick up in the air.

That alligator his eyes was redmeat hungry, and his mouth was hungry the same, and the closest one to him was Long Jim, and before anyone know'd what what, the both of them they was twisting and turning up under the brush and Long Jim he was hollering and some of them boys they was hollering back, and then three or four boys they done pull out some guns with that, only where them guns come from didnt nobody know cause they hadnt brought any with them, and Thaddeus he had a rifle in his hand hisself even he didnt own one his whole life, but all the same they had them guns in they hands, only wunt nobody know just when to shoot cause didnt nobody have a clear shot, and then Long Jim he was screaming for his knife, only there wunt no way he could get it cause it was strap down to his leg, and then they was both rolling down the sides of the bank, him and that blackblue alligator, all the way down to the black, black water cause that alligator he was dragging Long Jim to a hole. Didnt nobody wait no more after that they was all running for Long Jim and that blackblue alligator, and a couple they drop they guns for knives and was waving them in the air so Long Jim could see, they was saying say hold on Long Jim hold on, and Long Jim he was trying to grab at roots, only look like it wunt no use, and then them boys they done jump to the back of that alligator, and the two they was hacking at its backside with they knives, left them bury up to the hilt in that blackblue hide, and the others they done empty out they guns, one upside that blackblue belly, the other upside the head, but that alligator he wunt about to let go of Long Jim even there a hundred knife stuck out of his hide, and he wunt bother by the guns neither except to make him chew some harder, and there was all kind of steam rising up from his mouth and he was lashing back with his tail knock one of them boys to the ground, but the rest they was hacking at that blackblue hide some more, and empty out a couple three more guns into that alligator head, and then Thaddeus he step up with that babynew rifle of his stretch out like a arm, and he empty it out the same, and then wunt nothing heard but a click click click they was all squeezing they triggers dry, and with that the clock it done stop, and that blackblue alligator he was laying down the side of the bank, just laying, half-in, half-out of the bloodblack water, and was twenty or twenty-five knife bury deep in his hide, and maybe eighty ninety bullet been shot through his head and his belly, and wunt much left even butcher it up for meat, but wunt nobody thinking on that just yet cause that alligator mouth it was still wrap around Long Jim leg couldnt even see it, and when them boys they done pry that mouth open and slide Long Jim up, they done seen wunt much left of his leg neither.

Long Jim he didnt do nothing but moan, and every now and then he roll his head have a look at what left of his leg and then moan some more. A couple three they ease that leg up and wrap it with a croaker sack been cut into strips, and wunt easy cause some of the parts they kept sliding to the ground, and the rest of them boys they was butcher up all they could of that alligator meat, which was more than it looked at first on account of a thirty foot alligator it a lot of meat, aint no sense let it go to waste, and then they was all done with the wrapping and cutting and they pack up the gear and the meat and Long Jim and his leg, and they was heading back to the shack. The whole bunch was worry theyself with talk, and some was saying they aint never seen a alligator big as that it wunt no alligator must of been the devil hisself, and then they was praying some on account they wunt even close being inside maybe the devil he come back finish them off, and then a couple of lanterns swing through that black maybe see the devil coming only wunt nothing to see so they was praying some more, and then one them boys, was a bald, rumple-head man, he was saying say didnt nobody see the devil he didnt want to be seen what we has to do we has to fool the devil just set them two lantern up along the bank somewhere on a stump when the devil he come he see the light and that where he go only we long gone by then, and the rest of the boys they was nodding with that, and then they was all running like a pack of ghosts from the glow of them two yellow lantern wash down across the blackblue water and then they was up through the dark and over roots and dead logs and brush through the moss, and they didnt stop for nothing even they was lugging five hundred pound of alligator meat and Long Jim and his leg till they was up to the shack.

The first thing they done they was inside they fire up that small red lantern cause it been out a while, and then they was all flop to the floor for laughing relief, only they was still scare and tense from thinking on the devil, so it was a thin, stringy kind of laugh barely stretch across the floor. The only one wunt laughing was Long Jim, but every now and then he give another moan, which maybe sound a little like laughing you was just listening to it the way the air kept breaking up in his throat, but it wunt anywhere near to laughing you was looking at what was left of his leg. Then the laughing it stop, and they was all looking to Long Jim and his leg, look like something out of somebody dream the way that red lantern running its thin strings of soft-yellow light down across the shadow black floor, wunt hardly enough light see they own hands let alone who next to them, and then they was talking what to do, they voices stretch out thin in the dark of that shack like the light.

"What we do now," said the first.

"We do what we can," said the second.

"We doing that now," said the third. "Aint nothing to do. We aint none of we going outside. Aint nothing but trouble we go back out we all end up like him. Look at him, man. There death in them eyes."

"You all cant let a man die like that," say the first. "Leg chew up and spit out like tobacco. Could be you lying there on the floor instead of him."

"Could be."

"That what I said."

"Could be any one of we here, but it aint. It Long Jim no matter what we saying."

And it was just about then Long Jim he was clutching up at the air like he was thinking he back in the water with that alligator chewing his leg, and he done pull hisself up to almost sitting, he was prop against the leg of the pine-wood table, and then he was calling out for his knife again. Thaddeus he was the closest one so he take up a knife put it into Long Jim hand, and with that Long Jim he lay hisself down to the floor again and he fell asleep, a couple string of soft-yellow light stretch across his face.

"That man he need a doctor," said Thaddeus.

The rest of them boys they was looking to Thaddeus when he say that, most of they faces all wrinkle up with amusement, but some they was stiff with silent rebuke, and then they was all talking with theyself some more.

"What kind of doctor he talking about?"

"Aint no doctor on this here island. Have to head up the coast. Even then aint find many take colored folk, lessn they colored theyself."

"Long Jim he aint have to worry about that. He be dead before he cross the water."

"Man, he lucky we dont talk him to death here and now."

"Aint that the truth."

Then that rumple-head man, he'd been listening all the while from the dark of the corner, he give a jerk with his arms and roll hisself up to his knees, and with that he done corner the rest with his black-arrow eyes dart back and forth, and then he open his mouth.

"Aint no doctor ever cure a devil-bit leg," he said. "And that a fact. Only thing cure that is a conjure man, and that what Long Jim need."

And with that the rumple-head man he fold hisself back into his corner, he was waiting on what happen, cause he wunt the one go for a conjure man and everybody knowd that, but before he fade into the dark complete, one of the rest he was up from the floor and he was saying say he'd be back with the conjure man even he have to kill dead a hundred alligator to do it, only it didnt sound like he mean a hundred, didnt sound like he mean even one, but then he was through the door all the same and moving through the blueblack of the night. The rest they was left sitting in the middle of the floor, and they was satisfy they was doing all they could for Long Jim so they was busy now scrounge about for something to eat, maybe a cup of cold beans or rice go along with some ham, they didnt even think about some of that deaded alligator meat, and they was talking some more too, but it was about conjure men how most was good with colds and maybe fever and some could call the rain but only a few could bring back the dead they didnt want to come. Long Jim he done roll hisself up under that pine-wood table, maybe he was thinking he get away from that alligator in his head, and he done left a stringy blood-stain on the floor where his leg it been drag. He didnt hear a word was said about conjure men calling rain or how maybe one was coming, but it look like he was needing one soon by the way he was still calling out for his knife even he had one in his hand.

No telling how long they was waiting, but by and by them boys they was done with they food and they talking done drop to a slow, heavy roll around the room, like they eyelids, and they'd a been asleep another minute only was then the conjure man he come busting into the shack, and the other one what went for him he done slip in behind. The conjure man he was a big bone man the color of dark plum, and he was wearing a red skullcap and holding a small black bag in his hand, but he wunt looking too happy on account of he'd been woke up out of bed and rowed five maybe six mile through the backwater wood, but soon as he seen Long Jim laying there a smile come busting up on to his face. First thing he was over to the table he was sending Thaddeus sit by the door, and then he was hunch over Long Jim leg and he was mumbling to hisself and shaking his head, and didnt nobody have no idea what he was saying, but the meaning come through clear enough, and then the conjure man he was dragging Long Jim out from under the table scatter the rest of them boys up against the walls, and then he set Long Jim up in the middle of the shack. Long Jim he was moaning still, but wunt as bad as before, which was saying something about the touch of this here conjure man, and he even drag Long Jim by his chew-up leg too. Then he took out his chalk and make a circle up around Long Jim, and he done it smart, and then he done fire up some candles, one for the head, one for each arm, each leg, even the chew-up one, and then he was dancing around that circle and calling out to the spirits, and every now and then he'd reach into his black bag and pull out some chicken bones or some feathers and he scatter them down across Long Jim and his chew-up leg, but some was landing on the floor.

The conjure man he was dancing in everybody eye, except Long Jim eyes they was shut, and the soft yellow from the small red lantern it mix up with the yellow from the candles it was all dancing the same, but look like the conjure man he wunt having much luck with Long Jim and that leg no matter how long he dance, like maybe the devil he done eat up too much of that leg, but just then there come a dancing wind it seem to answer the conjure man call, and it come dancing in through one side blow out the candle light and the lantern light, and them chicken bones and them feathers they was swirl up, and then the wind it was dancing out the door take the door and the bones and the feathers with it, and then the rest of them boys they wunt watching the conjure man dance cause the wind it was coming back for dance some more, they was all hanging on to arms and legs keep from following after the bones and the feathers, and the conjure man he was watching the wind the same and hanging on to Long Jim, and then all of a sudden a smile come wind-dance across his face, and with that he was shouting out to them boys how this here storm was the spirits doing wunt nothing for them to do but wait it out. It was almost like being outside. With the wind come a couple crack of lightning so sharp was like a whip beat across the back of the sky, and then come the blood-warm rain through the holes in the roof, and it didnt let up. And every time that whip done crack, them boys they flinch up like it was they own backs been whip, and some it looked like they was bleeding real blood in that flashing light and then the light it was gone, and didnt none of them boys move at first cause they was too scare, but after six or seven stroke they was all moving for huddle up under that pine-wood table, all except the rumple-head man fold-up in the corner and Thaddeus by the door and Long Jim and his leg stretch out in the chalk circle. The conjure man he was the first one under, and he kept shoving the rest of them back into the rain saying they wunt enough room they wunt enough room, but just as he clear them out a fifth time the wind it come again and dance some with the pine-wood table, and that surprise even the conjure man, and then the table it was dancing out the door and down the bank to the water, only it have to go break-leg cause it was too big to fit through any other way, and with that the conjure man he was saying say now huddle round huddle round, which the rest they done it.

By and by the wind and the rain they blowd theyself out, and them boys they was shaking water out of they hair and wiping it from they eyes, and Thaddeus he was doing the same, and the conjure man he was looking to the still black sky from out the middle of that huddle of shaking hair, and his eyes they was full up with rejubilation, only then he wipe away his enthuse along with the water, and he was saying say he done his best he call the spirits down and they come wunt nobody say they wunt he been in this room see what we seen and wunt nothing more to do neither but wait on Long Jim see if he wake up come the morning sun or either gone off with the devil. With that the boys they was nodding they heads, even the rumple-head man in the corner, and some they was looking to Long Jim with respect or either scare, but wunt nobody saying a word just yet, and then the conjure man he was saying say he thought it looking pretty good for Long Jim, but he'd been wrong a couple time before only both time it been on account of a white man, and with that them boys they was all looking to Thaddeus they eyes slicing him up like he another alligator, and the conjure man he was watching satisfy he done made a name for hisself and then he fell asleep, and then one by one them boys they was all falling asleep, but they was mumbling to theyself the while, was all the same thing, they was saying say they go kill theyself one more alligator kill one for Long Jim they have to it the last thing they ever do, and maybe give Thaddeus another look, and seem like everybody say it five or six time, and then the mumbling it stop. The only ones wunt sleeping was Long Jim and his leg, and they was stretched out dead in the middle of the room, and the other was white man Thaddeus, and he was sitting up by the door and wondering what he was go do next.

Turn out wunt nothing else to do. Thaddeus he seen Long Jim wunt go be waking up anytime soon, and he knowd exactly what them boys would be thinking they wake up see Long Jim nail-dead on the floor, so what he done he took hold of Long Jim by his arms and he start dragging him to the door and he was praying some too maybe none of them boys wake up before he make it. It wunt easy cause Long Jim he was already stiffen up, and he have to almost break his arms to get him through, but then he was, and without thinking where he was going next he was dragging Long Jim through the thick green wet of the brush pile up from the storm, he was heading for the water, and all the way Long Jim his leg was bouncing side to side. Was then Thaddeus he seen the conjure man patch-up rowboat pull up to a tree, and the next thing he done he heave up Long Jim and roll him in, and then they was both in, and then Thaddeus he pick up the oars and push away from the bank and then he was rowing up through the backwater wood.

Thaddeus he still didnt have a idea where he was going, but he was going just the same, and every now and then he'd ask Long Jim what he want to do next, where he want to go, but Long Jim he was just laying low in the boat with his head flop up against one side, and his arm trailing low for ripple in the black, black water. Wunt too long Thaddeus he see the light of them two lantern left to fool the devil, and why they was still lit he couldnt say cause the storm must of swept up this way the same, but he wunt thinking too hard on coincidence he was thinking say it pretty dark too dark to be rowing aint some kind of light, and so he row on over to the edge of the bank, and he grab the two lantern off the stump set them down by his knees, and even they didnt give off enough light except for maybe light up Long Jim face, well Thaddeus he didnt mind, he was saying say light is light, and then he was rowing some more. He must of been rowing a hour fore he pull up his oar and toss the light of one of them lantern around, and he still couldnt see much of anything cause the warm wet dark it swallow up the light before it reach down to the water, but all the same he knowd it the right place, could feel it more than see it, could smell it, taste it maybe, taste like it almost a deep deep swampwater lake, and then he shine the light on Long Jim face give him one more look, and then the lantern it was down in the bottom of the boat again and Thaddeus he was shoving Long Jim over the side.

Soon as Long Jim he hit the water there come a rush of white water, and Thaddeus he hold out the lantern some more and he seen ten or twelve black shadows steaming for the boat, and they red eyes they was steaming the same, and Thaddeus he wunt about to wait for them to come up under the boat cause they was a swampwater pack of alligator and like to knock him in the water they trying to get at Long Jim, so he was pushing back quick with his oars give them alligators room, and then the alligators they was fighting theyself and bellow in the water, and there was red eyes everywhere dipping down and then back up again, and everything was getting wet, even Thaddeus, and he was fifty foot away by then, and then all of a sudden the fighting and the bellowing and the white water stop, and the shadows they was dipping down some more, but only to cool off they tempers, and there wunt nothing left to see of where Long Jim went under except maybe some steam rising up off the black, black water, and with that Thaddeus he was thinking to hisself say it wunt exactly what the conjure man done said, but wunt no one else gonna know, it was close enough.

By the time Thaddeus he coming back, the sun was coming up, and the blackblue of the backwater wood was drift up like a ghost. He didnt waste no time tie up the boat he was scramble up through the warm wet brush, and he was bringing the two lantern along, they was burn out by then, and he wunt thinking a thing except get hisself through the door, and then he was. Wunt nobody awake just yet they was all huddle up on the floor smell like wet mules been lock up a week or more, and then Thaddeus he have hisself a idea, and he set them two lantern where Long Jim he used to been right in the middle of the conjure man chalk circle, and he was dancing with a smile hisself he do that cause he could hardly wait and see everybody faces they wake up, and then he was laying hisself up against the pine-wood wall like he been there all the while, and he close his eyes like he asleep.

Thaddeus he didnt have to wait long before that huddle it shake itself awake, and didnt none of them boys say a word right away, and the conjure man he didnt say a word neither, the truth was they was all staring at them two lantern where Long Jim should of been. It hard to say how long nobody said a word, but they was looking more and more like mules too stupid even to kick, they wunt even blinking they eyes, and then one of them was saying say thems the lanterns they done left for fool the devil, and they was all nodding they head with that but didnt none of them ask how they got where they was, and then another he was saying say anybody see where Long Jim done gone to, and they was all looking around the room, only Long Jim he wunt there, and the boys they was looking impress and scare and hungry and tense, and all at the same time too, but the conjure man he wunt looking anything but scare the way his eyes going round and round that shack like part of him was wondering what it was he done only most of him didnt really want to know, and then another one of them he was saying say maybe the devil he carry Long Jim off just like the conjure man done said, and with that then the conjure man he done had enough he was up from the huddle and he was saying say wunt no trusting the devil wunt a hundred hundred men full up his appetite no sir we better make tracks fore he change his mind come back for more, and with that the huddle it break up and everybody scrambling around that shack, they was packing up the gear and the five hundred pound of alligator meat and they brand new but empty guns, they was packing up everything except them two lantern in the middle of the floor, they was worry about that, and Thaddeus he was scrambling right there with them, only he was having a hard time keep hisself from laughing out loud, and then they was all through the door into the leaf-washed light of the morning sun, and the conjure man he was leading the way.

-3-

The old man he still aint say a word about where we going or what we go do, aint nothing but the swish swish swish of them oar, maybe some tree-groan, some owl-shriek, but by and by he slowing down, and I sees we coming to a moss-cover bank with one black sycamore lean over the water. The first thing we do we sliding that boat up from the edge and tie it to that tree, and then the old man he saying say look up through them trees, which I does, and there a small tarpaper shack bury up in some dark-needle pine, and a deep red glow coming through a red-curtain window make the black of the wood look blacker still.

"That's where we spending the rest of the night," he say, and then he nudge me up the bank and up we go.

It the same shack he been with Long Jim, only there a couple of chair lean against the wall now, and someone been fix up the door and that broken-leg pine-wood table the same as new, and that deep red glow from the outside it yellow now we is inside and it coming from two lantern stand up on the floor and one small red lantern missing its glass its up on the table. There aint no blood-stain wood, no chalk circle, it all scrub bare bare, even the holes in the roof they been patch, only who done it and when and where he gone there aint no telling. Then the old man he look at me like he know what I thinking.

"Aint no one here, boy, except you and me," he say. "Aint no one else been here must be thirty year now."

How he know that make no sense cause I can see the door and the table and them three lantern, and who done lit them I aint know but must of been somebody. But the old man he aint bother about that, and then he pull out two green shoulder-pack stack up under the table, and he going through them see what there. In the one there some brown bread and a couple can of peaches and look like some cheese, and in the other there a couple of rib-tooth knife and some fold up croaker sacks and a couple three roll of twine, and the rest I aint see for the old man shadow, but seem he satisfy with what he see cause the next thing he do he sitting in a chair his hands a hold of his knees, and then he leaning out into the wash of the yellow lantern light and he talk some more.

"You gonna find yourself a mat over there in the corner. You get yourself some sleep as best you can. I aint never close my eye I been in this shack, and that almost thirty year, but that my problem. Tomorrow come we gonna pack up the boat and head out into the backwater hunt you up a alligator."

With that I moving to the corner and rolling out the mat, and then I laying down, I aint know what else to do, and the old man he aint move from his chair he watching me all the way, and when he see me looking at him he give me his waiting-smile. Then he turn down them lanterns, and with that aint nothing to see but three red fuzz ball floating in the black, and Im is staring at them fuzz ball and staring and then it like they all just one fuzz ball, and it look like the devil's eye for sure the way its hovering there and red like it is, and then just like that the shack and the old man in the chair and them lanterns, everything is gone,

and there I is standing at the bottom of some ghost-white stone steps rise almost straight up into the sky, and with that Im is thinking say maybe I dreaming, I has to be, but it seem too too real be a dream, and with that I aint know what to think I just standing there on them steps and must be four or five hundred folks standing there with me crab-stiff on them steps, they heads arch back and looking up cause it just starting to rain, and some they wearing black hats and black coats and some they wearing black dresses and holding black fans out from they sides, and then they all grumbling to theyself and checking they watches for the time saying say how long before the doors they open up aint they been standing long enough this unbelievable keep folk waiting round like this have to take this up with someone, and then the man a step above me he turn he saying say we all be here as long as it take but some folks aint happy lessn they something to complain about, and then he look down to me with his brown ball eyes and he take off a black bowl hat and give a patient, waiting nod like so, and then he saying say he only been waiting maybe five year but they saying some, the ones at the top, they been here over a hundred, and then he black bowl his head again and turn his brown ball eyes to looking up some more.

I aint even try to think what five year waiting feel like, but then it happen I aint have to worry none cause a sigh of repent and relief come roll down through that crowd of black-hat folks, and then we all is walking up. By the time we to the top of the steps the rain it gone, except some dripping down from the hats and the fans, and we standing up front of a ghost-white clapboard church, aint a whole lot bigger than Willies store and warehouse before the fire. The folks they passing through two polish oak doors and then they sitting down on some polish oak benches, only everybody hunch over a bit cause aint no backs, and then the doors they shut, and everybody restless and waiting. Aint nothing happen. And then a couple hanging lantern is fire up down front, only aint no one I see done it, then a couple more and a couple more all the way to the back, and seem like the air it burn red with smoke, so much so the peoples they mopping up they faces just to see, and then the smoke it clear some, and the red from those lantern come down to a glow, and a preacher he step to the box.

The preacher he wearing a fire-bright suit like he the devils own rooster, not even Willie has a suit like that, and his eyes they is fire-bright the same, and everywhere he look he burning something, three hat catch fire, a young womans dress crumble up to ash, a couple old grands they cant keep still they shoes is smoking, but mostly he burning out eyes till they nothing but empty white sockets staring back. Is then the preacher he talking, only it aint exactly talking, more like we is thinking what already been said, and it only one thing, start out a whisper, but it a growing thing too, over and over and over again, the words they saying say aint nothing be afraid of folks nothing at all, and then the folks they take up chanting them words, louder, louder, some they mopping they faces some more, some they slipping out of they coats, hats falling to the floor, a couple more dress ash-crumble, and all the while the preacher he keep time with his fire bright eyes.

Aint long and the church it full up with the ash from all that white-socket chanting, so the preacher he wave his arm once and he bring that chanting down, and then he wave again and the fire from them hanging lanterns is bleeding up along the ceiling and then down along the walls, and then *he out the box he wave a third time calling everyone to come on down the aisle, and then they doing just that, and the preacher he saying say what you afraid of, and I aint exactly hear what anyone say back, but it look like they all afraid of something cause they nodding they heads, and some even reach out to grab the preacher by the hand, and then they stepping past, only where they going I cant say cause there too much ash from the words and smoke from the fire to see, and then it my turn, and the preacher he saying say what you afraid of boy, and I know what it is, only I cant say it, and then the preacher he pointing to a big big kettle sitting up there past the steps, and a big big fire underneath, and that where all the people been going, only they aint people no more, look like they crabs been boil for supper, and soon as I see that the preacher he laughing, and the fire from that kettle it laughing the same, and then a hot hot flash, and just like that the church and the preacher and that kettle full of people-turn-crabs is gone, aint nothing left but some church-ash swirl up around my face, and that laughter echo round in my head.*

Well, with that I sure hoping this a dream. Then the ash it settle down, and the laughing too, and Im is standing in front of a black iron gate open up to a boneyard. There three black and scraggly sycamore huddle up in the middle of a small-hump hill, and four or five hundred cross pin-stuck in the soft black earth, and look to be some dirt-wash headstone lean up against a black iron fence one side, they am almost turn green for wait on the devil, and the other side there a one window slate-gray shed, only nobody home. Aint nothing more to do so I climbing over the gate for a look, and past the four or five hundred cross, and past the turn-green stones, and this been a dying place a long time in anyone rememory cause look like the names and the dates all been wash away, and I is just stop up under them sycamores time I hears a shallow scrape scrape scrape and then a rustle sound like wings.

I aint move or even breathe in the dead-leaf shadow of them three black sycamores, and it a lucky thing too cause from out that slate-gray shed come two singing men. They singing shovel songs, cause they both a shovel slung over they shoulder, and then they down the other side from them sycamores and they singing death songs, cause that what they shoveling, and one he doing most of the work, and by and by he a pretty good load of dirt pile up behind him, and the other one he doing most of the singing, but every now and then he shovel up some black and let go over his shoulder. Then they both done stop with they shoveling and they singing, and they leaning on they shovels for catch up they breath, and the one done the most shovel he mopping his sweat with a fade red rag and he brush away some of them green-eye boneyard snapflies, and the other one he aint so tire so he start up talking.

"Aint no need dig every man a grave," he say. "After a while it pretty hard tell one from another."

The first one he aint catch his breath just yet so all he do he just nod.

"The devil he aint mind who bury where. Come judgement day he go open up every grave hisself have a big old meal of bones. He aint look see he a old man elbow in one hand and a young girl ankle the other. He eat em all."

The first one he nod his head some more. The second one keep talking.

"No sir, the devil he aint mind at all," he say. "That why I saying say dont you bury me. Just throw me to the fire till my bones they crack and burn. Watch me stick in the devil craw then. Aint he be surprise."

And with that the singing men they laughing to theyself, and then the first one he say come on, and he shoulder up his shovel, and the second one he laugh and do the same, and then they both walking down to that slate-gray shed, and they singing a fool-the-devil song now.

Soon as they gone, I out from the sycamore shadow and down for look at the grave they been digging. There a bone -rot smell rise up from the hole, even aint no one in it just yet, and then Im is wondering who it for and how long he been died and what from, and then I sees the stone up one end, and soon as I see it I know there been a misunderstatement somewhere down the line cause that stone have my name burn into it, and then just like that I aint looking at the stone no more, Im is lying in the black rot of that hole looking up to ghost-white sky, and Im is trying to move my arms my legs climb out of that hole, only aint nothing work, and then I hears them singing men again, and sound like they coming back from the shed, sound like they singing some more shovel songs too, and then the singing it stop, and I sees the two of them standing on the edge of the grave, they shovels prop up on they shoulders, and they talking some more about fool the devil, only they aint look down and see me, and I aint know what all been happening or either why, all I know is I scare and confuse, and Im is trying to call out, only my mouth it aint work neither, and then the singing men they start up singing some more, and then down come a pile of soft, black dirt, and look like nothing go keep them two from singing and shoveling, singing and shoveling, and then everything goes black.

The next thing I know my eyes is open and I looking around the shack. The way the sky shine a deep blue through the cracks in the wall it look to be late evening, and I wondering where the old man is cause them two green shoulder pack they gone, and so is them two lantern for fool the devil. Aint a sign the old man ever been there. Then Im is thinking say its time I heading home, I sure as hell aint go spend another night in that shack, not with everything happen last night, even it was only a dream, I aint go stay. But then Im is thinking say if it was a dream, then who done send it, and why, one thing for sure, I go be on the lookout for a big big kettle. Then I aint thinking on nothing no more and I get up and head outside, and Im is standing up against the shack in the shadow of a couple of pine tree hang over the roof, and listening to the old man sing. He down the bank by the water, he stowing them shoulder packs in the boat and a couple of croaker sacks and then he reach over put something else in and then he looking around see if he sprung a leak, and all the while he singing about the devil and his daughter, how she was a pretty young thing had a way of putting men on they backs when they wunt looking and every now and then she'd up and marry one for spite only she wunt never able to hide nothing from her daddy. The old man he singing like he know the girl hisself, and I thinking say that does say a awful damn lot, only then the old man he stop singing and look up to the shack. He see me standing in the shadow of them two pine tree.

"It about time you get up, boy" he say. And then he say, "What you waiting on? Come on. Aint nothing left for you to do now. The boat it already loaded up." And he sitting on the side of the boat.

I aint feel like move, but I moving just the same, and then it seem like I scrambling down the side of the bank and clutching at roots maybe bust my neck, and the old man it all he can do not to bust out laughing. Then we both in the boat and the old man he push us away from the bank with his oar, and then we moving up through the blackblue water, and he singing some more about the devil his daughter, and all of a sudden it have a funny feeling, like all the time the old man singing Im is belly up inside a alligator, aint nothing to hear or either see except maybe the wind whistle down through some alligator teeth. Then the old man he aint singing no more. He just whisper some. He telling me to watch out now cause he can smell some kind of alligator lurk about in the water, or maybe up along the bank.

Well I looking with that. I looking so hard my eyeballs peel back raw like onions, only aint nothing but the deep blue shadow of pine and sycamore and cypress twist up on the blackgreen bank, and some they branch-nails digging into the water, and they all cover up with moss. But the old man he just tell me to reach back and pick up a gig, cause there no telling how many alligators go be swimming past the boat by and by. Then he dont say nothing, and I wondering just where it is we going there so many alligators, only then it come to me. The old man he taking me to where he dump Long Jim in the water. My whole self go numb with that, and it feel like I been there before, and then the old man he saying say ready with that gig boy say what you doing I said ready he go get away without even a scratch you dont hurry up.

The alligator he sunk low in the blackblue aint nothing but two red eyes bubble up above the water give him away, and then he rise up a bit in the water, look like he give a alligator smile, like he been waiting on us maybe his whole life long, and then aint nothing but a wind-ripple where he gone down and under. The old man he see that smile same as me and he shaking his head he saying say we in trouble now a alligator smile like that mean only one thing mean all you can do is watch and wait and the alligator he know that the same so he watching and waiting aint nothing go outlast a alligator and when you just about ready to give up then the alligator he come lash out of the water and before you know it you and he you both is fighting on the same terms. The old man then he looking to the water, he almost resting on his oar, and I looking the same, only it hard to rest with a gig in my hand, and I wondering if that alligator he as much trouble as the old man been saying, maybe he aint even coming back.

Im is just about settle myself he aint when the old man he up in the boat and shouting and the alligator he rising fast from the blackblue water, his two red eyes burning holes in the air, and Im is coming down with the gig, but everything moving too too slow, excepting the alligator, and all I coming down on is water, and the alligator now he twisting around in the water he curl his tail up around the boat, and the old man he shouting for me to watch that tail, and so I does, and then the tail it come smashing down on top of the boat, and before I done raise that gig again, it out of my hands and in the water, and is then I heading in after it, and the old man he heading in the same, and then we both sinking down in the water we alligator bait, only that alligator he aint bother none cause he too busy smashing up the boat with his tail. Im is trying grab a hold of something, even that alligator, only everything slip away, and the more and more Im is trying, the faster I going down, and deeper too, and then it seem like there aint no reason try any more, cause aint no use, so I stop, and the only thought what come to me it about Long Jim how he was eat up by a alligator and look like the same damn thing go happen to me. It hard to say what all happen next. First it feel like something grab a hold of me from behind, up around my collar, and I aint know exactly what to do with that so I start kicking at it, and I thinking say as long as I has both of my legs I be going down kicking, only it dont do no good, and then I feels the black of the water rushing up around my head, and then around my arms and legs, and I dont know ifn I at the bottom of that swampwater lake or either up in the belly of that rowboat-smashing alligator, and then the rushing it stops, and then it feel like I being drag up from the water and up along the bank through the wood, and then it feel like dry, stiff grass, and I aint know how long I been drag like that, or where to, but then the dragging it stop, and with that then I hear the old mans voice saying say

come on boy come on boy come on, and then he grabbing
hold of my legs and he pump them up and down and up
and down, and before I knows what what I coughing up
some swampwater, taste like I coughing up a couple three
barrel of axle grease, and then I open my eyes.

The old man he leaning over me and rubbing at my arms
and my legs, only all I see is a ghost-white shadow up
against the deep blackblue of the sky, and feel like I aint any
skin left he rubbing so hard, and all the while he saying say
that the biggest alligator he ever seen and he seen a few we
just lucky he wunt as smart as he was big that all he wunt
too smart must of got hisself a belly full of wood by now,
and Im is wondering if all that wood feel worse than a belly
full of water, and Im is hoping it does, and just then the old
man he stop with the rubbing and the words, and he give
me a pig-knuckle smile like he know all along what Im is
thinking about, and then he sit on back in the long dry grass
and he staring up at the sky, and his face it looking like he
done had all he want to eat and then some, and then it
sound like someone saying say I told you boy aint nothing
be afraid of, and maybe it the old man talking, and maybe it
aint, I aint hear just where the words they blowing from,
maybe it the wind.

. . . now when the next morning done come, along with it come a second man, and he wunt big big like the first, but he had hisself a long black knife hang down from his belt, and when he done heard that alligator roaring and roaring, he done come looking just like the first, and when he seen that alligator sitting on top of that log, he done smile wide he was saying say he was go teach that alligator what was what and then it wunt go be no alligator world no more, and with that the second man he was waving his knife around like he was trying to cut the air in two, and the animals up in them trees they was looking out through de moss same as before they was asking theyself what go happen this time hope this second man he do better than the first they been treed too long, and then the second man he done jump on that alligator back he was holding his knife up against the hot yellow sun and riding that alligator like he on the back of a horse, and he kept trying to stick that knife somewhere in the alligator head, only it wunt as easy as he thought on account of that alligator was thrashing this way and that, and snapping at the air every time that knife come down, and after a while it look like that second man go ride that alligator three hundred day if that what it take, and the animals they was cheering him on like the three hundred day almost up, but then the alligator he was up in the air roll back like he done the first time, and then the second man and his knife and the alligator they was all tumbling into the water, and the second man he was twisting around look see where his knife was at, only all there was was the blackgreen water full up with a bluegreen alligator, and with that he didnt know what to do, so he start swimming for the bank, *only he wunt much for swimming so the alligator he aint have no trouble come up from behind grab hold of a leg, and before the second man he even think to give a kick, that alligator he done gobble him up same as the first, and with that he was back on his log and he was roaring and roaring say just me and my world, and this time he done roar all the way through the night, and the animals they was shaking they heads some more they was saying say they wunt ever go get out of them trees, and it was looking like they might be right . . .*

Songs

-1-

A great deal of time has passed, almost without his noticing, which is, perhaps, not so unusual for a man who has lived his life outside the normal bounds, outside of time, so to speak. So there he is now, sitting inside his cabin in the summer-hazy isolation of an old man. It is a too too hot evening, early evening, and also moist, and the sky is a heavy, sickly green color, which means that from somewhere a storm is coming. But Thaddeus does not bother about the storm. He seems almost oblivious to its coming. He is sitting there with the windows closed in spite of the heat, and he is shivering slightly even as he is perspiring in the closed-window stuffiness of the cabin, and he wonders how it can be cold in August, but he does not really mind. He is sitting at the table eating crabs and the lamps are not lit and the sickly green light from outside does not seem to penetrate the hazy, enveloping dark of his eating, and he does not mind this either. Then he looks to the window and blinks at the dying green light which does not come in and he thinks that even the sky is dying and then he looks away from the window to the crab bones scattered carelessly about the table, finds one with a scrap of meat clinging to it, gnaws on it, chews the meat, and while he chews he begins reliving his life, though quite without meaning to, from the time of that visiting Reverend's daughter to the time of Kilby and the crabs, but it's all mixed up in his head, fragments, parts left out, the confusion of a dream, as if the life that was is slowly merging with the life that is, the inevitable mingling of the past with the present. . .

O come and join our boisterous band,
Our women and wine we'll share;
We soon shall reach the promised land,
And drink whatever's there.

We'll grab a jug, it wont be long,
We'll empty it by and by;
Then arm in arm we'll sing this song,
And laugh until we cry.

The show had not yet begun, and a young Thaddeus was thinking about the girl from Charleston, he'd been looking at her a while but he didn't know what to say it was like his mouth didn't work and that troubled him and then today she'd come up and they started talking and then she said why didn't the two of them get together after the meeting her daddy had gone down to Jasper county for a couple of days there wasn't nobody to bother them, and Thaddeus he had said that he would. He was part of a group of men standing outside the tent, but not really a part, and the men sang and laughed and whistled at the pretty women who flashed by on their way into the tent, and some not so pretty. They sang mostly taproom ditties, although when the more prominent of the town passed by they dropped the words and it sounded a little like they were humming hymns, and when they whistled at the women they made suggestive gestures with their hands and laughed when these were noticed and then abruptly ignored.

One of the men, grizzled, whiskey on his breath, an old brown coat in spite of the warmth, nodded at Thaddeus and asked if he'd heard this here preacher the last time he come to town, they had themselves a real good time then, why the sheriff himself he had to come all the way out break things up, of course everyone knew he would, the sheriff, he didnt hold too much with tent preachers, especially those that liked to sing and dance and maybe have a drink, not since he was married he didnt, his wife she believed in a dry state, at least ever since they passed the Prohibition.

Then the grizzled man laughed.

"Them deputies gonna have a hell of a time tonight if the sheriff sends 'em over this way," and he pointed to a single car parked on the other side of the road maybe a hundred yards away, the car turning black in the late evening light, a couple of deputies sitting on the hood. Then he laughed some more.

Thaddeus looked to the deputies, two skinny men, each a shadowy reflection of the other, like twins, black hair, not so tall, unshaven, guns stuffed loosely in their belts, looked to be talking quietly, not paying much attention to the men and women gathering beneath the large white tent. Then the others started talking, laughing.

"What you wanna bet that young Sheriff Aikens come busting in by nine o'clock," said a longnosed man in mudgray workpants and a faded yellow shortsleeve. "And his Uncle Walter in the crowd too."

"You mean the Judge," said a man with bigred ears, bigred hands.

"That's the one."

"He'd be crazy bust in on the Judge."

"He would at that."

"But it'd be something to see now, wouldn't it. Like two pigs in a poke. I'd pay five dollar see something like that. Cash money too."

"I'll bet you five dollar the Sheriff dont do nothing," said a man in corduroy pants smoking a Pall Mall. "He probably home right now busting into that pretty young wife of his?

You ever see the way she wiggle her hips when she walk down the street? Man, I wouldn't let nothing get in the way of me and them hips."

The men murmuring with enthusiastic agreement, laughing some more, the possibility of encountering the softwiggling hips of Mrs. Albert Aikens eclipsing all thoughts of a nighttime raid. At least for the moment. Then a puzzled voice coming from the man with the bigred ears, bigred hands.

"What he doing with a wife like that?"

"Not enough, that's for sure."

"You think he know that?"

"Hell, no. He too busy busting up revival meetings."

The men laughing some more, then the longnose and the Pall Mall man giving five dollars each to the bigred to hold, then shoving their dollarempty hands in their pockets, fat, wagerhappy smiles spreading across their faces.

"They gonna have a hell of a time," said the grizzled man, and then he turned to Thaddeus and asked if he wanted a snort, and when Thaddeus shook his head the grizzled man smiled, relieved perhaps, slipped his hand into his coat and pulled out a jug of whiskey, uncorked it, took a snort, corked it and then back into his coat. Just in case this show wasnt as good as the last one he said, and then he smiled again. Then the men sang some more.

Again Thaddeus looked to the deputies and wondered how long it was going to be before the sheriff arrived. He remembered the last time they played Barclayville. Someone put a couple of shots into the Conover piano and an old woman in the front row fainted from the excitement. Thaddeus laughed to himself. Then a blackbooted usher stepped from the tent and announced that the meeting was about to begin it being eight o'clock or close enough and anybody who wanted a seat better grab one now there wasnt gonna be no one putting out more chairs, and with that Thaddeus and the barbershop four of his waiting there lilted into the tent and sat down in the back.

The crowd did not quiet down immediately, did not really ever quiet down. Some were singing taproom ditties not unlike the song which the grizzled man and his friends had sung outside. Some were drinking on the sly, look about to see who was watching, then a snort or two, just in case. Some were laughing, and every now and then a woman would cry out stop that, and the laughter would swell. Then the grizzled man poked Thaddeus in the stomach. "We're gonna have a hell of a time tonight, deputies or no deputies" he said, and Thaddeus nodded politely, noncommittally, but all the while he was thinking he sure as hell hoped so, but he was thinking of later, then the grizzled man took another snort from his jug and Thaddeus looked away, waiting, then looked to the platform. The Reverend Jacobs was sitting there, an inscrutable calm about the man, and beside him sat the other one, the one not gone to Jasper county, his hands fluttering about uselessly, from fear of crowds, perhaps. Then the aging, genderless one behind the piano struck a note, and the three pearl-throated women and the four soft-singing young men of the choir behind them began to sing a Presbyterian hymn, though at first the song was barely audible on account of the boisterous almost savage nature of the crowd. But soon the music began to swell and the crowd grew silent with anticipation and the air grew still and it seemed for a moment that everyone was holding their breath.

Then the Reverend Jacobs was standing at the podium and he motioned to the choir and the singing stopped, and everyone exhaled, slowly, but the Reverend did not speak. He looked at this crowd of withering expectation with the practiced eye of a dealer in horse flesh. Then he pulled out his black leather bible, held it high in the air as if it were a ringleaders whip, and then he snap snapped it with a supple jerk of his wrist, and the men and women in the crowd jumped. Then he spoke in a low, gravelly voice.

"Ladies and gentlemen, I have not seen, I say I say I have not seen such wickedness in a congregation as I am witnessing here tonight. Not in forty years, ladies and gentlemen. You ought to be ashamed of yourselves. But you are not. You ought to bow down before the Lord and ask his forgiveness. But you will not."

And he stepped into the crowd and shook his black bible fist at the people.

"You will not, and do you know why you will not?"

The people shifting uncomfortably in their seats.

"Do you know why you will not bow down before the Lord? Yes, you. And you. And you. You will not bow down before the Lord because you have made of your world a new Sodom and Gomorrah. Yes you have, ladies and gentlemen. You all are living a life of depraved and repugnant excess."

And the Reverend held in his gaze the pale faces of those he had pointed out with his bible, and the others in the tent tried to look away, to either side of those flashing, bible-black eyes, to avoid, perhaps, being pointed out themselves. But they could not look away.

"But you will not escape the vengeance of the Lord."

Then the snap snap of the black bible whip and the crowd jumped a second time and the good Reverend was now roving back and forth through the crowd, a contorted leer of satisfaction and contempt on his face.

"Yes, ladies and gentlemen. I say, I say you will not escape. No one escapes from the vengeance of the Lord. But you, you are like a man I once knew, all of you are. He thought he could escape. This man I once knew, and he was a giant of a man, stood well over seven feet tall, he thought he could escape. But he could not. He lived a life of the wildest, most beguiling depravity, and thought he was a world unto himself. But he could not escape the vengeance of the Lord."

And the men and women beneath the white canvas bigtop began to sway back and forth, back and forth, listening to the words of the ringling Reverend Jacobs with the rare and even unsettling attentiveness of those hypnotized by the mystique of the center ring.

"But let me tell you, ladies and gentlemen, I say I say let me tell you now all about this man I once knew, so you may judge for yourselves the truth of what I say. He belonged to a circus, but not just any circus. No, indeed, ladies and gentlemen. The show of shows, the sign said, a panorama of the uncommon, the unusual, the unheard of. It was a scene of the most profligate extravagance to rival anything the ancients had ever experienced. This was a show you did not want to miss."

The image of the circus beginning to take root, the men and women longing to witness the show of shows.

"And this man I once knew, he was the most uncommon of them all. Yes he was , ladies and gentlemen. He claimed to be the world's strongest man, yes he did, and the most beautiful as well, and so he was, a seven foot colossus of the modern era to rival the likes of Hercules or Apollo himself. And some wondered why they were not as strong or as beautiful, and they despaired, they looked deep down into their immortal souls and they thought the Lord had done them wrong."

A flurry of soulful, despairing looks.

"And the most beautiful women in the world would throw themselves at his feet, and he would devour them, as a savage beast devours its prey."

A few in the crowd getting down on their hands and knees, becoming savage beasts themselves, looking for something to devour.

"But they paid their dollars. I say, I say they paid their dollars to see this man who was a beast. They paid their dollars to partake of the savage and yet beguiling depravity of that circus among circuses. Yes they did ladies and gentlemen."

Snap, snap, snap.

"And afterwards some were invited to go still further, for every night these people of the high wire threw an after-midnight extravaganza in honor of their seven foot savage, and always on board their libertine circus train, a train over one-thousand cars long, a train which never went anywhere more than once, a train of consummate excess."

Snap, snap, snap.

"And for a single dollar, ladies and gentlemen, I will show you what they saw. Yes I will. For a single dollar I will show you this man who was a beast and everything he was a part of. I will help you feel what they felt. And all for a single dollar."

"A single dollar single dollar single dollar dollar dollar."

And the crowd of men and women were overwhelmed by the words of the Reverend, or so it seemed, and they roared in uninhibited appreciation, the ringling Reverend smiling again, the satisfied, leering look still perched on his face, and then he cracked his blackbiblewhip and two ushers in black ties and black jackets got up from each end of the platform and made their way down the sides of the tent to the back, each with a large golden plate in hand, the genderless piano player playing an earthy, eager, almost unrestrained rendition of *Where Cross the Crowded Ways of Life*, the pearl-clad choir joining in, and the men and women of this circus-train congregation rummaging madly through their pockets and purses and wallets and then piling dollar after dollar upon the passing-by plates. Even the sour -smelling, grizzled acquaintance of Thaddeus added to the pile. And when the last of the money had been collected, the ushers hurried to the platform, the plates piled high with single dollars and their hands on top, the ringleader Reverend now smiling a broad smile at the dollarempty faces of the men and women, at the two ushers, at the plates, a carnival barker smile, a get-what-you-can-while-the-gettings-good smile, smiling and nodding and smiling,

this is it ladies and gentlemen

snap snap snap

i've seen you looking at me

the moment you've all been

you've what

waiting for

i've seen you, but i don't mind

now you will see for yourself

you don't

he's got them now, the young man thought to himself, it's gonna to be one hell of a show

snap snap

unh-uh

snap

and he wanted to join in the fun, for there was something compelling about what the Reverend promised

now my daddy would mind

one hell of a show

but i dont

you don't?

i've been looking at you too

but he did not join in

snap snap snap

The ringling leader Reverend now whirling his way through the crowd, up towards the platform, towards the podium, and then back the other way again, and all the while cracking his blackbiblewhip, and the crowd ducking with every snap snap snap of his arm, and some howling, the rage of bestiality in their eyes.

"See the longest circus train in the history of circus trains pull out from the city of Charleston, over one-thousand cars of the most scintillating entertainment found anywhere in the civilized world. The greatest assortment of man and beast ever assembled."

From somewhere there was the sound of a train pulling out.

"Hear the howling of the monkeys, the growling of the lions caged in the rear, the rumblings of the elephants as they stumble against each other, the coarse shrieks of the majestic birds of prey. Yes, ladies and gentlemen, I said, I said hear all these strange and exotic sounds, and many more besides, direct from that darkest of continents. The faraway continent of Africa."

"The darkest of the darkest of the dark."

More men and women becoming beasts.

snap snap snap

"See the seven foot colossus, the wonder of the modern world, upon that very train. See him walk from car to car, the cloak of a sheik upon his back, a willing throng of men and women following his every move. And see him remove that cloak."

And it seemed to the men and women who were beasts that the good Reverend removed his own heavy black coat and hat as he spoke, and also the too too white shirt underneath, and then everything but his socks, and with that they fell upon each other, ripping shirts from backs and skirts from hips.

snap

"See the women of his harem dance rings around his nakedness, their hands upon his chest, his arms, his legs, his body rubbed with oils from arabia, his face smiling the smile of a sheik, then this majesty of the circus train taking the women one by one."

snap snap snap

And the men and women howled with glee, for they were all of them beasts now. The lust of the ringling Reverend's words danced within their newly naked souls. Or so it seemed.

"See the men of this traveling-by-rail sheikdom taking those that are left, one by one then none. See the unbridled lust of men and women become savages, the naked arms, the naked legs, the naked breasts, the naked hips."

snap snap snap

"Yes, ladies and gentlemen, yes."

(And the ringling Reverend snap snapped his whip to the rhythm of his words and the men and women who were beasts squirmed faster and faster)

snap snap snap

(their naked bodies squirming in the grass beneath the white canvas bigtop)

snap snap snap

(and then some up on all fours and howling and barking as if they had treed the devil and then back down in the squirming seething grass of the Reverends conjuring)

snap snap snap

(the whip of the ringling Reverend urging them faster and faster and faster)

so you

snap snap snap

so you doing anything tonight, i mean after the show

no i, i wasn't doing a thing

snap

i was hoping you'd say that

snap snap snap

(then the naked bodies of the men and women who were beasts lay panting on the grass under the large white tent their backs bared to the good Reverends stinging blackbiblewhip)

ladies and gentlemen

(the ringling Reverend back at the podium now and he snapped his whip and the men and women who were beasts became men and women again)

i said i said ladies and gentlemen

snap snap snap

(and then the men and women sat down on the benches still naked still panting and they saw that the Reverend was fully clothed)

ladies and gentlemen just look at yourselves you ought to be ashamed

snap snap snap

you are just like that man i once knew the man on that irredeemable circus train well let me tell you what the good Lord had in store for that one let me tell you about the vengeance of the Lord for when he looked down upon that train he saw the very wickedness of sodom and gomorrah come to life a second time and he could not believe his eyes so he called a council of angels and they looked down from heaven and they all agreed that such a phenomenon was most unquestionably unnatural was in fact a natural impossibility and should therefore be destroyed immediately and the Lord agreed and commanded that the train be struck from the tracks

(the men and women moaning with despair at the thought a protracted ohhhhhhhhhhhhhhhhhhhhhhhhhh whirling around the tent or maybe they were just shivering in the nakedness of their no longer being beasts)

and when the Lord had spoken a single angel departed from the host and came down from heaven an angel of the most prodigious muscular capabilities why his right arm alone was thicker than the mightiest of the great cedars of ancient Lebanon and the angel held aloft a mighty sword a sword forged in the fires of a time before man a time before time a time of volcanoes and molten rock this sword a sword of fire itself and when the angel neared the train he heard the sounds of that most primordial passion and down came the mighty sword and the sound of steel on steel echoed throughout the land

(and the moan again for the nakedburning men and women could hear that coming down sword)

some thought those terrible giant lizards of a thousand millennia past had reawakened from their paleozoic slumber deep within the darkest catacombs of the earth and walked again across the continents of the modern world

ohhhhhhhhhhhhhhhhhhhhhhhhh

(the Reverend thinking of an even larger second collection)

and some thought the incandescent immortality of the sun had collided with the earth that the end had most assuredly come

ohhhhhhhhhhhhhhhhhhhhhhhhhh

and some thought they heard the raging voice of God as if God himself had descended in judgment upon all mankind yes indeed ladies and gentlemen the sound of that sword upon that train was unlike any sound heard within the memory of man

snap snap snap

but what of us what of us what of us us us

(and the ringling Reverend heard their words the leering satisfied look expanding and he spoke again)

i see a most sombrous sight awaiting you a most sombrous sight of carnage and destruction yes i do ladies and gentlemen for like that man i once knew you are also riding that circus train yes you are you are all riding into the railway darkness of sodom and gomorrah see the naked corpses of men and women scattered across the side of a mountain their bodies twisted beyond recognition amid the wreckage of wheels and twisted iron

snap snap snap

(the men and women saw the wreckage)

see the stunned survivors looking from body to body in a naked disbelief most profound

(the men and women looking at each other in the nakedness of disbelief)

see the savage beasts of those darkest of jungles acquire a most immediate taste for human blood

snap snap snap

(the men and women shuddering)

see the majestic lions of africa run down the shrieking sheiks

(and some heard the roar of the lions prowling outside and ran from their chairs and hid beneath the platform and some did not know where to hide and some just fainted)

see the hordes of howling monkeys feast upon the flesh and bones of the dead and dying

(and some heard the howls of monkeys echoing in the air above and fell to their knees)

yes indeed ladies and gentlemen see a sea of cataclysmic upheaval a scourge of dynamic dimensions yes indeed a veritable rain of fire and death fallen upon the immoral heads of the wicked each and every one

snap snap snap

(and with that the men and women who were no longer beasts cried out in earclutching prayer)

save us Lord save us from the fire of the howling sword of the monkeys prowling in the fire of the fire of the save us from the lions of the Lord

(then the ringleader Reverend snap snapped his whip a final time and those who were not kneeling joined those who were and they all bowed down their heads before the imagined incendiary might of the Lord all of them naked still even the grizzled man who had offered Thaddeus a snort went to his knees though he seemed more concerned with the whereabouts of his somehow missing jug than with the possibility of death by fire but the young man name of

Thaddeus was not kneeling not praying he was thinking again about the girl from Charleston so he stood up and walked out through the flap a pause then one more look and then he turned from the nakedglow of the men and women at prayer the dollarglow of the two reverends on the platform then looked out into the darkness of the night and he saw the black shapes of wagons maybe some trucks moving in from the road towards the tent they were moving and he walked to meet these wagons these trucks a step or so he walked and then he stopped watched waited then the wagons and the trucks slowed and then stopped a dozen or so in all each with a dozen or so men and then the men climbed out down a joggle of arms and legs assembling in the grassy heavy heaving dark then the joggle marching towards the nakedburningorangeglow of the tent bubbling up against the dark dark sky the joggle marching with the rigid yet nervous dignity of men who carried guns but had never had the opportunity to use them)

snap snap snap

(and as they neared the tent a thin wiry shadow separated itself from the group and then a thin wiry voice)

load em up boys goddamn jaybird naked evangelists load up as many as you can get a hold of

(and with that the dozen dozen men ran past the watching Thaddeus and into the bubbleglow of the tent some waving their guns in the air and shouting and some not and then came the thin wiry shadow and Thaddeus saw it was the sheriff though not so tall not so old not the kind of sheriff one expected in a small South Carolina town the sheriff watching his men and then smiling at Thaddeus giving him an elbowpoking angled up)

thems good boys to have at your back

(then the sheriff laughing a thin and wiry laugh also then running into the nakedbubbleglow of the tent himself)

load em up boys load em up

(and the men and women saw the dozen dozen running wild through the flap the sheriff running also the men and women no longer praying no longer contemplating the incendiary might of the Lord or so it seemed and the Reverend saw them also him kneeling by the plates and stuffing his pockets with dollar bills and then looking out again and the other one the one not gone to Jasper county still sitting in his chair not sure just what a reverend should do during a raid his hands still fluttering about uselessly and the men and women now scrambling over chairs and under them the men and women naked still some hiding beneath the platform some of them sifting through the mostly abandoned clothes on the ground then grabbing whatever they could the grizzled man sitting on the ground between two chairs at the back of the tent sitting on the folds of his coat the missing jug in his hand and all the while the piano player was playing though the choir had fled and the sheriff and his boys riding herd through the crowd their guns waving wildly in the air a couple of shots then a couple more then a shout and then grabbing at this arm at that some of the men and women struggling and some not and some not knowing what to do)

load em up boys loademup

snap

(and then some of the men and women were edging under the sides of the tent then running into the night the tent stakes popping loose behind them the tent collapsing the white of the canvas settling down upon the ground like a shroud down upon the naked men and women and the still-playing piano player and upon the dollarhappy reverend and the other one his hands fluttering still and upon the sheriff and his boys and their guns and the young man name of Thaddeus scrambling away from the settling shroud back through the dark moist grass of the field then stopping looking to the ghostly white of the canvas spreading out upon the ground the sound of the piano drifting above it all like the very soul of those beneath the sound escaping up into the next world or so it seemed then the voices of those underneath the men and women shouting)

this way no this way no this way no this

(then the sheriffs thin wiry voice)

we got em now boys we got em now

(then some laughter then a shout then a gunshot then a gruff and gravelly voice)

you best tell your boys to let go of my arm Albert

(then silence)

(then the sheriffs voice a bit thinner now)

that you Uncle Walter

you heard me

yes sir Uncle Walter sir you heard him boys say let go of his arm that Uncle Walter

and while they at it you tell em to let go of the rest of them folks then head on home

you heard him boys we done enough for tonight

(then the ringleader Reverends voice billowing up and out)

bow down your heads i said i said bow down your heads

this way no this way no this way

(then one by one the voices slipping out from underneath the edge of the tent some becoming naked men and women some clutching clothes in their hands some not then off into the dark then some becoming the deputies no longer waving their guns in the air no longer in pursuit then to the black of the wagons the trucks one becoming the sheriff another becoming the sheriffs uncle a large pink man pink ears a pink belly a white but bootstreaked shirt the sheriff hanging on to the uncles elbow the uncle buttoning up his shirt tucking it in his pants) i sure is sorry about all this Uncle Walter i mean i mean i sure is sorry

come eight o'clock tomorrow morning you best be at the courthouse you hear me Albert

yes sir Uncle Walter i will i mean i do i mean yes sir yes sir

(then the uncle rolling his pink ears his pink belly buttoned now into the black of a carriage then hip switching then off into the black of the field the sheriff watching him go then into an old ford the sheriff nodding firmly to his boys a time-we-went-home kind of nod then the rest of wagons the trucks rolling off into the black of the field also)

-2-

He had felt the island before he had actually seen it. And then it loomed before him, a gray lump spreading out against the heavy, black horizon. He rowed towards the shore, and then he felt the rowboat scudding over the sandy bottom and he got out and pulled it up onto the narrow stretch of beach. The moonlight glinted off the sand, and Thaddeus thought to himself, it is more like I am dreaming now than when I first saw myself coming here. Yes, this is the place. And he was certain of himself this time, for he had been to several islands the past month, many islands, or so it had seemed, each one rising up out of the seagrassy sea of that beckoning voice and then he would be standing on a beach and watching the seagulls and the fish that had washed up or he would see the hazy, early morning silhouettes of people in the distance but when he got closer the people would be gone or maybe he would stumble across the twisted remains of a dock half-buried in the sand and that's all there was, but none of these islands had measured up to the image from his dream, none had felt right, there had been a vagueness about them, an emptiness, an incompleteness, and then the voice would start up again and he would get back into the boat and try another island. But he felt a completeness here. He felt like he had come home. The voice from his dream would bother him no more. Then he left the boat and went dripping across the mooncooled sand and up into the long grass of the dunes, but not far. Stretching out in the sandy, grassy earth, his heels digging in, he fell asleep. But he did not sleep long, and when he woke he heard the sound of men talking, and the spit and hiss of a small fire. The men and the fire were very close.

"What you mean about de devil?"

"He dont mean nothing. Willie here been talking bout de devil since before you was born."

"What you mean?"

"I mean I seen him dat's what I mean. I was out here one night was after midnight, must of been dis very spot too, and I wunt doing nothing jes sitting thinking maybe looking to de dark blue waves come rolling in and den from out de dark I done heard de slap slap slap of a oar and den in come a old patchup rowboat look like it was about to sink. It was den I done seen a man standing up in de bow of dat boat, only he wunt no ordinary man, no sir, looked like de devil hisself come to life."

"How'd you know he was de devil?"

"I jes know'd, dat's all. He was wearing a black coat, a black hat, had hisself a gold chain hang round his neck, a couple of gold ring, and he was holding on to looked like de staff of Moses only it had de head of a snake on it, and all de while he was riding in dat boat he was staring across de waves his eyes looking straight at de island, and red too, like he was trying to burn everything down. De next thing I know'd he was out of dat boat and we was standing face to face down de beach a ways, and de devil he give out a crooked kind of laugh seem to be coming from everywhere, and den he done said it was about time he made my acquaintance, and den he done stuck his Moses staff in de sand like dat and den everything bust loose. De snake head it open its eyes and start twisting and turning and flicking its tongue and den it give a hisssssssssy sound like it dying, only it wunt, and den a red fire come out of its mouth burn a circle in de sand, dere was fire all de way around, and me and de devil we was standing in de middle of it, and den de devil he grab hold of my shoulders toss me to de sand and we was wrestling like we both born to it. Some of de time de devil he was up on top and some of de time was me, legs and arms and shoulders and hips churning up de sand, de sand flying dis way and dat, de hot of dem flames burning red across my face across de devils face almost looked like we was wrestling wid fire, and den de fire it was gone, and de devil he was standing by his boat been pull up on de sand, only he was looking too spit and polish to been wrestling like he was, wunt even a button pop off his coat, and den he done look me over and he said de night was almost over but he'd come back some other night and we'd wrestle some more, and den he give me his crooked smile again and step into his boat, and den he was gone. And dat de truth."

"What kind of truth you talking about?"

"Truth is truth."

"He was gone cause he wunt never dere, and dat de real truth."

"Truth is truth."

"Say Willie, when you think de devil he go come back and wrestle wid you some more?"

"Dont know for sure. De devil he didnt say, and no way of knowing neither. I expects I jes has to keep my wits about me. De devil he show up any time he feel like it."

Thaddeus was sitting up now on the grassy slope of the dune, but the three men had not seen him in the uneasy glare of their talking and the glow of their fire against the night. They had been there only a short while, but already there were scads of empty beer bottles scattered about. But they didn't bother about these. They laughed and talked and drank and tossed a few more empties to the sand and then they talked some more. The one doing most of the talking sat furthest from the fire, almost in the shadows, the bald arc of his head glistening with only the faintest flicker of light, the posture of a prophet, or so he seemed to think. And the one doing most of the listening did so with almost ritual misgivings, a little round face leaning forward, slowly, looking into the fire, then to the other two, then leaning back and looking to the jagged darkness beyond with pleading, perspiring, round-faced eyes and the unexpressed but religious hope that dawn would come suddenly and brightly. And then there was the one doing most of the drinking, a heavy-set man in a faded, grease-soaked baseball cap, a lazy dignity in the way he leaned back on his side, drinking, looking up at the other two, and every now and then a word of advice.

"You suppose he go come tonight?"

The voice belonged to the little round-faced man, and he hunched up closer to the fire. The bald-headed prophet smiled. The man in the baseball cap looked up from his almost empty bottle and shook his head.

"Man, I told you Willie here he jes talkin. Aint no devil comin back. Tonight nor any other night."

"But jes supposin he do?"

The bald-headed prophet smiled again. "Ifn he do he do. I aint seen de devil but once in my life but I done held my own. I expect I can do de same again. Ifn he do."

And with that Thaddeus slipped from the grassy dune of his concealment to the sandshadows of the beach and into the light of the small orange fire. The three men stopped laughing, stopped talking, stopped drinking, their eyes fixed on this figure of their superstition come to life, their eyes brittle like church glass, the unanimity of their silence like church glass also. Thaddeus cocked his jaw as if to speak, but he didn't, and then he sat down. For maybe five minutes he stared at the silent, waiting, firesinged men, and they stared back, but they were looking through him more than at him, as if the reality of what they saw was still sitting back among the shadows of the dunes. He smiled at these three unmoving almost shadows of men, but still they did not respond. His face was beginning to sweat in the orange glow of the fire, and he wiped the sweat from his brow and his hand on his pants. Then he thought perhaps he would become the devil for these firewaiting silencesinged men, a thought so random and absurd he almost burst out laughing, and yet it was also intriguing. Then he smiled a second time.

"What are you boys all doing out here?"

The three men said nothing.

"You dont mind if I join you, do you?"

The three men still said nothing, their eyes filled with the image of a squatting, sandspitting devil, their eyes about to burst into a thousand pieces, a single image becoming a thousand then a thousand more. Then Thaddeus looked into the kaleidoscope of their eyes.

"I come over in that rowboat over there?"

Thaddeus nodded towards the gray, shadowy heap of the rowboat several yards from where they sat, the boat turned over and pulled up from the water, but not all the way.

"I've been going up and down the coast in that goddamn boat for how long only the devil knows. Seems like I aint been on dry land in a month of Sundays. You all have any more of that beer? I could sure use a swallow."

But with that the eyes like church glass broke into a thousand thousand pieces. The little round-faced, round-eyed man was the first. He looked from Thaddeus to the gray, heaping shadow of the rowboat and the waves lapping there to the one named Willie, the little man's round face getting rounder, and then he scrambled to his feet, kicking sand into the fire, and then he was gone down the beach. The one in the baseball cap was next. He looked first to the not-yet-empty bottle of beer in his hand, then to Thaddeus, to Willie, and then he dropped his bottle and scrambled after the first one. Willie was the last. He looked from the orange-glowing fire to the seemingly smoky silhouette of Thaddeus squatting in the sand to the heap of the rowboat and the swelling memory of his story and the devil he had fought and finally to the shallow craters where the other two had been, a look of fat desperation dripping down the sides of his face, unwilling to believe, it seemed, in the efficacy of his own bald-headed prophecy. Then Thaddeus moved closer to the prodding warmth of the fire and looked up and grinned, but before he could say another word, the prophet named Willie was running after the other two.

Within weeks of Thaddeus coming to the island he had seemingly forgotten about the Reverend and the girl and even Gabriel and the grave beneath the fallen cedar and how Gabriel's life had been a warning to his own. The delirium of his sudden banishment and the time spent with the chain-bound trumpet player, all of that seemed now like some fragment from a childhood nightmare, and so he had put it aside. Even the dream that had brought him to the island he had forgotten. Instead, he abandoned himself utterly to the unthinking festivity of Pappa Toms, and so it was that ten years quickly passed. Grab a beer and sit down. Talk to the girls and watch them bounce up the stairs and the men following and then fuck like the devil and then bounce back down. And sometimes he'd pay a dollar himself and go up the stairs and some of the ones he paid for would ask if the stories were true and he'd say what stories and they'd say the ones about him turning into the devil soon as he got home they'd always heard about the devil and how big he was but they didnt know maybe it was all talk, and he'd say there was only one way to find out and then off they'd go for a couple of nights, maybe even a week. And when ever there was a new girl, Pappa Tom would point her out and Thaddeus would think up some excuse to go talk to her, though these conversations never lasted more than a couple of beers. Of course Thaddeus had no single criteria for the women he selected, though being young and new was certain to rouse his interest, and he did have a thing for blue blue eyes, or at least eyes that could be mistaken for blue, but he never became emotionally involved with any of them, he was against that. Women were something to be enjoyed, he thought, like the beer. But he'd be damned if he'd let them sneak in and take over his life. His life was not to be like other lives. It hadn't been. It wasn't. The ramshackle cabin of his indifference and the black squirrels nesting in the eaves above or the raccoons in the crawlspace below, and every afternoon catch some crabs, and make a few dollars that way, and then head on down to Pappa Toms and buy a girl. Or maybe she didn't even need to be bought. He hadn't bought half of them, they'd just come up on their own and opened up their legs. He didn't mind. But none of them had ever said a word about the primitive, earthy, dissolute squalor of his existence, not the ones he'd paid for, nor the ones he hadn't, and god damn anybody that did. His strength lay in the doing of things his way. And that was that.

Then he met Kiri Girl. For almost ten years nothing had happened to challenge the dissolute squalor his life had become. And now there she was sitting there in the orange-gleaming light of Pappa Toms, the two of them sitting at a small table shoved up against the stairwell and the shriek and smash of laughter all around, like the sound of bottles breaking. Her sitting directly across from him but looking away, and him not remembering when she sat down but wanting to ask. But he said nothing to Kiri Girl. Not at first. Which was goddamn odd, he thought. But it seemed that his mouth didn't work, and he vaguely remembered the same thing happening one time before, one time before a woman had troubled him, or perhaps it was a girl, but he couldn't place the other one, and so he just sat there, staring at this woman, this girl with blue blue eyes. And there she sat with an air of noble almost scolding indifference and those blue blue eyes staring off into space, and it wasn't just Thaddeus she ignored, but the sounds of the piano and the laughter and the dancing and drinking, all of this whirling around her and she did not respond. And then it came to Thaddeus that maybe this girl was not a girl, maybe she was a work of art, even her face had the finely cut precision of a marble statue, and with this in mind he leaned up over the table and peered closely at the finely worked skin of this unmoved and unmoving beauty, so close he could almost taste it, feel it, yes, he thought, she's one hell of a statue, his hands moving up to confirm his suspicions, and then quite without his expecting it, she did move, sharply and suddenly, and he blinked some and sat back a lump in his chair. Yes, once before he had been troubled by a girl, but in the nearness of this sculpted work of art, he had forgotten. Then Kiri Girl spoke to Thaddeus, though even he did not see her lips move.

"What you want from me."

He coughed some and blurted out a response.

"You want to dance some?" he said.

"That what you want?"

"Yes."

"That all you want?"

Again the coughing.

"Yes."

And then his throat was clear.

"All right by me."

So they stood up in the smoky light of their watering eyes, the white and yellow string of bulbs flickering from the rafters, on then off then on then off again, an unending barrage of shadows flickering across his face and hers, or perhaps they were smiling at each other, but who could say. But they did not move from the table, and all the while they stood there they were looking at each other, eyes hooked into eyes, as if the piano and the music and the others dancing and laughing and drinking did not exist, as if all that they did not see were but a dream, and all that they did see were the only reality. They stood and stared at each other and then each became an image in the others eye, an image of a time that once was, like each was a mirror of the past, or at least she was, an image of youth, of beauty, an image of the sacred, and then the images were gone, and all that remained were the mirrors, empty mirrors waiting for some new image to fill their frames. Or so it seemed.

"You sure."

"Yes."

The music of the piano slowed, no longer a racing staccato now, it was something smoother, like the gentle roll of the black tidewater, and the dancing shadows of the others also slowed, even the walls were now rolling with the tide, a lazy black tide it seemed, hips curling around hips, arms curling around arms, and Thaddeus and this girl who was taken for a work of art waded into that black and rolling tide, arms curling around arms, hips curling around hips, then they were lost in the sweaty, heaving, swelling blackness, hallelujah. Later they had gone up to his cabin, though who had suggested it Thaddeus could not remember. But there they were, sitting at the table shoved up against the half-open window and the heavy, warm dark from outside coming in. The faint, faintly warm, yellow glow of an oil lamp showing itself in streaks on the table, and also faintly on the face of the girl.

But Thaddeus was turned away from the lamp.

"You know about me?"

"I know what they been saying."

"And what's that?"

"They been saying you is the devil."

"What do you think?"

"If you wants to be the devil that all right by me. Maybe I like the devil."

What she saw in this man who might have been the devil she never said. And he never asked. But there was something there. It was in the way she spoke, the coppery insistence of her voice, and also the way she moved about the room, a haughty indifference in every step, and yet also a measured willingness. Then they both moved from the table and the lamp to the darkness of the back room and the sagging, gray shadow of the bed and the lamp light not reaching there, but they did not mind. Then they were in the bed.

"So how bout I show you what the devil can do?"

Kiri Girl smiled. "What ever you want to do you just do it."

And then he was finished he rolled off the girl name of Kiri Girl lay back in the sagging bed of his exhaustion his head to one side to her side propped up on his elbow he looked into the blue blue of her eyes brightly shining blue even in the dark and saw himself his nakedness shining wet in the darkness of the pinetimbered room a languid lover

now the girl name of Kiri Girl looked up and smiled her
nakedness shining in the darkness also she smiled again and
for a moment the darkness was gone as if her whole body
had smiled with the light of the moon or of the sun her
whole body the pliant curve of her neck to her shoulders
and arms the slippingaway arc of her breasts slipping up
then down with every breath the gentle slope of thigh to
knee to calf her whole body smiling with the light of the
moon or of the sun and yet he did not return her smile to
do so would have been to risk eternal damnation he felt
certain of that in this moment of his conquest to do so
would have been to tear off a little piece of his soul and
give it to the devil yes that was it soon he would have
nothing left and the devil would have it all yes of course
there was nothing wrong with taking a woman to bed
especially one as willing as this one it was perfectly natural
an urge but nothing more and there was nothing wrong
with giving in to those primitive urges nothing wrong with
worshiping the sun or the moon yet a man could only go so
far yes there was no use getting emotional over such a thing
as a woman and for a moment the memory of the other
one took root in his brain and it was sharp and piercing and
he winced and then the memory was gone and it was Kiri
Girl once more yes, there was no use getting emotional no it
was better to curtail the emotional part get rid of it entirely
or if that was not possible then give his emotions to
something else yes that was the trick let her stay as long as
she liked but not give in to the emotions of it yes yes but all
the same he better watch out with this girl if he didnt well
God only knew what might happen if he didnt then the
man name of Thaddeus watched the girl name of Kiri Girl
and he fell completely into those blue blue eyes and he
knew that everything he had ever thought or felt or hoped
for up till that moment had been a lie she was the light of
the moon or the sun and if she wanted his soul it was hers

for the taking and so he watched her lying there next to him until he was no longer sure why he was watching then the girl smiled once more curled her hip around his and closed her eyes and with that the light of the sun was gone or perhaps it was the light of the moon . . .

Ten months have passed in an instant. Or so it seems. Ten months which he thinks he's just forgotten. Like the ten years before Kiri Girl and before that the dream of his banishment and before that and before that and before that. The years gone by in a shimmering, weaving blur like rain. Or maybe the past never was. Yes, that's it. He has always been here, the living of his life and the salt-sweet smell of the ocean and the breeze coming in and the nights with Kiri Girl, and the mornings too. This is all he has ever wanted. He does not remember anything else. Him standing there at one end of the porch. At the other end a clump of blacks huddled together, a lantern hanging above them, the lantern lit, swinging gently in the night air, the yellow light mixing with the shadows.

No it hurts noit hurts noithurts noithurtsnoithurtsnoithurts.

The voice of a woman screams through the cracks of the pine-timbered walls and claws at the ears of Thaddeus and the blacks. Then Thaddeus moving to the window, and the heavy silence that comes after such a scream, but still it is there, the scrape and wretch of it, in the pit of his stomach. But he does not show it. His body does not even flinch, though this could be just a trick of the light, the lantern flashing across his face, and then shadows. He puts his face to the window and it sticks there. He sees Kiri Girl lying in bed, the brown bubble of her stomach half-hidden by the white of the sheets spread across her knees, her skin glowing with the heat of perspiration. A covey of blackwomenfaces hovering around the bed, the girl, folding and unfolding sheets, the women boiling water on the top of the black stove, stroking her arms her legs her brow with a cool, damp cloth, singing softly, slowly, then rising, almost moaning, a song about the birthing of babies. Thaddeus listens to the words a moment, the song lingering. Then he turns from the window, absently, helplessly, and waits for the next scream.

Then the blacks at the other end of the porch, talking softly.

"She sure can carry a tune."

"She sure can."

"Aint like any music I ever heard."

"What music you talking about, you damn near deaf, why if you done cover up you ears with you bigknuckle hands wouldnt make no bit of difference."

Then the one who had spoken presses the flat of his hands against his ears and opens his mouth in silent song. The others laugh, a knowing laugh, some looking to the open-mouthed jester in their midst, some looking to the door, the windows of the cabin, and some looking to Thaddeus, a solitary figure leaning against the unfinished cut of a corner post, and then the laughter lessening, lessening, then lost in the darkness beyond the porch. Thaddeus puts his pipe to his mouth, strikes a match against the post, then brings the match to the pipe and inhales, the flame catching, the smoke rising, a cloud of white above his head. Then the woman screams again. And the blacks turn from the scream, some rubbing their ears, and talk some more.

"Sure hopes she has dat chile of hers soon enough," says one. The others nod, some still rubbing their ears.

"It aint hers," says another, the voice almost inaudible.

"Dont care whose it is. I cant be listening to dat singing of hers much more."

"I said it aint hers."

"What aint. What you talking about?"

"If she keep singing like dat much more my ears they go fall off land on the floor."

"Mine too."

"I said de chile it aint hers."

The voice speaking with the determined assurance of a prophet, the absurdity of the statement obscured by the faintest possibility of its being true. Or so it seems.

"What you mean by dat?" The others nod, no longer rubbing their ears, puzzled, intrigued. "She giving birth to it right now."

"She givin birth but dat chile aint hers. Aint hers. Dat chile de chile of de devil hisself. You mark my words. De devil he jes using dat girl bring his chile into dis here world. You mark my words."

The clump of blacks huddle closer together beneath the light of the lantern, the blacks marking words perhaps, the voice of the prophet drawing them in. The prophet stands motionless in the middle of the clump, his bald head shining in the swirl of light and dark. Then the voices of the others break from the huddle, a swirl of light and dark, also.

"How you know dat Willie?"

"Yeah, how you know dat?"

But the prophet name of Willie simply raises his hand and the swirling voices stop. Then the prophet speaks again.

"De devil he done come among us. So says de Lord. De devil he done come to take our women for hisself. Jes like de serpent done in de garden of Eden. You all know what Im is talking about. He been doing dat ever since he done come to dis here isle and we been let him too. Is time we done put we heel to his snakeuglyhead and give we heel a turn. Dat de only way deal wid de devil I know of."

And with that the prophet name of Willie retreats into the comfortable shadows of the porch, the trace of a smile spreading across his face. The clump of blacks huddle closer still, no longer needing to mark words it seems, some looking to the man name of Thaddeus who has now become the devil, some looking to the cabin again, to the girl inside giving birth to his demon child, some hiding their faces in the shadow of Willies smile, all of them aware of the presence of the serpent at the other end of the porch, the serpent coiled around the corner post, all of them grgrgrinding the cups of their heels into the soft wet pinewood of the porch, the grinding unconscious, perhaps, instinctive, the heels turning faster and faster and faster. The man name of Thaddeus turns at the sound, looks to the clump of heelgrinding blacks beneath the lantern, but says nothing, smokes on his pipe some more, and then the tobacco is used up. Then the blacks become frightened and turn to the bald head of their prophet once again.

"What you mean by we heels?"

"What we supposed to do?"

And the prophet hears the words of their fear and for a moment he does not answer. There is no answer, it seems. And the blacks wait for the prophet to confirm their suspicions. They wait a moment longer. And then the woman inside screams a third time and the silence of the prophet is forgotten.

"There she go some more."

"Aint she done?"

"Sound like she done hit the highest note on de scale."

"Sounds like it."

"Sounds like she done, you mean."

So Thaddeus turns from the darkness beyond the porch when the woman inside the cabin screams, turns once more to face the window, the door, the smoked-out pipe in his hand. Then the scream fades and he opens the door and steps inside and makes his way over to the woman and the bed and the child. The clump of blacks clump in behind him, silently, as if they are a reluctant shadow, and then they spread out against the wall. There is a heavy, warm, stifling stillness about the cabin. And also an emptiness. Kiri Girl lies in the bed, the sheets pulled up to her shoulders, she is sleeping now, the rhythmic rise and fall of her applehard breasts barely noticeable, a testament to the pain of giving birth perhaps. And the women who eased her pain stand stiffly behind the bed, almost bitterly, the hollow of their eyes looking through him, he thinks, as if he were a doorway to some other world. And then the door closes and he sees the child, a small blueblack raisin of a child in the arms of one of the women. The child does not move. And then Thaddeus is holding the child, he looks at its wrinkled face, its wrinkled hands, and does not move either. The child of the devil, the voice says. A whisper from the shadows on the wall but Thaddeus does not hear the words. The face of the devil. The hands of the devil. Then the voice stops for a moment and Thaddeus steps with the child to the door and then they are outside. The shadows on the wall become blacks again and clump through the door and stop beneath the light and dark of the lantern.

Then the voice begins again.

From that moment on Thaddeus did not speak to the girl named Kiri Girl, or even really think of her until after she abandoned him to his misery of solitude some five years later, and then when he did think of her in later years it was with bitter, halting recollection, not because she had left, but because he could not separate the memory of her being there from the unbreathing quiet of his still-born son, and he did not speak to any one else either, except for maybe a few words to get his crabs sold, and that went on until after the end of the second great war. But it was those first few years that were the worst. He expected biscuits for breakfast, and coffee, though how they came to be on the table he never bothered to ask, and then he would spend the day up along the ocean side of the island and maybe catch some crabs, at least that's what she thought he was doing, but he rarely came home with anything but an empty basket. At night he would grumble over the beans, but never a word directly her way, and then he would grab the small red lantern and light it and off he would go down the hill and vanish into the black black wood. She used to stand there sometimes on the porch and watch that red bead of light as it bounced along, smaller, smaller, and then it would be gone. And sometimes she was still there in the morning when the light broke up from the beach and settled in a soft, hazy blue about the cabin, and there he was coming back up the hill, and the light in the small red lantern was out. But most of the time she was asleep. And then this was always true. Of course she often wondered where he went during the night, and sometimes she would wake long after midnight and feel the stifling emptiness of the cabin closing in and she would imagine her Thaddeus had gone to the devil, but most of the time she figured what he did was his business and let it be.

The only thing she never forgave him for was taking the child without her say-so. Even if it was dead it had been her child as much as his. More so, she told herself, it was my stomach it done come out of. He didn't do nothing but stand on the porch and wait it out. But he never told her what he had done with it. And she never asked him. And then one day Kiri Girl decided to leave. Why she had stayed so long in the silence of his misery even she did not know. Perhaps she had no where else to go. But she left all the same. She watched Thaddeus go off with his basket and his net and his pail of rotting chicken heads, and then she packed up her suitcase and headed into town. And when this old man of her last day came back later that afternoon, and he was an old man by then, or at least he looked it with his suddenly white, stringy, tangled hair and his black, black eyes of hunch-backed bewilderment, he hardly noticed she had gone.

-3-

"What you think he doing"
(dreaming)
"What you think"
(or not dreaming)
"Maybe he dead"
(his eyes closed)
"Maybe he aint"
(or half-closed)

But Thaddeus did not move. Perhaps he could not move. He had not moved in almost twenty years, or so he sometimes thought. The birth of the stillborn child had robbed him of his strength. But even though he did not move, he watched with growing interest these two adolescent boys of his half-dreaming as they ran up along the sunwarmed beach and then stopped to have a look at this old man sleeping in the sand. They looked carefully, suspiciously at the sunwarmed but strangely white white face. As boys will when meeting a would-be devil for the first time, a mixture of awe and fear shaping their features. And then they were the ones not moving. They looked from the devilmaybeface of the old man to the basket of crabs by his side to the pattern of sticks and strings inching across the sand to the murky yellow-green of the tidewater channel. They saw fishheads drifting in the shallows. Or maybe chickenheads. They saw a basket of big blue crabs, the crabs fighting for a place in the sunwarmed basket, the click click of their claws sounding harsh, discordant, alarming in the warm, sunny air. Then the smaller boy seemed about to run off with the basket of click click clicking, and the bigger boy was about to follow, but then they stopped. The smaller boy now with a smile stretched across his face. And all the while the watcher watched.

click click
you see em
click
yousee

For a moment time stopped. The ripple of the murky, yellow-green waves became like glass, a glass of possibilities, perhaps. And the two adolescent boys looked into this glass and saw themselves, but were unaware of the possibilities, or so it seemed. Then they looked beyond themselves and they saw four giant crabs crowding around the remains of a chickenhead, blue crabs, each as big in the eyes of the boys as the sun or the moon or some other celestial body, a phenomenon caused, no doubt, by the refraction of light in water. Then the glass became a ripple of yellow-green waves again, the tidewater rolling in over the crabs, the chickenhead, up the sandy bank, and then back out, the crabs eating undisturbed, and now the bigger boy down in the sand, taking hold of the string, winding the string around his wrist, winding slowly, slowly, the chickenhead moving through the sandsifted water, and also moving slowly were the four crabs, still undisturbed, following the half-eaten head, the smaller boy so excited now he could fly to the moon, or to the sun, then the smaller boy shouting to the bigger boy, the bigger boy blinking in the sudden glare of shouted words, and then shouting himself

wheres the wheres the
click click
wheres the net
im is looking im is looking

wheres the

click

the smaller boy wondering where he was going to find a net, wondering if the old man had one, was sure he must, and the old man no longer sleeping, suddenly rising from the hardpacked sand, his eyes burning with the white of the sun, or the moon, then shouting about his crabs, his basket, the bigger boy not moving, not saying a word, as if time had stopped once again, the smaller boy turning, heels sandkicking, the smaller boy then moving through time, or so it seemed

cmon

not a word

you click click boys think you can rob a man of his click click crabs and click click like that

what you

not a word

what you waiting for

you boys got a thing or two coming ifn thats what you click click think

not a word

cmon

then the smaller boy was running down the beach as a smaller boy will run when being chased by something larger older the devil perhaps and the bigger boy eager to follow tearing string from wrist then up and after but catching his foot on the old mans basket the bigger boy down in the sand a second time the basket sandtwisting the once imprisoned crabs now rolling towards the sea clickety clickety clickety click the bigger boy wondering what the devilmaybefaced old man had in store for him the boy watching the blue crabs vanish into the waves him wishing he could set free the crab part of himself locked inside and then vanish in the waves also as if his true soul were that of a giant blue crab a kindred spirit to those vanishing in the haze of the tidewater refuge then the black of the old mans shadow looked down on the boywannabecrab then down came the net on the bigger boys head bigger but not so big and whoosh his eyes went wide with the fear that comes from being netted . . .

Several hours later, after the boy had left his cabin for home, Thaddeus stepped out onto the porch. There was still the smell of beans in the air, and he breathed that in, and then there was the night and it had come in heavy and dark and there was the promise of a summer storm and he breathed that in too, but no storm came. Then Thaddeus went back inside and fumbled a bit with a kerosene lantern and lit it and then came back out, but the lantern only made the darkness seem darker. So he stood there a moment on the porch in the gently swinging glow of the lantern light and watched the orange sparks of the fireflies blurring and weaving their way through the tree shadows along the bottom of the hill and then fading in the deepening gloom, and ever so faintly he heard the sound of the sea. He started off down the hill and moved through the black of the trees and the moss slapping him in the face and the low-waiting branches whipping back and stumbling over roots or almost and also the gnats. He moved through all of this, though just where he was going even he did not seem to know, away from the faint sea-sound and the porch and the smell of twice-cooked beans, and then the air was still and hot and had the feel of being dead.

It was good, he thought, that thing he had said about fear. He hadn't known just what to say to the boy, all the way he'd been dragging him up through the marsh grass he'd been wondering what'd he say and how he'd say it, give him a thing or two to think about, that's what he had told himself back at the beach, which caught the general drift of his mood concerning the boy but it didn't help much with the particulars, and then he'd been sitting on that Co-

Cola crate and getting worried by then but he figured he might as well give the boy a couple of good whacks for the crabs and get something to eat, and if he didn't think of anything by then he'd maybe give him a couple more. But then there was the way that boy looked when he ate up those beans, like they were the last beans he was ever gonna eat, him spooning them in as fast as he could but his eyes weren't watching the beans, that's when it had come to Thaddeus, him now remembering the words   *most folks is so afraid of living they cant wait to go to war and they is so afraid of dying they cant pass up a church without going inside*   But that boy didn't show the same kind of fear most people had, hell no, not the way he kept to himself and his eyes always watching, why he didn't even cry out from the hickory, he just stood there waiting for more, not insolent or defiant, just detached, and for a moment Thaddeus had felt he was looking into his own eyes.   This is what Thaddeus was thinking when he looked at that boy.   He could still see him eating there and those eyes above that spoon. Goddamn it, and he was laughing to himself now, I bet that boy would've been shitting beans if I'd of taken up that stick again. Then Thaddeus laughed out loud, but then just as suddenly became quiet again, thoughtful, for it seemed to him a profound wisdom he had spoken to the boy.

Then the thinking was done, but Thaddeus was still walking through the black black woods. He walked in stiff, unthinking silence, and then he came to a small tar-papered shack overlooking the black black channel water several yards below, and he went inside. The very same shack where more than thirty years earlier Long Jim had bemoaned the loss of his leg and the two lanterns had been left. But it was dark now, for those lanterns had long since expired, and Thaddeus set his own on a chair by the door and then took a stick and lit the two still there on the floor, and also a small red lantern in the middle of the table, and then he sat down in another chair. The last time he had been there was eight or nine years after the child and he had made a new door out of a piece of pine and dragged the broken table up the slope and fixed that too, but he hadn't done anything about the chalk circle. It had seemed almost burned into the wood slats of the floor. And so he had left it as a reminder, a marker of sorts, though of just what he had only vaguely articulated to himself. But in time even this circle had disappeared from the floor, and everything was as it had been before Long Jim and his leg, except for the two lanterns.

It's been a too, too long time, he thought, and then with unhurried movements he reached underneath the table and pulled out a canvas backpack and opened it and pulled out a can of peaches, or maybe it was pears, and a can opener and then opened the can and sniffed at it and it seemed tolerable in spite of the years so he slurped down the fruit and then the sweet, sticky juice. Then he left the empty tin on the table and put away the can opener and the backpack, and then he picked up the small, red, now red-glowing lantern and was out the door, glancing but briefly at the dark gash of the backwater channel below and then making his way around to the rear of the shack, and there he stood a while contemplating the dark, sloping grade of a small rise, and then beyond that it dipped away. Then he started up, the dim yellow glow of the tar-paper shack unfelt against his back, but he was walking more cautiously now than when he had come up through the wood, more slowly, almost not moving at all, as if in nearing his purpose in coming to this place he had suddenly changed his mind, or forgotten what it was, or was by some invisible, oppressive hand being forced to a stuttering, halting, but inevitable abnegation of things. Of himself, perhaps. Of the way things had been the past twenty years and him not giving a goddamn. From somewhere a wisp of wind fluttered against his face and for a moment he thought he could smell the sea, and then the wind and the sea-smell were gone and he was standing at the top of this small rise and looking down into the spreading darkness below him. He knew near enough where it was, but he couldn't see it in the dark. Thinking *damn, I should of been back long before this, what if something dug it up, what then, or maybe there was water got in and floated it away, this goddamn swamp you cant keep it in one place before its bubbling up somewhere else, goddamn it, what the hell I been doing.*

Uncautiously now, he trundled through the darkness, the small red lantern bobbing its light this way and that in enthusiastic but silent accompaniment. But the dark did not give way, and seemed even to suck up the light as he reached the bottom, so he ranged back and forth through a dark, thickening clutch of willow oak and some bay, and there was also a tangled, viny mass of muscadine and wisteria, all the while punching at the darkness with the lantern, his free hand pushing through the branches and the vines, and then dragging himself through. He was no longer merely a watcher of things, or so it seemed, but was once again a doer. And then suddenly he found it, a small clear patch among a few pine, and he set the lantern down and knelt and pulled at the vines that had crept over the mound and the three flagstones he had put there to mark the grave, and the vines came loose and he brushed them away and also the loose dirt and then re-stacked the flagstones neatly one on top of two, and then he was satisfied and sat back some. Still he kept his eyes on the grave, an intent, silent, aching, but also bewildered look about his face, as if he had suddenly and unexpectedly seen his own newly-dug grave in the now soft, humming dark. Thinking *I should of been back long before this, but I've been here some and that's more than she can say, hell, she didn't come even once, she didn't even ask, and it was hers as much as mine.* And from a distance there was only the small lantern glowing like a red bead against the night, for the old man had seemingly vanished into the moist, enveloping shadows. But still sitting there. Thinking *but maybe she didn't want it, that would explain it, maybe she even wanted it born dead and that way she wouldn't have to bother.* And then *hell, it wasn't hers at all, not ever, it was always mine, only and always.*

And then even the light from the lantern was gone.

-4-

And then he had come to the end of it. The end of a life and the death that was to be. And he was not afraid. In the brutal solitude of his old age he had come to appreciate the directness of death, the unblinking honesty of dying. He thought of death and dying as he might think of a quiet conversation with an old friend, no eye of God watching over your every step, no hand of the devil trying to trip you up, just two old friends talking for eternity, an endless stream of words what you doin here i been riding in this here car for more years than i care to count on account of these chains on my feet i been riding around hope to come across someone help me break free is that what you doin here is you the one

He tossed the overgnawed crab bone to the pile of white at the center of the table the bone clattering among the many bones. Then he stood up from the table and walked to the door the walk of a man having eaten too much each step somewhat rounded him moving to the openness of the porch he stopped a moment the sickly green sky having become a deep heavy purple the storm beginning now the first few drops of rain pelting the ground and him listening to the rain, and the mingling of past and present was complete, or so it seemed, him looking over to the boy whyunt you just pull up them pants and sit yourself down i aint gonna eat these goddam beans all by myself   and then he saw that the boy had finished with an endless stream of big blue crabs had finished the last of the words his words and then the boy was gone and instead he saw himself in the deep of the backwater wood the black shadows of the water oak and the pine and the redbay becoming a single shadow the wink-on-wink-off-wink-on-again light of the fireflies patches of bright yellow flitting from branch to branch wink on wink off like the souls of the dead flitting from the here to the hereafter lost souls perhaps wink on wink off and the man name of Thaddeus followed the winking dead through the trees follow me follow me follow me a thousand voices winking a thousand and a thousand more the voices winking with laughter in the dark dark follow me follow me follow me and he followed the patchwork of beckoning laughter then the bright yellow dimming the laughter growing softer and softer with every step and the laughter was gone and he saw the wrinkled face the wrinkled hands of a small child a small blueblack body in his arms the child not breathing the fingers curled toes curled and there he was in a small clearing him now laying the child of his devilmaybesorrow by his side him then remembering the voices on the porch and her pain and then the silence then him digging in the earth the warm soil moist in his hands digging deeper and deeper the weight of the earth the weight the click click click of crab toed feet then the black boy almost a man inside the cabin his face pressed up against the glass of the window and then he Thaddeus kneeling before a small black hole him breathing hard his lungs filling with the quiet dirtdamp air then him laying the child in the hole and he had wanted to give this child something of himself a sense of life and some words to live by but there were no words now not for this blueblack child and him feeling wordless voiceless but only for a moment the grief the inadequacy the fear then pouring out up and then the body of the blueblack child changing then changed the blueblack white the white white of the moon it seemed the wrinkled face not wrinkled the fingers the toes not curled and him sprinkling the black earth upon the body sprinkling slowly the whiteness of the child rising up to fill the hollow places in the sky then the whiteness gone him kneeling before the mound of a newly filled grave him kneeling now in prayer the voice of his grief and the whiteness of his words rising up to the sky also you there and then im here and then i do not understand and then you were not meant to understand and then why did this child have to die and then what child and then the child buried in this grave my child my flesh my blood my bone and then i do not know children are born children die i do not know why there is no why only living and dying and then but why this child i do not understand and then you were not meant to understand there is no understanding you must root out the memory of the living child from the hollow black of your brain and bury that memory alongside the body and then it is more than memory and then then you must become the child and take your place in the grave and the child will be of no more consequence   that all you want yes all right by me   and for a moment the past became the past once again and the old man name of Thaddeus found himself standing on the edge of the porch still standing there still looking to the stormy blackness of the sky but he did not seem to notice it the harsh pelting of the rain now against his face but he did not seem to feel it him moving now to the cabinside of the porch a lantern hanging from a hook above the door him lifting the glass of the lantern taking a match from his pocket then striking a flame the light sputtering a moment in the breezy stormy dark then catching then filtering through the yellow yellow glass and mixing with the dark him stepping from the lantern and the swirling light and dark and sitting down in a cane-back chair the rain sweeping across the edges of the porch now but not where he was sitting him sitting there listening to the voice of a child the child singing then the last of the earth would fall upon him and he would be surrounded by its blackness its warmth and the singing would the singing would him taking his pipe from his pocket putting pipe to mouth the pipe unlit him listening to the words of the song what was now is what is now was an endless stream of words

. . . but the very next morning, along come a third man, only he didnt look like much, he wunt big big like the first, and he wunt wearing a knife like the second, and the animals they thought they done seen enough they was just shaking they heads some more they was saying say it wunt go be long fore this one in the alligator belly just like the rest, but the third man he didnt pay them tree-sitting animals no mind, maybe he done heard that alligator roaring and roaring and come looking the same as the first and the second, but he wunt coming too fast or either bold, and he wunt talking neither, cause he knowd a alligator wunt nothing fool with, all he did he just stop along the edge of the swamp and he was looking to that alligator sunning hisself on that log, and next he pull out a piece of rope he make hisself a noose and that was it, and all the while that alligator he was waiting on the third man same as the rest, and he was waiting and waiting and waiting but wunt nothing happening, and by and by the alligator he done look to see what was what, and all he seen was a man with a rope aint make no move, and the alligator he wunt sure what to think with that, and the animals up in dem trees they wunt sure neither, and then it seem like the end was coming cause the alligator he wunt go wait no more, he was sliding from that log into the water he was go show that man whose world it was, only before that alligator make it halfway up the bank, the third man he done slip a thick thick noose around them alligator jaws and pull it tight, and with that the alligator he wunt able to open his mouth, and he was shaking his head this way and that try to shake hisself loose, only wunt nothing he could do, and the more he was

shaking, the more tire he was, and pretty soon all he wanted was to slip way into the cool of the swamp maybe hide in a hole, but the third man he didnt let go, and when the alligator he done tire hisself out, the third man he done pull on that rope some more, and then he tied it off, and before that alligator he knowd what was what, the third man he done grab him by the tail and he was swinging him round and around and around, and when the third man he done let go of that rope, that alligator he went rising up through them trees, and then the alligator he was gone . . .

The Storm

It been three week since I seen the old man, not since he pull me out from that alligator, which it just go to show how Willie and the rest of them they all been wrong. He aint no devil. The truth is most people just dont know him, and he dont care. Then Im is thinking say just why it is I aint seen him and what it is he been doing, and soon as I thinking that it have the feeling like the old man he waiting on me this very minute, and then it aint the old man at all it like I is supposed to go do something or something go happen, and then it the old man again. It sure is strange thinking like that the way it shift back and forth. Then Jonas Lee he come hobble along on his crutches and I aint thinking on nothing no more and Jonas Lee he look like he some kind of crab the way he moving through the dust of the street, and then he go through the gate and bang it shut, and before I can say a word he sitting next to me out the front stoop.

The first thing Jonas do he smile he saying he another idea, and that the last thing I want to hear, but aint nothing I can do cause Jonas he already talking. Jonas he saying say he wanna head on up to Pappa Toms maybe slip inside and he aint wanna go all the way by hisself maybe I come along, didnt I always want to stick my head on the inside, of course I did, didnt I know the same stories, I'd heard them too, anyways what was I doing round here the middle of the afternoon, wunt nothing for excitement like Pappa Toms, so what I say. Is just then my mama she call out from the back of the cabin she saying say I best get inside help her tie down the windows aint I look to the sky there a big big blow coming look to be here a couple of hour maybe three, and mama she right about the sky it a pale graygreen stretch out to the south, but there aint much wind yet, and there aint no rain far as I can see, and before she open her mouth call out again Im is walking up the street with Jonas Lee.

The whole way we walking Jonas Lee he telling me about his brother B. J. how he done walk in all by hisself the first time he ever been to Pappa Toms, how the lights they was burning low from the walls, and was all kind of grease-heads and chaw-talkers from over the coast sitting at some darkwood tables and drinking rye or whiskey and laughing and humming and talk about the girls, and some of the girls they already found theyself a partner they was dancing out front or maybe up the stairs they already had enough to drink, and there was a whole lot more waiting to wet they throats, but B. J. he couldnt move even to lick his lips. Was then a couple of them girl they done come up to him, and they was giggling say what was he doing there didnt he want to come upstairs or was he nail to the floor, and B. J. his eyes they was smiling up and down them girls he looking to catch some skin, and then they was moving up the stairs, the two girl in front they was wiggling they hips side to side, and B. J. his eyes they was wiggling side to side the same, and then they was up in some room and the door shut, and every now and then they voices was drifting down, first was B. J. saying say he ready he waiting, and them two girl they was giggling, and then B. J. he was saying say what they do like that for there room enough on this bed for three, and then them two girl they was giggling some more, and the next thing what happen them two girl they was running down the stairs and out the front and then they was gone, and B. J. he was at the top of the stairs and shout about them two girl he was saying say they done rob him stole his pants off the chair, and sure enough, he wunt wearing nothing but his shoes, and the dancers and the drinkers down the first floor they was all laughing out loud, and some what knowd B. J. was calling out say how you like you first taste you must of liked it a whole lot cause look like you hungry for more, and then everybody was laughing so much was hard to think, and B. J. he was down the steps, he took them three at a time, and then he was out the front the same as them two girl.

Pappa Toms it shining with a couple hundred orangewhite light strung along a black shingle roof, they winking on and then off and then on and then off again, look like fireflies floating up in the black of the wood, and there a heavy crowd of peoples going up some blue blue steps and across this low hang porch, and there a fat head he be nodding evening from top of a blackwood stool and he saying say hope you all have you some kind of ruckus tonight storm or no storm for blow, and the peoples they all nodding they heads, only some they turning they eyes have a look at that graygreen storm-coming sky, but only a moment, and they all going through a couple of blue blue door, and then they gone.

Me and Jonas Lee we watching from back in the hammock, and Jonas Lee he saying say the only way we moving past that nodding fat head is through the back door, and with that we moving down a narrow blackwood walkway stretch around to the backside of Pappa Toms. We moving up along from the water, past a couple three rowboat tie down in the water and something else look like a barge, past some old wood boxes and some empty bottle toss down in the grass, and then we sliding inside of a black screen door almost fall off its hinges, and the next thing I knows we is sitting at a two-chair table shove up in the corner, and aint nobody seen us come in. There sure is a lot going on. There a couple three talking heads sitting next to us, they saying say there be some storm coming tonight and that the truth, and then they laugh, and then they drinking they beer. Most the mens they drinking bottle beer and some they drinking whiskey or rye, and some they sitting hunch over they tables slap anything on the behind it come for wiggle by, and some they just tapping they feet to the music, and some they wearing white string ties and stub toe shoes and they out there on the dancing floor they saying say come on wind come on rain aint nothing look bad you riding a train, and a whole lot of other things aint make no sense, but them girls they giggling no matter what they say and moving up close, and then the mens they all shouting some more. All this happening to the sound of a brown-bear piano man sitting up front at a tin pan piano and bang away at the keys, and he smiling like he a whole other piano stuck up in his mouth, and his head it bobbing back and forth with every note, and the music it swell up in the smoke-yellow glow of the lights, bigger, bigger, and bigger, and them dancing people they moving faster and faster and faster, pretty soon aint nothing to see but arms reaching up and legs kicking out, how nobody been kick I aint know, and me and Jonas Lee we watching like we watching a movie.

Is then a long-legged woman come walking into the roadhouse up front she move across the floor, she wearing some kind of gold wrap around her body and she has two yellow-brown eye match her yellow-brown skin, and a long thick braid of hair hang down her back, and everybody they staring at her the way she moving through Pappa Toms, they aint dancing or either drinking, they aint doing nothing no more, and she swishing this way and that like she some kind of river, and then some they start up when she pass by, they saying say look at that Jordan she the only woman in this place, she the land of milk and honey come to us, aint no river you need to cross you on top of her, but the woman she just smile and dont say nothing, and all the while me and Jonas Lee we just four blinking eyes, and wouldnt it be something talk to a woman like that, only what you go say, and then wouldnt need nothing to say, just looking at her all I want to do, and all of a sudden it look like she coming to me and Jonas Lee, only what she go do that for I dont know, and then she standing right there, she looking me up and down and smiling, and I wondering what Jonas Lee go think only just then Jordan she leaning down real close, and the way she smell, like apricots or something, it knock Jonas Lee out of my head, all I care about is breath that Jordan in, and all the while I breathing, that gold wrap it going swish swish swish, and then Jordan she running her fingers through my hair and whispering in my ear, she saying say come with me sweetie you follow me aint nothing you need to worry about I only go show you a thing or two maybe you like it, and the next thing I knows she kissing me on my neck and then around to my mouth, and the way she smell like apricots and her tongue curling up around mine, it almost knock me out, and then she pull away and she pulling me away with her, and she saying say, come on sweetie if the rest of you move like that we go have us some sweet time.

First thing Im is thinking is I aint never been on a dance floor before, and all that twisting and grinding and kicking and shouting, well I just dont know, but just then that brown-bear piano man he slowing things down, he playing a grief-song now about some girl been left by a railroad man but then she marry his brother, and maybe I can do that, only Jordan she must have some other idea cause we moving past the dancing and the heat of that sad sad song, and Jordan she saying say come on sweetie aint too long now, only she aint say where we going, and the next thing I knows we heading upstairs, up these rickety old steps been cover by an old blue rug, and Im is looking back at the dancing and the piano man and Jonas Lee he still sitting at that two-table chair in the corner only look like he have his own trouble cause a couple girl they got a hold of his crutch, aint nobody let go, and then Jordan she saying we almost there it wont be long, and we moving down a lamp-lit hall.

I aint never seen a hall like that. The lamps they aint giving off much light, it like walking through a blueblack cloud, and there doors all over the place, and Jordan she trying every door she see, but they all lock, and Im is trying a couple myself, and one door it do come open, only out come a bony arm man, and he waving a bottle of rye in the air and he saying when the fire too hot the wick most likely go soft, and then he rattling with a bony-arm laugh, look like he about to head downstairs, and then a voice come calling out say I aint mean it Horace you come back now, and Horace he wink at me he saying happen every time, then he back inside and shutting the door. Is then Jordan she calling me from the end of the hall and she saying she found one aint too big she hope I like it, and with that Im is following her through the shadow and into the room. There only one window, so it pretty dark, and look to be getting darker too cause the graygreen sky outside it almost black now, and the rain it running up against the window, and every now and then the wind it blow like a freight train coming through. Then Jordan she turn on a floor lamp bring a little light, and then she slipping out of her clothes, and I aint know just what to do she do that, maybe look around find a towel to give her but there aint even that, and Jordan she laughing all the while she saying say she aint mind that storm even it blow the roof away, and then she spread herself out on a rumple sheet iron-post bed, and the soft yellow light from the lamp it running up along the inside of her legs and then down again, it all I can do keep from staring with my mouth.

Well, I aint know just what I doing after that, and then Jordan she saying say come on sweetie she only go bite a

little bit, and then she laugh, and before Jordan she say
another word I climbing up beside her on the bed, and
where my pants and shirt they at I cant say for sure, I aint
remember taking them off, but somehow Im is still wearing
my shoes, and that some comfort, only Jordan she see that
and she laughing some more she saying she aint heard of
nobody keep his shoes on his feet, only what she have
against shoes she aint say, and then she reach up pull me on
top, and her legs climbing up around mine, and Im is
thinking to myself aint nobody downstairs dancing this close
when just then that freight train storm come slamming itself
into the side of Pappa Toms. With that then the window in
Jordan room it bust into a couple hundred piece slice
through the air, and then the stormwater rolling in come
roll across the floor knock the floor lamp out then on to the
bed, and me and Jordan we aint wait around see what
happen next, we scrambling through the door and out into
the blueblack of the hall.

Looks like there water everywhere, but me and Jordan
we the first ones running down the hall, and some they
peeking out from they blueblack doors see what what they
saying say Lordy they aint never seen so much water full up
a house before where it all coming from sure hope them
people downstairs they all know how to swim, and then
everybody out in the hall and everybody naked too, and
we all running for the stairs, only we run smack into them
downstairs people they running up, and someone say aint
nothing down there except you a fish, and then everybody
stop, aint nobody know just what to do, and all the while
the water in that hall keep rising, it up to our knees now,
and then another voice call out he say there some stairs the
other end of the hall go all the way up to the roof, and then
everybody they off running again, aint nobody even mind
some is naked and some aint, and a couple three more they
even taking off they clothes as they go just to be polite, and

then everybody up on the roof come face to face with that freight-train storm, and there so much water now Pappa Toms look like a raft, and some of them peoples they aint wait for the water get any higher, they diving off the roof maybe swim to a tree, but the rest they just huddle up hold on to anything they can, and me and Jordan we doing the same, and then all of a sudden there a stormwater wave come roll over that roof wash everything clean.

-2-

The next thing I know, the storm and the water and Jordan and the trees and Pappa Toms itself they all gone, aint nothing but a black, black haze cover everything up, and I cant move about see anything different. If that aint dead I dont know what. But maybe it aint so bad being dead, it aint like people been say, seem like it go be a comfort just lie there all day all night aint nothing more you has to think about, not the old man and everything he been saying and doing and is he waiting on me and what I suppose to do, and not Willie and all his devil talk and how he aint never go stop till he meet up with the old man face to face like two railroad trains run smack into each other, not worry about what you go do next and is you afraid or aint you, all of that you done with when you is dead, and all the while I is thinking like that, the black black haze it lifting, slow, slow, and then all of a sudden there a nighttide sky with a bright blue moon, and I is walking through the thick of the wood, brushing past moss and branches, and climbing over the wet of dead logs and up around the ghostdark of palmetto stands, only where exactly I is and where I going I cant say, and by and by I sees a small blue

fire burn in the distance, and then from out the blueblack of
the wood I hears some voices and they talking about all the
crabs they done caught and how they done shell a couple
three thousand they done boil them and eat them up and
my oh my how soft and sweet that crab meat is it aint never
taste so fine before what they go do they run out, and then
they cackling like they knows they aint never go run out of
crabmeat, and the cackling it getting louder and louder, and
it must be coming from some witches cause who else sit
around under a blue moon munch on a couple three
thousand crab, and the next thing Im is standing on the edge
of a small clearing, and there am three witches sitting up
around a smoky blueblack kettle with a small blue fire up
under, and the witches they all wearing black tatter skirts,
black tatter shawls, but they eyes bright as smoke, and all
they all doing they eating and talking and grabbing for crabs
out of that kettle, and they look to been eating crabmeat
maybe two three year the way there crab bones pile up all
over the ground, and look to be some stony chip crows
poking they beaks through them piles turn over the bones,
they scrounge abouts theyselves looking to eat some scrap
of crabmeat and clawing at each other they find some, and
then they looking to them witches they blue bead eyes full
up with hungry and crow-squawking sound like throw
down some more throw down some more throw down
some more, and them witches they acting like they aint
heard they just keep adding to the pile, but every now and
then they squinting some then fling some crabmeat to the
crows, and with that the crows they flapping they wings
some more and snapping at the meat in the air, and it gone
before it ever get to the ground, and with that Im is
stepping back slow and easy, the last thing Im is wanting is
them witches see me hiding in the trees, and I just about to
turn and run off into the dark when them witches they stop
they cackling and turn they smoke bright eyes to the wood,
and the crows they turning they eyes the same.

"Aint nothing you need to worry about, honey," say the first. "We been expecting you."

The other two they be echoing the first one words, and then they all cackling to theyself, but it aint seem like they know exactly where I is the way they looking out through all them pile of bones and into the blue black of the night, which all right by me, but why I aint even think to run I dont know why, and then the witches they all calling out they saying say now honey come on now honey come on, and it all I can do be resist with that, and then they aint saying now honey no more, and the first one she raise a bony white hand and she snap her bony white fingers in the air crack crack like she cracking the bones of one of them crabs, and with that then them crows they up from they piles they flapping they wings and squawking some more, only this time it sound like break all his bones break all his bones, and then they swooping up through the heavy black shadows of the trees, and the witches they cackling some more, only they more appetite in they voices now, and Im is wanting to run, only them crows they closing in they smoke eyes burning aint no where to go, and then the witches they saying say here he come he coming now, and the next thing I knows Im is floating in that smoke black kettle, only how that happen I aint know, and the crows they sitting down around the edge of the fire they in a stony chip ring looking up to them witches they all expectation like maybe there some crabmeat coming to them by and by, and I looking to the crows, and then to the witches and them piles of crab bone, and what I go do now I aint even know where to begin, and the witches they cackling say wunt too many boys running round the wood in nothing but they shoes, and then they laughing for feel the pluck of my arms and legs with they bony white hands, and then they cackling some more they saying say what a fine figure of a boy, fine figure, he almost a man, you feel that juice, we having we some kind of feast tonight, we is, more better than all that crabmeat, even the bones, they aint go be hardly nothing left for the crows eat up, nothing, but that the way it go sometimes, and then they asking me say they hoping the water it hot enough, and I saying say it is, feel like the meat of my bones been boil away for soup, and I knows I dont find me some way out of this pot I aint go be fit keeping company with even them crows, only seem like Im is all lock jaw cause I cant move for even pray, and then the witches they dancing around that kettle they cackling some more and singing and chanting,

> The devil he dance for eat them bones,
> See he dancing in a brakemans shack,
> Then the devil he done and going home,
> Pick his teeth with a wooden jack.
>
> Up and up and up the smoke,
> See the kettle boy start to choke,
> Time he done it time for eat,
> Aint that kettle boy tasting sweet.
>
> The devil he say he coming back,
> All he find is a empty shack.
> Been twenty year that kettle boy gone,
> Been twenty year we sing this song.

And the words of that song they rising up with the steam from that kettle, sound like someone ringing a bell, and then the steam it burning white and whiter, and pretty soon that all there is, and from out of that white come a voice, sound like it me talking to myself, and the voice it saying say them witches they done spend they time getting fat off the bones of dead folk only I aint dead so what I doing I want to end up a twenty year kettle boy course not then what I afraid of

233

aint I enough sense know what to do aint I the sense God give a bean there aint nothing be afraid of just do what you have to, and with that then the voice it gone, and Im is climbing up over the side of that kettle, and then Im is running from the smoke smell rising and them stone-chip crows waiting around to eat and them piles of crab bones scatter in the grass and them song-singing witches the same, and I knows I been that close to dead, only I aint, and then just like that I is running up along the beach, feel like I been running three whole day too, and look like it close to supper time the way the sun hang low in the sky, and the next thing I know I aint running no more, Im is looking to the dark blue water, and aint nothing run through my mind now, it gone numb, and then Im is sitting stretch out on the cool cool hardpack sand and feel the waves wash around my feet.

It take me a while know just what I go do next, feel almost like I done crawl out the blue blue water instead of sitting there looking at it, and then I is thinking on what done happen to me, only I have no idea, but I too too happy I aint dead to worry now, I go figure it out soon enough, and then I is asking myself say when the last time I been eat, been too long aint it, wouldnt some of Tramsee peach pie hit the spot, maybe she cook up some of her fried chickens go with it, and with that then Im is heading for Ty and Tramsee shack, almost taste that sweet peach pie, and then I there. Look like no one been out since the storm to put it back together, look worse than the last time too there boards bust up all over sticking out of the sand, a iron post bed turn over its side, a couple pillow and the mattress fold down a top of some sea oats, some pots and plates and spoons and soup cans and empty bottles and magazines and shoes and a old tire too, they all scatter up one dune and down the next, and then off to one side, look almost like a photograph, there Ty he sitting in a cane bottom chair sea weed all up around his feet, he wearing the pants from a blue serge suit, and a cotton shirt, but he done forgot about his socks and shoes, and all he doing he looking to the sea and working on a bottle of rye.

Ty he aint see me yet, so I walking up to the chair and come up behind, and then I saying say what you waiting on Ty, only loud enough in his ear give him a jump, only he dont move, he just sit there mumbling to hisself, he going on and on, how there must have been a couple hundred peoples moving through the backwater wood and all the way down to town they looking for somebody, only who it is he aint say, and some they was busy dragging chains through the blackgreen water and the heavy heavy hammock and every now and then they was calling out to stop and have a look and then they was shaking they heads and dragging some more, and some they was flipping through what left of Pappa Toms, which Ty he was saying there wunt enough Pappa Toms left sell for kindling, and then Ty he going on about how it was too too hot so hot feel like the air itself melting and most everybody was too too tired go on with them chains, and then Ty he talking how Willie come up the road just then and Willie was saying wunt nobody go find nobody that boy he must a been eat up by the devil that wunt no natural storm that was a devil-come-take-me storm and that just what the devil he done too he done take that boy for eat him up wunt nothing left to do now but go to church Sunday give that boy up to God that the only thing help him now, and then Willie he was heading back to town and everybody else was going with him, and with that then Ty he start whispering now, he saying say get ready, it almost time, it almost time they done move it up, it aint go be Sunday, it be this here night, Friday night, then we all go see God face to face, and then Ty he just stop like that, he looking straight into my face like he just seen me then, only he dont say a word, he just clutching that bottle of rye, and the next thing happen he up from the chair and he stumbling across the sand.

I aint know what to say the way Ty he run off. Im is standing next to that cane bottom chair and thinking say it something what a bottle of rye can do, but that aint right, cause Ty he aint never act that way before even he drink a hundred bottle, but it sure hard to say just what he talking about, and then it come to me say I aint wearing nothing but shoes, what else a drunk man say and do a naked boy come at him from behind, and with that I kicking the sand and laughing, and then I is looking through what left of Ty and Tramsee shack maybe find me something to wear, only aint nothing but more shoes, aint even a hat, and the next thing Im is edging down along the beach make my way to town, aint no telling how many peoples eating they supper or either done and sitting on they porches talking some or maybe just watch the red of the sky fade a deep blackblue, and what they go say they see me jaybird naked I aint want to know so I best find me a place hide out till they all go to bed, and then something inside me say hide out in the church, which it make the most sense, cause aint nobody go to church on a Friday night no matter what that crazy old Ty was talking about.

I aint been long inside when the church bell it start ringing out, and what that mean I aint know, and I trying to think, only nothing come, but the church is the last place I want to be that bell keep ringing, so I back to the welcome room and open the door, only it too too late cause the whole town they walking up the street, look like they all mules been tied to a plow they walking so slow, but they coming all the same. Nothing to do but crouch down back of some old sofa been left inside for waiting, pray nobody think to look my way, which I does just that, and then the door open and in come the town, and the mens they in they Sunday black suits and Sunday black hats even it only Friday, and some they wiping they faces with handkerchiefs and talking grim and low, and some they kicking the dust off they shoes and straighten up they ties and they aint saying a word, and the womens they in they Sunday black dresses and hats the same, and some they reading out from they black bible books and they walking with they words, and some they singing, sound like grief songs, and some they just talking to hear theyself talk.

"What a boy like him doing a place like that I like to know," say one.

"Hell, he a boy like any boy," say a second.

"One thing for sure," say a third. "There plenty of worse ways to spend your last day on this here earth."

"Aint that the truth," say the second, and then they all laughing low and looking to sit theyself down maybe somewhere in the back, and the next thing I know everybody inside and they sitting down the same, but just who they come to see off I dont know, and then it come to me maybe it Jonas Lee Porter, cause I aint seen him come in, only what he get hisself kill for, he know more better than that, but then I is thinking maybe Jonas Lee he aint dead like everybody think, maybe he playing the devil go fool everybody else, and if that the case then the peoples eyes they go jump soon as he walk through the door and this I has to see, and with that then Im is up from that old sofa and edge up along the welcome room wall go take me a look inside.

It sure is something to see. The church it lit up with oil lamps burn from one side and the other, but they aint give off a whole lot of light, mostly shadow. There aint been so many peoples stuff up in there since Mister Baxter his funeral, and was so many then must of been thirty or forty pass out on the floor. The only thing different there aint no coffin, which it only make sense cause Jonas Lee he aint dead, but all the same the peoples they aint know. Some they bending they heads most down to they knees they moaning and rubbing they eyes, and some they singing more of them grief songs, and some they looking to they black bible books they saying say sweet Jesus sweet Jesus over and over. Even Mama and Tramsee they sitting up front they holding each other hands and they aint saying a word. Seem like nobody see it coming but me, except maybe Ty, he know something up cause he sitting back of Tramsee whisper something in her ear and then she push him back and he look around like he waiting on a ghost.

Is then the Preacher Barnes he stepping down from the reading desk, he look like a shadow float through the gold flake lamplight, and he walking back and forth across the front a while, like he thinking on what to say, and then he turn face out to the peoples, and he open his mouth. It have the look like he about to swallow everybody there.

"We all know grief, brothers and sisters," he say. "Aint none of us strangers."

And a couple womens they calling out they know honey they know.

"We all go miss that boy, been missing him already, but he in a better place, I knows that been told by the Lord."

And some more they praising the Lord sweet Jesus thank you thank you. Then the Preacher Barnes he start talking a narrow, harsh voice.

"Aint all of us go be so lucky though," he say. And them praising voices they saying no sir we aint no sir.

"I knowd of a railroad man he been work the boiler of a engine up and down the South Carolina rail line must of been thirty-five year and he wunt so lucky. Every time the Lord call him he turn the other way face the devil."

And then them voices again.

"Sweet Lord Jesus no."

And the preacher he stepping down the aisle now, and he a black bible in his hand, and his voice it like a knife-thin whisper cut to the bone. "That right brothers. That right sisters. He turn to face the devil instead of the Lord."

"Sweet Lord Jesus."

"Then one night the devil he give him his due. Railroad man he was having some trouble with a pop valve talking so much steam it was slowing things down, and hot too, but it wunt no ordinary trouble, brothers and sisters. No it wunt. A railroad man he know how to deal with ordinary trouble. No brothers and sisters, the trouble he face was the devil working his devilment."

And a couple women they fainting with that, and a couple more calling on Jesus save em save em now, and the Preacher Barnes he keep talking, only now his voice it rising with the steam from that boiler.

"The engineer he kept on calling back for more steam, and the railroad man he was trying, he done about everything he think of, only it wunt no use. That pop valve kept on hissing, that hot kept on burning, and wunt long before the railroad man he done lost his head and pick up a shovel and he knock that pop valve hard as he could, only time he do that the steam from that boiler it done bust loose and burn him dead."

And there voices come from all over the church with that they saying say Lord a mercy Lord aint nothing help him now sweet Jesus dont let that happen here sweet Jesus Lord, and then the Preacher Barnes he pull his voice back a bit for everyone to hear.

"That railroad man he just like we all right here we done turn face the devil instead of the Lord and the devil he go give us our due we dont turn back."

And some of the peoples they nodding they heads like they know they been facing the devil but they ready to turn the other way, and some they saying, "No sir, no sir, we aint been face the devil, no sir" and then the Preacher Barnes he waving that black bible book of his in the air.

"You want to turn from the devil?"

And a whole lot of voices saying yes they do.

"You ready turn from the devil face the Lord?"

And them same voices saying they ready they ready now.

"Then this here the ticket take you where you wanna go, this here the fire of Jesus words, the fire of his name come burn away everybody sin, you wanna turn from the devil face the Lord you gotta have this ticket, then you be riding a train all the way to the promised land."

And the Preacher Barnes he walking back up the aisle now and he saying say aaaaaammeennnnn brother, aaaaaammeennnnn sister, and the peoples they saying aaaaaammeennnnn back and swaying with the hum of them preacher words, sound like he the train he talking about, and it coming closer and closer and closer,

and then all of a sudden Im is standing on a platform my face up against a crossstitch iron gate for wait, and there am all kind of people they waiting with me we all naked as the devils daughter, and we all waiting on a train, can hear it coming, only aint no one know just who go get on board, and then this wrinkle old man dress down in black bib-overalls and a black cap he stepping across the black of the rails, he a blue ball lantern swing loose by his side, and then he up on the platform the same, only he on the other side of the gate, and then he fixing that blue ball lantern on a hook and he waving his cap in the air, and with that a blackblue train move up along the platform, its wheels they whining angry with the slowdown, and then there a cloud of steam come hissing up from under, it curl up hot and heavy and roll up through that gate, but the people dont seem to mind cause maybe it go be more heat where they going they miss this train, and then everybody looking everybody else they thinking now who got a ticket, and some they rifling through they pockets they almost cat-crying say where they done put it where it at and then my oh my oh my, and then down on they knees and cat-cry some more, and some they looking to buy, but aint nobody want to sell, and some they shaking they fists in the air they saying they go ride that train even they aint got a ticket, and some they just staring into the white of all that steam,

And then the Preacher Barnes he back at his desk and he waving his bible some more. "But dont you miss that train. You miss that train you go be left to the devils own, that right brothers and sisters, and then the devil he go feast on your black barbecue bones hisself. But if you hear the good Lord call out you name, then you get on board, brother, you take your seat, sister, cause you in for a gospel feast for all eternity sure as you been born."

And with that the rumbling words they stop, and the peoples they up from they benches they shouting halleloo halleloo halleloo, sound like a couple hundred bell ringing round and around, and some of the people they laughing out loud, and some they clapping they hands, and some they burst out singing a heaven-train coming song, and then everybody dancing, they dancing on the floor, they dancing on they benches, they dancing up the aisle to the reading desk, and the Preacher Barnes he dancing just the same, he waving his black bible book in the air, look like he dancing with that book, and then the Preacher Barnes he start up shouting and singing, and then the peoples they shouting and singing to match the preacher, and he shouting and singing some more and they match him some more, look like the whole church been set on fire by the hand of God, and before I know what what Im is shouting and singing and dancing with all the rest, *and then the next thing happen Im is back on that platform and staring into the white of all that steam, and the conductor he standing on a black block step out front of that train, and he calling out names from a book and nodding his head at the old man in the black cap to let them through, and the rest aint been called they all hoping so hard look like the gate go break, only it dont, and some they take to praying, only no sound coming out, and some it look like they ready to kick something, only they just wait and see, and then the conductor he done calling out names and he close up his book, and then he step up into the train and then he gone, and with that the peoples been left they rushing the gate try to force they way through, only the old man in the black overalls he working to shut that gate fast as he can and beating back arms and legs all the while with his cap, and then the gate it lock up tight and the blueblack train give a sharp blast of its whistle and then it pulling out, and some of the peoples they reaching they arms through the crossstitch like they trying to catch hold of that train, and some they trying to climb over, only it too high, and some they mule-kicking anything get in they way, and with that a couple three fight break out and people losing teeth, and some like me, they aint saying a word, they just staring after that blueblack train, and then it give another sharp sharp whistle blast and it round the bend and then it gone, there nothing but a blueblack shadow hang dead in the air,*

And with that Im is standing in the middle of the church, and aint nobody dancing and singing no more, look like they all turn face me instead, and some they falling to the floor right there it like they dead, and some they crouching down by they benches they holding they breath, aint nothing move except they black beetle eyes rattle round in they heads, and some they talking to the Lord like he hiding up in they hats, and some they just angry and take a couple three step closer, like they done miss that heaven-bound train wanna take it out on somebody, and then from out the black gold gloom of the church come a black beetle voice, and it rattling like some of them eyes.

"What it . . . what it is you want?"

The voice it coming from the Preacher Barnes, he leaning out from the shadow of his reading desk, and I aint know just what to say cause aint nothing I want, and then it come to me how it aint Jonas Lee suppose to been dead, only where he at I still don't know, it was me all along, I is the one been dead, only I don't know what to say about that neither, so I dont say a word, and the preacher he pause and bite his lip, then he rattle loose some more words.

"We done . . . we done everything we could. You been dead three whole day. What you . . . what you wanna come bother us for? Aint nothing help you now you but the sweet Lord Jesus."

The preacher then he pull his head back into the turtle-shell dark, and some of the rest they pulling they heads in the same, but aint everyone scare of a three day dead naked island boy suppose to been dead but aint, and some they stepping closer almost crowd around to find out, look like they thinking on make me a ghost ifn I aint one already, and with that Im is looking to the reading desk and all around maybe find somebody help a poor naked boy aint wanna be a ghost, only aint nobody want to bother, even my mama she see me looking she duck her head, and I saying say mama what the matter with you I aint no ghost, and mama she saying say course you aint child you just go right on with what you is, and then she ducking her head some more she wait and see what happen next, and them stepping-closer faces they just about staring me eye to eye, here go, only just then everybody suck in they breath, and them stepping-closer faces move over to one side, and up step Willie, and the next thing happen his voice it come hissing out through the gaps in his teeth, and he asking me what I is ifn I aint no ghost then why I running around without any clothes it sure do have the feeling like I one of the devils own, and Willie now he standing tall in the gold black gloom of the church, and he shaking his arm in the air along with his words, there just a glint of gold dance from his teeth, and he saying say it dont matter you dead or not cause either way you been seen with the devil you been seen following his hand I seen you we all seen you but he been using you boy try to turn you against you own people, and the peoples they all rising up, they eyes glowing with the gold black glint of them Willie words they move to hear some more, and Willie he saying say it about time we done rid us of that old man devil, he been bringing fire and storm to this here island long enough, burn my store and warehouse down, been turn our children against us then eat they bones, the old man he been after this here boy for eat him up, try to eat the other one too, but he done got away, only cost him two broke legs too, but them boys they only recent, aint none of we forget what the old man done he get a hold of a teenage girl, even it a hundred year ago, we a long memory of that time, and most the peoples they closing up around Willie they looking up to him too cause Willie he look to be standing twenty foot tall, and some they saying they aint never heard it told that way before, and some they saying well it the truth any way it told he must of turn fifty girl against they own, and some they aint saying a word they just waiting for Willie tell them what to do, and then all of a sudden Willie he grab hold of someone black bible book, and he standing up front by the reading desk now, and he saying say all we need is the word of God to chase that devil man off of this island, like we chasing him with fire, and then Willie he open up the fire of one of the church lamps and he dip his black bible book in the flame till it catch, and then he raise it up above his head he

saying say this here fire this the ticket we go burn that old
man out, and then he waving his black bible torch in the air
for everybody to be doing the same, this here the ticket, this
here the ticket, and most they eyes they glowing with the
bright red of that Willie torch it cut like a switch through the
deep deep dark, and then they taking they own books and
they leaping to lamps, and before long there burning books
anywhere you look so many the church it full up with
smoke, and from out of that smoke come Willie chanting
some more he saying say this is it this is it, and then the rest
they all chanting the same and waving they black bible
torches in the air, and it looking like some wild hoodoo
dance, only it aint no dance, and then it like everybody
been caught up in a picture and there a voice up inside my
head it saying say *aint I enough sense know what to do the
old man waiting on me now this very minute this here what
suppose to happen so you go do what you have to do what
you suppose to do aint nothing be afraid of just go*, and then
the voice it gone, and everybody dancing and chanting and
waving they torches some more, and they heading for the
door now they saying say burn him out burn him out, and
the next thing I know I is through the church doors and
running for the old man's cabin, fast as I can go.

-3-

Is like death itself when I get there. Aint even the sound
of the wind. There a yellow ballglass lantern hang from a
porch hook up by the door, and the old man he sitting in
the soft shadows on the far side of the porch, only he aint
sitting, he laying back in a cane-back chair like he done fall
asleep, his feet prop up on a crate, and then Im is up by the

door, and the hot of that yellow lantern light it burn against the back of my head. Willie he always been after the old man, and now he coming with a pack of black bible revengement, but maybe the old man know what to do, and then we go see. But its then I see Thaddeus he aint been sleeping, he been dead, and except for the lantern been lit just a little while, look like he been dead a couple three day cause aint nothing been clean up after the storm. The next thing I do I is reaching over turn the old man chair around face the light, only somehow he still in the shadow, and Im is thinking say what that mean and staring into two black eye look like holes the way they sunk in, and then all of sudden I hears the old man voice, sound like it coming from everywhere, and the old man he saying say   *it about time you done got here what been keeping you boy it sure as hell been getting cold sitting up in this here chair I wunt gonna last much longer*   and then it seem like the old man he blink them black, black eyes of his and then he sitting up and then he saying say   *this is yours now you keep it maybe you see me again maybe you dont you go on now go on they almost here*   then he hanging a chain around my neck, it the one with that alligator tooth he been talk about, and then it like he aint move at all, and the last words he saying say he sure go miss the devils daughter, and he laughing some, and then the old mans voice it gone and I is thinking about that alligator tooth around my neck and how the old man done said when it was his time he want to go up just like old Elijah, and before I know what what Im is lifting the old man from out that chair and bring him inside the cabin lay him down on his bed, it almost look like he smiling, and then Im is down under the sink lay hold of a kerosene can and empty it out on the floor and some on the bed and then all over, and then Im is grabbing hold of that yellowglass lantern off the porch, aint much light left but it enough, and it almost like the old man he laughing again, and then I done throw that lantern through the door watch it bust up under the old mans bed, and with that there fire everywhere, it roll through the cabin like a stormwater flood, and Im is standing by the door watch the tide of that fire roll up and over the shadow of the old man, and all the while Im is thinking say what everybody go do now the old man dead, well theres one thing for sure, aint nobody go blame they troubles on the devil and look the old mans way, and then Im is thinking on why the old man he give me his alligator tooth, and I is sure I dont know, but all the same it have the feeling like maybe I suppose to take over where he leave off, only what exactly that go mean, well I aint know that neither, and then from out the fire the old man he laughing some more, and then the laughing it gone, and the shadow it gone the same, aint nothing left but the smoke of burning wood, and then Im is turning from the cabin I go leave it burn, only there is Willie and the rest of them book burning people, they faces rising up slow from the black of the hill and the grass, they eyes glowing bright with the red of the cabin fire, and what happen next Im is saying say the old man he dead already you all just be putting up them books aint nothing more to do you all just head on home, but aint nobody move, at least not at first, and some of them wild-eye people they looking up to the fire maybe wish they had a part in it, and some they looking to they black bible books, only them books they aint nothing but charred black paper now, and most everybody they looking to Willie they aint know what to do, only Willie he aint know what to do neither, and then a second time Im is saying say the old man he already dead aint nothing more for them to do, and with that the people they shaking they heads they saying say if that dont beat all, and then they turning one by one from Willie and the fire and they walking to the black of the hill and the grass and the sky, and some they tossing they black bible books to the ground, they aint hardly worth reading no more, and then they all gone except for Willie, and Willie his eyes they still burning bright with the red of the old mans fire, and he looking at me like he has to burn something even it me, but that Willie-look it dont bother me none at all, and then one more time Im is saying say the old man he dead he already dead, and with that the fire from Willie eyes it gone, and then Willie he turn away a slow slow turning, and then he walking into the black shadows of the hill and the sky, and he holding a charred black book in his hand. . .

. . . and with that the third man he was walking from the swamp and the log and the animals up in them trees, he was walking into the bluegreen haze of the wood, and the animals they was all laughing to theyself, and some was saying say it wunt the alligator world no more that for sure, and then they was all climbing down from they trees and going about they business.

April 20, 2010
Peter Damian Bellis